**With Shocking Force and Tortured Beauty
the Sea Can Live and Fight and Die
Like Any Man!**

Beneath the raging mists and whips of spray, down where boats and bathers never go, lives the last frontier and the first womb of life, a world as primitive as nature and as eerie, as eternal, as outer space.

Here is more danger than can be found in any land, more horror, more evil, more mystical joy. Here is a dimension uncharted in fact or in fiction, where all life floats and glides and weaves, and where the strangest of creatures meet the bravest or most doomed of men.

Here is the savagery and splendor of the earth's own secret galaxy, and a science fiction writer's most spectacular debut—

WAVE RIDER

HILBERT SCHENCK

WAVE RIDER

PUBLISHED BY POCKET BOOKS NEW YORK

The following stories were first published in *The Magazine of Fantasy and Science Fiction:* "Three Days at the End of the World" (September, 1977), "The Morphology of the *Kirkham* Wreck" (September, 1978), "The Battle of the Abaco Reefs" (June, 1979). "Wave Rider" was first published in *Chrysalis* (December, 1979).

POCKET BOOKS, a Simon & Schuster division of
GULF & WESTERN CORPORATION
1230 Avenue of the Americas, New York, N.Y. 10020

ISBN: 0-671-83265-4

First Pocket Books printing January, 1980

10 9 8 7 6 5 4 3 2 1

Trademarks registered in the United States and other countries.

Printed in the U.S.A

CONTENTS

Author's Preface   7

The Morphology of the *Kirkham* Wreck   11

Three Days at the End of the World   51

Buoyant Ascent   99

Wave Rider   159

The Battle of the Abaco Reefs   177

AUTHOR'S PREFACE

Imagine a spectrum of story collections, starting at the left end on your shelf with a wholly random distribution of unrelated yarns and ending at the right end with a complete and continuous narrative, broken down into discrete parts. The five stories comprising this collection fall to the left of center, perhaps halfway out to the fully-randomized group.

Taken in order, these independent stories involve a time span of about one hundred years in the history of the oceans; a one-hundred-years more important, alas, than the last twenty million.

The first yarn about the *Kirkham* wreck deals with a true hero, Walter Chase, and a real rescue, the last and greatest of its kind, just before technology made such efforts redundant. The Abaco story that ends the book comes about one hundred years later and tells of an ocean controlled and passive, a tool for those who choose to pick it up.

"Three Days . . ." belongs to us, today, and suggests just one of the infinity of environmental pollution realities, most of them either reasonably plausible or already frighteningly evident.

"Buoyant Ascent" and "Wave Rider," like the *Kirkham* story, pit man against a stormy sea, but such a struggle today is more technical, politically and morally more ambiguous.

There are differences between the stories that flow out of the time in which they take place. But they are knit together in many ways too. For example, if the collection has a single theme, and I think it does, it is simply that if you intend to work in and with the ocean, you must start by knowing what you are doing. This was true when the Greeks sailed for Troy three thousand years ago, and it has never been truer than today.

—Hilbert Schenck

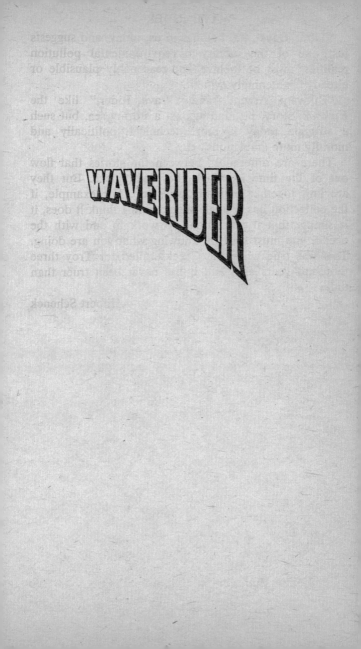

The Morphology
of the
Kirkham Wreck

"The Riches of the Commonwealth
Are free strong minds, and hearts of
    health;
And more to her than gold or grain,
The cunning hand and cultured brain."
    Robert B. Thomas,
      The Old Farmers Almanack,
    1892, William Ware & Co.,
      Boston, Mass.

When the three-masted schooner *H.P. Kirkham* stranded on Rose and Crown Shoal southeast of Nantucket Island on January 19, 1892, the Coskata Life Saving Crew, led by Keeper Walter Chase, responded. The ensuing rescue attempt involved alterations in the local time flow of magnitudes never before observed within this continuum. Evolutionary physical forces were changed beyond the control of time-using peoples, and a fundamental question was introduced into the information matrix of this continuum, having, apparently, no resolution.

Time-using societies had always recognized the possibility that energy-users might attain significant mastery of time manipulation. Indeed, even occasional members of Keeper Chase's world group had, under the impetus of some violent or emotional event, been able to perform some limited and simple feats of time engineering, usually associated with mood and incentive control of others in the immediate situation. What became evident when the *Kirkham* stranded was that extreme-value probability theory could not set a limit on such activity by an energy-user totally motivated and having what Keeper Chase's peoples would incorrectly call a high level of "psychic" ability but what in fact is simply the ability to make information transfers within an altered time domain.

The northern gale blew shrieking along the back of Great Point, driving the spume off the wave tops and over the bitter beach. The patrolman crouched behind a sand hill, hunched to keep an occasional swirl of snow out of his collar, staring dully out at the white and grey sea. The wind had built up through the night, and now the shreds of dawn were blowing south over Nantucket, and the wind spoke continuously of urgent death.

The beach patrol, a hulking dark figure, turned to put the blast behind him and started back towards the station where watchers in the cupola could relieve him in the light of day. It was twelve degrees above zero with the wind gusting over forty.

Inside the Coskata Station the dark, shadowed paneling glowed faintly pink, reflecting the luminous brilliance of a huge coal stove in the center of the big common room. Nyman was cookie that week, and the wheatcakes were piling up on the cook stove in the small galley under the stairs. Four men sat silent, waiting for their breakfast, not trying to speak against the whines and rattles of the wind gusts. Yet they clearly heard the telephone tinkle in the cupola. A moment later, Surfman Eldridge appeared at the top of the stairs. "Skipper? It's Joe Remsen at Sankaty Light."

Keeper Walter Chase rose in the dark glow of the station; a giant, almost seven feet tall, his huge shadow startlingly flew up to obscure the walls and ceiling as he moved in front of the ruddy stove and up the stairs.

And Surfman Perkins, toying with his coffee mug, listening to the wind snapping and keening around the station, knowing that dawn calls from the lighthouse meant only one thing, suddenly realized for the first time in his life that he might die. He coughed, sharp barks of sound contrasting with the heavy, measured tread of Keeper Chase mounting the two flights to the cupola.

"Walter Chase here. Is that you, Joe?"

"Walter!" An urgent tone. Chase sensed that time was beginning to run away from him. "Masts on Bass Rip. We saw a flare last night late, but couldn't tell where. She's leaning some. Seems steady, but it's awful far to tell."

"What's her true bearing, Joe?"

"Just about due east from us. That would put her on the north end of Bass Rip."

Keeper Chase consulted a chart and compared angles. He looked out over the station pointer with powerful glasses. "Joe, I can't make her out. She *has* to be further out. We've got forty feet here and I could sure see her if she was laying on Bass Rip. She's got to be on Rose and Crown. South end from your bearing."

A pause. "Well . . . I don't know, Walter. I doubt

we'd see her so clear that far. She may have lost her topmasts."

There was no point in arguing. Chase knew the wreck was fifteen miles out, on Rose and Crown Shoal. A sudden gust blew through the stout, government sashes and swirled its chill into the cupola. The little tower rattled and shook. Walter Chase looked out at the ragged dawn, across at Eldridge, then down at the phone. "Joe, hang on. I'm getting the surfboat ready. We'll haul to the backside and launch there. I'll be back to you before I leave the station." Chase rose, ducking his head instinctively in the small room, and slowly climbed down the ladder, his mind fragmenting, working the launch, estimating the tide rips, laying beside the stranded vessel. "Eat quick!" shouted Walter Chase down the stairs. "We got a wreck on Rose and Crown!"

The difficulty in predicting improbable, time-controlling events by energy-users stems from these peoples' unlikely and illogical motivations and perception. One might assume that Keeper Chase's need to "defeat" the seas of the Nantucket South Shoals flowed from some sense of vengeance or hatred on his part resulting from the loss of a loved parent or a woman in some sea disaster. In fact, Keeper Chase suffered no such loss. Distant family members had, through the years, died on various whaling and trading voyages, but they were only names to Keeper Chase with little emotional attachment. Yet where the winter storms easily broke and ruined other capable men, for Keeper Chase the natural variation of wind and sea, so implacable and daunting to most of Chase's world group, only resonated with his self-image. In essence, Chase did not strongly believe in the "God" concepts so typical of energy-users, but he strongly believed in a "Devil," that is, the continual temptation of his world group by easy choices and safe paths. Keeper Chase saw the variability of the ocean as a natural test of behavior, as a kind of "Devil's assistant." That this naive motivation coupled with his great physical strength and the urgent and marginal situation at the stranded *Kirkham* should have produced such an unprecedented control over time flow cannot now be understood. Keeper Chase's meaning and purpose in this continuum thus remains inexplicable, as, in fact, he himself was to realize.

Surfman Flood ducked around the corner of the station, finally relieved of the wind blast at his back. He saw the stable door was open and, in the dim interior, Perkins and Gould were fastening a long wooden yoke across the neck of the silent ox. Harness bells tinkled, sound pinpoints in the rush and scream of the wind. Flood's heart seemed hollow. "Where's it at?" he asked at the door.

Josiah Gould peered from under his slicker hat. "Rose and Crown."

Flood sighed. "Fifteen miles downwind."

"Ayeh. Better get some breakfast."

Flood pushed open the station door and felt the relative warmth and stillness of the dark interior suck at his resolve. Nyman was steadily lifting forkfuls of flapjack into his mouth, alternating with steaming coffee from a huge cup in his left hand. Across the table was Flood's place set with a heaping meal.

"We got some rowin' to do, George. Better feed your face quick," said John Nyman. As they ate, rapidly and silently, the two wide doors of the apparatus room opened on the other side of the station, and swirls and draughts of chill rushed everywhere. They heard the shouts and tinkles as the stolid ox was backed over the sills and the harness lashings connected to the surfboat cart.

"Gawd, John, hit's just awful on the beach!"

Nyman grinned and winked in the dark, chilling room. "The govinment only pays you to go out, George," he said, quoting the old wheeze. "You got to get back any way you can."

"Fifteen miles to windward! Hell's delight, we won't row a hundred yards in this smother!"

They heard Keeper Chase's deep voice in the apparatus room as the creak of the wheels signaled the surfboat's movement out into the wild dawn. He came into the common room and looked at the two men. "You fellers follow across the neck when you're finished and bring back the ox. I'm going to call Joe Remsen at Sankaty and have him order a tug from Woods Hole. We hain't going to row very far in this blow after we get them fellers off the wreck."

"Amen," said Surfman Flood under his breath. The wind was penetrating everywhere in the station and the commotion was restless and insistent.

Walter Chase climbed back up into the cupola and cranked the phone magneto.

"Sankaty Light, Keeper Remsen."

"Joe, Walter Chase again. We'll be launching pretty quick. Can you still see her out there?"

"Hang on . . . yep. No change in her heel, as far as I can tell."

"Joe, will you call the town and have them telegraph Woods Hole for a tug. I think this storm's got another day to run, and we just hain't going to row back against it."

"Walter, I'll do my best . . . them salvage fellows . . . they're hardly what you'd call heroes, you know."

Walter Chase grinned in the dark tower, which was suddenly shaking like a wet terrier. "Rats, vultures, buzzards, and skunks is what I usually hear them called, Joe. But we'll get back. Listen, Joe, I'm taking a line and drail. Might be some squeteague in those shallows in this rough weather."

But Joe Remsen made no sudden answer. He had rowed in the surfboat with Walter Chase under old Captain Pease when the Coskata Station had opened eight years before. Together, they had worked the wreck of the infamous brig *Merriwa,* manned by a crew of New York City thugs who attempted to shoot up the station soon after they were landed. Walter Chase and an ax handle had secured the pistols, and then he and Joe had gone with them, now drunk as lords, to town in Wallace Adams' catboat. And Joe Remsen, feeling the tough and solid tower of Sankaty Light vibrate as a thin scream of icy air pierced the solid masonry, smiled in spite of himself, remembering the lunch at the American House. One of the drunken hoodlums had shoved his hand under a waitress's dress, and she had let him have a full tray of food plumb in the face. Back-to-back, he and Walter Chase had fought the six of them, chairs flying, crockery smashing everywhere. Joe Remsen's throat had a catch. He had to say something. "Walter . . . old friend, take care . . . God bless."

The walk across the neck took only a few blustery minutes, and Walter Chase met Nyman and Flood midway in that walk leading the ox home. Chase strode through the tidal cut between two high dunes, and the full wind caught his slicker and blew it suddenly open so that for a moment he seemed impossibly huge in the grey, fitful light. The surfboat lay above high water, and the men around it huddled together, their backs against the cutting wind.

Surfman Jesse Eldridge was Number One in the Coskata crew. He walked, hunched and stolid, to

Walter Chase. "It's going to be a tough launch, Skipper. Them waves are running almost along the beach," he shouted.

Chase nodded. "We're getting some lee from Point Rip, Jesse, but we'll have to launch across them, hold her head to the east. Otherwise, we'll be back ashore before we know it." They watched the breaking curls running toward them from the north.

Nyman and Flood came back, and the men, three on a side, began to shift the surfboat into the backwash. The wind blustered at them. "We got to go quick ... when we go, boys!" shouted Walter Chase.

The blow was slightly west of north, but the waves were running directly south and meeting the beach at a sharp angle. "Take her out about nor'east!" shouted Walter Chase. "Ready .... Now, jump to it!"

The six men lifted the boat by its gunwales and ran into the waves. A large group had passed and now the nearshore was a confused and choppy mess. The leading surfmen, Cathcart and Perkins, were almost up to their waists, and over the sides they vaulted, lifting and dropping their oars in the rowlocks. Now Gould and Nyman scrambled in, then Eldridge and Flood. Walter Chase pushed the surfboat out alone, deeper in, and now a curl appeared more from the east than the others and slapped the surfboat's bow to port back towards shore. Walter Chase moved his right hand forward along the starboard gunwale and pulled sharply. The twenty-three-foot boat gave a hop and her bow shifted eastward again. Then Chase was gracefully over the stern and the men were rowing strongly while he put out the long steering oar. They were clear of the shore break and moving into deeper water. Yet, even here, the waves were huge, rolling by under the boat and now and again breaking unexpectedly under the keel or beside them as they pulled together.

George Flood, cheerful and round-faced, was rowing port oar next to Jesse Eldridge. "Say, Skipper," he shouted up at Walter Chase. "I'm sure glad your ma never stinted you food. We must have been in a fathom of water before you climbed in."

Walter Chase thought a moment. "Actually, George, I hain't all that big, as Chases go," he boomed. "My great uncle, Reuben Chase, was harpooner with Cap'n Grant on the *Niger*, and he went over seven feet. They claimed he could play a bull walrus or a whale on a harpoon line like you or I would a blue or striped bass." Chase paused, then . . . "Course, that would be a *small* whale, you understand."

Josiah Gould, seated directly ahead of Eldridge, lifted his head, his huge mustache blowing every which way. "Hain't that awful!" he yelled. "He's not just taking us out here to catch our death from pee-nu-monia, but now we're going to listen to more of them Chase family lies too!"

Flood grinned over his shoulder and shouted back. "Them's not exactly lies, Josiah. Them's what's called 'artistic license.' "

Walter Chase looked benignly at Flood, his small eyes bright and his sideburns wild and full in the whipping wind. "I wisht I had your education, George. It's a plain wonder how you fellers with schooling can call one single thing by so many names. Now my daddy always said there was just three kinds: plain lies; mean, dirty, awful lies; and what's in the Congressional Record."

Gould and Nyman looked sideways at each other, winking. If they could get Skipper Chase going on them "govinmint fellers," it would be a short and cheerful run to Rose and Crown.

But the wind was worse. They were completely clear of any lee from Great Point. Even Chase's huge voice would be torn away and mutilated. "We're . . . far enough . . . out! Get . . . the sail up!" The four stern oarsmen continued to row, now more northerly into the teeth of the blasting wind. Cathcart and Perkins brought their oars inboard and wrestled the sail, tied in a tight bundle, out from under the thwarts and up into the wind. With Gould's and Nyman's help they finally stepped the mast and then unfurled and dropped the small, lateen rig. It caught and filled with a snap, and Walter Chase wrenched the steering oar so hard to port that it described a long arc between the water and the steering notch in the transom. The boat darted off. Eldridge manned the sheet, and the other men huddled on the floorboards, their heads hunched inside the thick issue sweaters and stiff slickers.

Chase, at the steering oar, and Eldridge, on the stern thwart, had their heads close together; and now, running with the wind on the stern quarter, they could suddenly speak less stridently.

"I'm going to head for the lightship south of Great Round Shoal, Jesse," said Walter Chase, his arms in constant motion. "If it comes on to blow worse, we'll just have to go on board her. If we decide to keep going, we'll lay off sou'east and run down to Rose and Crown."

Eldridge was silent, then: "When do you figure we decide, Skipper?"

Chase looked at the jagged seas, whitecaps everywhere to the horizon. "Much beyond the Bass Rip line, we could never fetch the lightship. This lugger hain't much to windward."

The two men looked out ahead as the surfboat, heavily driven, wallowed and yawed and fought the pull of Walter Chase and his tough hickory steering oar.

Now they were three miles out, and looking south,

Walter Chase saw that Bass Rip was clear and that the wreck was certainly on Rose and Crown. "We got to decide, Jesse," said Walter Chase.

Surfman Eldridge looked down at his high gum-rubber boots and nodded. "It hain't got worse, Skipper."

Chase's small eyes glittered. "Let out the sail, Jesse," he said, and the surfboat bounced and slapped and rolled, but now it was better for the waves were astern. Off they dashed southeast, surfing down the long rollers in the deep water, then struggling up the shifting water hills. Between the Bass Rip line and McBlair's Shoal, Walter Chase first saw the masts of the wreck. She was at the south end of Rose and Crown, probably in that one-fathom spot there, and leaning to the south perhaps twenty degrees. He headed a bit more southerly and they left the choppy white smother of McBlair's Shoal behind.

Now the three masts were clearly visible. The vessel lay roughly east and west with her stern to Nantucket. She had struck and then bilged, and now the waves were breaking cleanly over her. They had driven the hull over to starboard so that a spectacular line of surf would suddenly appear all along her port side that canted up to face the seas. They were too far away to count the men but Chase could see dark forms in the ratlines. He peered intently at the wreck. Was it shifting now? It was a bad stranding! If she were facing the seas, even quartering, but broadside they were wrenching her. And the tide was coming. The seas would enlarge and she'd be hit even harder. Chase peered and peered at the wreck, and the surfboat drove along the line made by his eyes.

Chase Two was aware of the *H.P. Kirkham* in a total sense. She was not going to stay together any longer. Chase Two detected unbalanced forces within the ship-sand-wind-water field matrix. He penetrated the force structure around the *Kirkham*, but there was no TIME! The surfboat was running down the seas. The *Kirkham* was twisting as the combers, steepened and shortened by the shoal, boarded her with shuddering blows. Chase Two clenched, and time flowed more slowly. The waves moved like molasses. The shocks were stretched out, and he could trace the force imbalances. SLOWER! He could not speed the finite duration of impulses flowing between his billions of neural cells, but he could slow time and process data that way. Fiercely he clenched. Time, he realized, could be traded for information. He saw the *Kirkham* completely, and yet simultaneously, in every relevant detail. The mizzen mast was shaky, split. Not much had shown on the mast's surface, but now the stick was resonating with the wind, and the splitting was worse. It would soon bring down the main and foremast, and the men as well.

There was no solution within the energy matrix alone, and neither time nor information domains extended directly into the energy system. The mast would have to be replaced.

Chase Two stooped like a hawk down the *Kirkham's* time line. He saw her leave Rose and Crown Shoal and flow backwards to Halifax and leave her lading. Then faster, backwards to other voyages in her brief year of life. Now the masts were out and the hull was coming apart on the stocks of a boatyard near the tiny town of Liverpool on the south coast of Nova Scotia. The masts suddenly grew branches, and, in a twinkling, Chase Two watched a French timber cruiser looking up at a tall pine deep in the Nova Scotia forests. The cruiser turned to his associate, the shipyard boss's young son on his first wood-buying trip into the woods. "By gar, dat's one fine tree, eh?"

The young man nodded. It was the tallest in the area. But now Chase Two showed the Frenchman something he had not seen before, that other time. The tree had been struck by lightning. The scar was grown over, but you could just make it out curling from the top and disappearing around the trunk.

"Look," said the timber cruiser. "Dat tree been struck. We walk around." And on the other side they saw the faint scar traveling down to the ground. "Risky, dose ones," said the Frenchman in a superior way. "Hmmmmm." And as he looked around, Chase Two showed him a shorter but perfectly branched mast tree on the other side of the clearing, and the French cruiser pointed and smiled. "Not so beeg, dat one, but plenty tough, I teenk."

And back down the time line, Chase Two dropped like a stone. He saw the new mizzen erected on the Liverpool ways, then, faster and faster, the loading and unloading and movement until the *Kirkham* again struck on Rose and Crown Shoal, bilged, and lay through the stormy night with her men in her rigging.

When Keeper Chase learned that informational and temporal entropy flows could be interchanged, his power to influence events grew at an unprecedented pace. In the course of replacing the *Kirkham*'s mast, Keeper Chase solved a variety of hydrodynamic and structural problems of extreme complexity and entirely by inspection and processing of data. Much more significant, he dealt surely with the philosophical and practical problems of time-information interchange and realized that if time flow could be slowed, it could be controlled in other ways. His ability to arrest time flow within his local region was now so pronounced

that a detectable chronologic entropy gradient existed
within the entire continuum.

The surfboat blew down on the stricken schooner
from the north, heading directly for her battered port
side where white spume flew up twenty feet or more
when a big wave took her full on.

"You bow men," shouted Walter Chase. "Get the
anchor ready." The positioning had to be done correctly the first time. There would be no clawing back up
from the schooner's lee to reanchor if they did it badly.
Walter Chase watched the choppy, surging space
shorten between the surfboat and the schooner. The
current was running to the northeast with the wind
a bit west of north and the waves about from due
north. He decided to anchor upwind of the vessel's
stern and then lay back south and easterly to come
under the mainmast and her center ratlines where the
crew was now clustered.

Chase's small eyes gleamed in the grey, dull light. He
watched the distance shorten and the schooner widen
and her masts grow up and, in them, the men now
clearly seen.

"Watch your head, Jesse!" shouted Walter Chase.
"We're rounding up now!" He put the steering oar hard
over, and again it formed a bow of iron-hard hickory,
arched against the forces that drove the boat halfway
around, heeling and wallowing wildly until it faced
the screaming wind and sharp seas. "Anchor over!"
shouted Walter Chase, then, "Oars out, all of you!"

They were up on the thwarts holding her head
against the wind as she slipped back with Perkins paying out the anchor line over a smooth, maple cleat.
The surfboat lay on her tether about southeast, and
Walter Chase guided her back and back until they
were a few yards from the schooner and just beyond

where the big rollers broke and shuddered the vessel all along her length. The surge was ten feet or more. The surfboat lay down in a trough, and they could look up and see several feet of the schooner's side, then up until they were above the rail and a great wave was sliding out from under them and creaming white and lovely over the vessel's port rail in a burst of foam and a sound of roaring and groaning that made Walter Chase flinch his cheek muscles, for he knew how weak the schooner was.

Chase cupped his hands and bellowed directly into the wind. "Perkins, throw them the heaving stick."

Perkins heard and readied the stick and its loops of line. The surge picked the surfboat up, and as they came level with the schooner's rail, Perkins hurled the stick into the rigging, with the thin line paying smoothly out behind in a graceful arc. One of the crew crawled up the ratlines to where the stick was entangled in the shrouds and turned towards the surfboat.

"You . . . bend a line on that! Use your topsail clew line." The roar of Walter Chase's voice flew downwind, and, in moments, the clew line was fast to the stick, and back it came, hand by hand, through the smother to Perkins, who bent it on the same cleat as the anchor warp.

The other end of the clew line was in the hands of the sailor and two others who had crawled over to join him. Walter Chase shouted again. "Tie that line to a shroud, you men!"

They stared stupidly at him, and sudden spray flew up in their faces. Walter Chase turned back to Perkins. "Start to haul in on that slowly. You rowers, ease us towards her side."

But the schooner's crew had waited long enough and they, or three of them, began to pull fiercely on the clew line themselves. Walter Chase felt the boat jerk roughly towards the schooner and begin a deep roll broadside in a trough. He crammed the steering oar violently over and spun around, pointing at the schooner. "Stop hauling! Stop, I say! Make your end fast. If you make one more pull on that line, we'll cut it!" And as he spoke, Chase pulled a big clasp knife from his slicker pocket and opened the blade with a snick that pierced the duller voice of the gale. Then he passed the big silver knife forward to Perkins, who brandished it above the clew line. The men on the schooner saw the great dark figure with the knife and heard the huge voice driven down by the wind, and they tied off the line and huddled, dully watching the Coskata crew, using both rope and oars, begin to move towards the wreck.

Suddenly, the schooner shuddered and, inexplicably, rolled to windward. She came almost upright and then went back over to starboard, stopping her breathtaking swing at the same list as before. The mizzen gaff snapped off and fell, thudding against its mast on the way down. The schooner began another roll to port, and Perkins looked directly at the men in the ratlines, and his eyes and theirs met. He remembered a Sunday six years ago when, after church, he and his mother had driven in the wagon over to Little Mioxes Pond where, everyone said, a large vessel had blown ashore. They had spent the day with hundreds of others watching the men in the rigging, too weak to grasp the lines shot over the vessel by the Surfside crew, falling one after another into the raging sea. The vessel had stranded well out so the crew were only small black figures and they did not move very much when they fell, but Perkins never after that time shot another crow or grackle with the .22 Winchester pump that his mother had saved for a year to buy him. Even if they were just birds, they fell the same way, black against the far sky. And now these men were about to fall, blackly still, but he would see their eyes clearly this time.

"Gawd help us, Skipper! She'll shake her sticks out!" shouted Perkins in a choking, coughing voice, strident with terror.

Walter Chase had followed that roll with bright, keen eyes. She could not withstand much more of that! "No!" he said sharply.

Chase Three surveyed the flow field under the wreck and processed the observations. He clamped intensely on the time flow, and the *Kirkham* was motionless in a sea of stationary fluid and a sky of stationary wind. He explored the flow characteristics of the near shores in every particular, considering the special character of the *Kirkham*'s fields of forces. The current, shifting clockwise during the flood as it did in the area, had undermined the sand bed on which the *Kirkham* lay. But worse, the current, now running more and more counter to the wind, was moving the hull as well.

Chase Three considered how the force and energy relationships could be corrected. The wind was beyond manipulation, deriving as it did from such a disparate mass of variables as to make significant time-based alteration impractical. But the flows of gravity and wind-driven water were another matter. As Chase Three studied these fields of flow, he gradually realized that the natural relationships allowed a bifurcation within the viscosity functions. There were at least two flow-field configurations that had equal probability and, most important, either could exist with no change in total energy level within the continuum. The present field system allowed a strong easterly current to move in over the shoal against the *Kirkham,* but with the alternate field the flow would be slightly damped and diverted more northerly, and the wind force on the schooner would be sufficient to hold her against the sand and damp the roll forces.

Since there was no energy gradient involved, Chase Three immediately altered the continuum to the new flow field, this information gradient being offset by the altered time flow in the local area. The *Kirkham* shuddered but did not roll again.

With his introduction of the Chase Field into the information matrix of our continuum, Keeper Chase was reaching the peak of his astonishing powers. That any alternate description of the fluid-dynamic field existed was not even known, and that Keeper Chase should have found a solution at equal energies was quite marvelous. He did not, when utilizing time-information entropy balances to make the shift, consider that these same laws govern the development and evolution of galactic and supra-galactic motion and that the field shift must occur there as well. Thus, Keeper Chase, in addition to sustaining an extraordinary temporal gradient within the continuum, had now inadvertently but irrevocably altered the way in which the energy universe would develop. Those time-using peoples who existed outside the gradient now convened and considered the immediate situation. We too could work within altered time, but the randomness of what was occurring put us beyond normal information transfer procedures. The storm on the Nantucket South Shoals had spawned a gradient storm in time itself. If the rescue attempt should become unlikely within any statistically allowed alternate energy structure, we would have to consider Keeper Chase's reaction to that perception and what an impossible, but certainly powerful, reaction by Keeper Chase to breach the energy-time-information barriers would cause within these boundaries.

Perkins, bent in a fit of coughing, saw that the schooner was stationary again. "Cathcart," shouted Walter Chase. "Bend a bowline in our painter and get ready to heave it over."

Now they edged closer, hanging like a lunging pony against the whipping anchor line. "Throw!" shouted Chase and the line flew across. "One man at a time," shouted Chase down the screaming wind to the schooner. "Put that bight around your waist."

A large, hulking Negro who had caught the painter passed it to a smaller figure, evidently the cabin boy. The youngster put the line over his head and waited, staring frozenly into the wind.

"Now . . ." and Chase's voice boomed under and around the wind's cry. "When I say jump, you come! You hear!"

The boy nodded, staring out at the marching lines of water foaming towards them.

"Cathcart, haul us in a bit. . . . Now, steady, boys!" The surfboat was caught by a comber and lifted, up and up, and the wave was pushing the boat towards the schooner. They were on the peak and the curl was slipping past.

"JUMP!"

The boy flung himself off the ratlines, his legs flailing. Cathcart and Perkins handed in the painter as he fell, thudding, into the space between the bow and center thwarts. "Ease that bow line quick!" shouted Walter Chase, and the surfboat lay off to the east before an early break could turn them over at the schooner's rail.

The boy looked up from the floorboards, his ankle hurting, his teeth chattering; and over him loomed a gigantic figure, sideburns wild and blustery, eyes small and intensely bright, beacons against the wild grey sky. "We count six more, son. Have you lost anyone yet?"

Somehow the boy was able to speak. "Nossir. Seven in all. The cap'n . . . the cap'n ain't so well. We . . . we been in the rigging since eight last night. Gawd, it's . . ."

"What ship?" asked George Flood, turning suddenly around.

"*H.P. Kirkham,*" said the boy. "From Halifax with fish. Bound to New York."

Walter Chase stood up. "Let's get the next one. You starboard rowers, bring us in slow. Cathcart, bring her head in."

Each time, they approached the *Kirkham* and waited for the proper wave to lift them up and slide the boat close. Then a black tumbling figure would come into the surfboat every which way, limp with fear and exhaustion and dazed by the sudden, unexpected hope.

Now there were three left and the surfboat rolled more heavily and more water slopped over the gunwales. "Sir," shouted the cabin boy. "I think the cap'n's coming next. They're going to have to sort o' throw him."

Walter Chase peered at the three figures in the ratlines. The wind had slackened a bit and it seemed brighter. He could see an old man, conscious but unable to hold his head up, supported and held against the ratlines by a huge Negro and another big man in bulky clothes. "Josiah . . . Johnny . . . get ready to help when this fellow comes across."

The center rowers shipped oars and waited. Cathcart carefully pulled them in, a bit at a time. Then he cleated the clew line and hurled the painter back across the foamy gap. They put the loop over the old man's head and shoulders. The boat was rising. "Get ready!" shouted Walter Chase to the three men. "Now!"

The two men threw the captain feet first into the boat. He came down crossways, catching John Nyman across the cheek with his fist as he fell. His head thumped a thwart and he slumped, a bundle of rags, into the bottom of the boat.

Walter Chase quickly knelt and lifted the old man's head. "Keeper Walter Chase. Coskata Life Saving Station. Can you understand me, Captain?"

The old man, his whiskers white with frost and brown with frozen tobacco juice and spittle, stared back unseeing. "Aye. Captain McCloud, master, *H.P. Kirkham* out of Nova Scotia. Thank God. . . ."

Chase's eyes pierced the old man's own eyes, and he nodded. "Captain McCloud. We cannot save your vessel. She is breaking up and this storm will grow worse by nightfall."

"I know," said McCloud and his head fell forward and his eyes shut and he shivered in cold and pain and despair. Then . . . "This bloody, foul, awful coast!" His eyes briefly lost their dullness. "Worse than Scotland! Worse than the Channel! These rotting shoals stick out so bleeding far . . . God Almighty . . ." The effort exhausted him. He did not speak again.

The next man was the first mate, hard, grizzled, Cockney-tough enough to sit up after his jump and stare at the young, slender Perkins, bent over in a fit of coughing. "Well, you blokes don't look like bloody much, but you bloomin' well know your business out here!"

And on their final surge up over the schooner's rail the huge black crewman flew between the great and little boats with a sudden grace, and he, like the mate, sat up immediately and peered about from huge white eyes. But he said nothing.

"Now, lads," boomed Walter Chase, as the surfboat lay off easterly, bobbing and pitching in the smother like a logy cork. "Oars out. We got to clear this shallows afore the wind comes on. Lively now."

The four stern oarsmen pulled mightily while Perkins and Cathcart heaved on the anchor warp. Slowly they moved to windward, their efforts sending rivers of sweat inside the heavy sweaters and slickers in the twelve-degree, forty-knot blast.

"Anchor up, Skipper!" shouted Cathcart while Perkins suddenly bent double, both hands over his mouth.

Walter Chase looked back, his side whiskers black spikes, his huge slicker masking the *Kirkham.* He hated to give the gale an inch, but to get past her stern to the west would be a near thing, and the wind was rising again. He put the steering oar over and they fell off on a big soft wave to starboard. "Pull, boys, we got to stay ahead of these combers."

They rowed eastward, then more southerly and cleared the *Kirkham*'s smashed and sagging bow by forty feet. Walter Chase put his oar to starboard and they pulled under the schooner's lee. It was easier there. The schooner was acting as a breakwater, taking the big ones before they reached the surfboat, and they pulled strongly to the west, the wind hard and vicious on their starboard quarter and the sea confused and breaking everywhere, an endless mouth filled with shifting teeth.

But once beyond the schooner's length it was impossible. Chase put her more towards the south, taking the wind on the beam with the current still northeast and running those great, curling rips in the very shallow spots.

"Jesse," said Walter Chase, leaning forward. "We got to clear this shoal afore the high tide this afternoon. Them rollers'll start to break and we couldn't lay at anchor. And the wind's making up again. Them clouds are coming back."

Jesse Eldridge only nodded. He was pulling too hard to talk. They were moving southeast, but only barely. The *Kirkham* was close behind them and the surfboat was slopping about, taking splash on every wave.

Walter Chase looked at the men they had rescued. His little bright eyes fixed on the first mate and the Negro, their heads buried in coats against the chill. "You fellers. Yank that sail and mast out of there and pitch it over the side. Our sailing days are done!"

The men moved slowly, as best they could, helped by a hand from this or that rower, and finally the outfit went over the side in a piecemeal fashion, trailing astern and finally pulling loose.

George Flood looked up and winked at Walter Chase. "Skipper," he panted, "how you going to explain throwing that valuable govinmint property over the side to the inspector?"

Walter Chase, at that moment fighting a great, half-breaking wave that threatened to broach the surfboat, suddenly winked a gleaming eye back. "George, I'll just tell that feller that we met this here bureaucrat adrift on his very own desk looking for Washington, D.C., and we just plumb did the Christian thing and loaned him our sail."

Charles Cathcart, leaning intently forward as he pulled, burst into a roar of laughter. "Hell's fire, Skipper! They'd just say you didn't get him to fill in the right forms."

Perkins' oar trailed astern and he leaned over the side, vomiting and coughing great, deep, sharp barks above the gale. Cathcart reached toward him, and the surfboat lost way and began to bounce and shift southerly into the troughs. Walter Chase looked piercingly at his men. They *must* clear the shoal now. It would only get worse.

Chase Four entered Perkins' continuity of self-awareness. The boy was sick, probably pneumonia, for his lungs were very wet. He was beaten. The cockney mate's praise had got him through the anchor recover, but now he was completely involved with his cough and nausea.

Chase Four dropped down Perkins' time line seeking a point that would reverberate with the *Kirkham* rescue. . . .

Each year on the last day of July along the islands, the life-saving crews return from a two-month off-duty period to a ten-month routine of patrols and watches. On that night the previous summer, the Coskata crew had produced their usual party. They had hired a banjo and violin from town, asked their wives, relatives, friends, and suppliers to the festive evening, and cleared out the dark apparatus room of its large gear. Colored streamers hung from the suspended life car, and festoons of buoys made arches beneath which the dancers turned. The girls, slim and pretty in ankle-length dresses, puffed sleeves, and swinging hair ringlets, smiled at the tall men in their government blue. Before the light went, they trooped outside to the breeches buoy training tower, and the girls climbed, one above the other up the ladder, and all looked back smiling while George Flood pressed his Kodak button and gave a happy shout.

But the prettiest there was Abigale Coffin with Roland Perkins. When the others returned in the dusk to the laughter and screech of the fiddler's bow, he caught her arm. "Let's go look at the ocean, Abby," he said. She was the nicest girl in the town, always smiling, her eyes so bright and full; and as they walked away from the station, Perkins could barely breathe, his chest was so full of love and hope. "Abby . . . could I . . . would you . . . ?" and he leaned toward her and brought his other arm up behind her back.

Chase Four did not wait for the sharp and hurtful reaction; he had skimmed by it once. Instead, he showed Abby Coffin that Roland Perkins was actually a fine, handsome boy. As she looked at him, she realized how sensitive and brave he would always be, how good and gentle his thoughts were toward her. She turned her face upward and they kissed. Later, under a bright moon, she said breathlessly, "Yes, you can touch me there, Roland."

Perkins, his coughing fit mastered, nodded at Cathcart and began to row strongly. Walter Chase urged them on. "We got to make some depth, boys." Perkins, grinning to himself, pulled and pulled. He knew they would get these men back. Chase was too good a boatman to fail, whatever the wind. They would all get government medals. And he thought of Abby and the medal and how she would hold him when he told her. Slowly the surfboat left the *Kirkham* behind.

George Flood's eyes popped open. "Look back quick, Skipper!" he shouted. Walter Chase spun around. In that instant, the *Kirkham* was dissolving. Her foremast was halfway down, with her main following. The taut and snapping shrouds ripped the quarterboards completely off the starboard side, and the deck buckled in several large pieces. The mizzen fell, and before it struck the water, the entire hull had disappeared. She had gone like smoke in a gale. Flood looked up at Walter Chase. "Dang lucky we didn't wait for another cup of coffee at the station, Skipper!" he shouted.

Walter Chase, fighting the steering oar continually in the heavy and confused seas, still stared back at the unchecked rollers now streaming over the *Kirkham's* last berth. They had taken the last man off less than an hour before. His eyes narrowed and he wondered about the rescue. Everything was so damn near, so chancy.

The Coskata crew rowed and rowed on Rose and Crown Shoal. Sometimes the boat moved west and sometimes it paused and pitched. Noon was past and the sky had darkened again. The wind was rising with the tide, but they were slowly getting into deeper water, into the twelve-fathom channel that cut aimlessly between Rose and Crown and Bass Rip. The waves were longer and not so steep, but the wind was too heavy. They were hardly moving and the men were exhausted. And the current had revolved almost due easterly and was actually setting them back away from Nantucket. This would have to do for now.

"Cathcart! We got to anchor. Handy now!" They lay back with the winds hammering their starboard quarter, all the scope they could muster laid out to their biggest anchor. The men slumped over their shipped oars while Walter Chase shoved the steering oar this way and that, using the current run to steer his boat up and over the combers. The wind was building again and its scream and slash was icy and terrible. Jesse Eldridge, hunched in a nest of sweaters and slicker, looked up at Walter Chase. "Skipper, we didn't even make a mile in three hours. You think that tug'll get out here?"

"I figure he will as long as he thinks there might be some loot on the schooner, Jesse," said Walter Chase. He sensed, in fact, that the tug would not come into these wild shoals. Bitterly he thought of the wonderful strength of her cross-compound steam engine driving that big powerful screw. Yellow, rotten cowards! What was the point of even building such a vessel if you could not find men to man it? The surfboat jumped and tugged at the snapping anchor line. While the crew bailed as the spume and spray came in on them with every wave, Perkins and Cathcart gently tended the anchor line, wrapping it in rags, shifting it a few inches now and then to relieve the chafing.

The sky grew darker as the afternoon wore on and the wind built up again. There was so much agitation and violent activity, so many unexpected swoops and thumps, so many waves that appeared from odd directions and with surprising steepness.

Chase pulled and fought the oar, staring out at the screaming bowl of energy around him while a coldness and fierceness steadied his heart and mind. He would bring these men home, all of them. Nothing anywhere was more important than that. The tug, the life-saving service, the men at their desks in Washington and Boston, the sea and its commerce, the life cars and motor-driven surfboats, the rescues of the past and future, men adrift on the seas of the world and foundering forever in the gales and currents along the coasts, meant nothing beside these few in the Coskata surfboat. He focused his great strength on this single purpose and found a balance between the forces of the storm and his own resolve. They pitched and waited in the freezing blast for the tide to turn.

Dusk comes early to Nantucket in January, and it was almost dark by the time the surfboat had swung clockwise on her tether and now lay a bit west of south. Chase knew they had to go whenever the tide could drive them, and he shouted and joshed the men. Tiredly they put out oars, pulled up the anchor, then struggled off to the west. Chase used his rowers to hold a northerly set, counting on the southeast current to give them a general westerly direction. They took plenty of slop with the waves on their starboard bow, and Chase urged the *Kirkham's* mate and her black crewman to bailing. The boat moved into deeper water, and as the night came on, Chase suddenly saw, on the very rim of his world, the tiny, flashing point of Sankaty Light.

"Hey, boys!" he shouted. "There's old Sankaty and Joe Remsen having fried bluefish for supper with a bit of Medford rum and lime in hot water."

"Dang me, Skipper," said George Flood, "I wouldn't mind the rum, but Joe can keep the bluefish."

"George," said Walter Chase, shaking his head sadly, "I can't make out how you fellers can call yourselves Nantucketers when you like that awful, smelly cod better'n a little fried blue."

This discussion, which ebbed and flowed at the station depending on who was cook that week, somehow cheered Jesse Eldridge immensely. "Walter," he said, loudly and firmly, "even them rich Boston summer folk won't give a nickel a pound for blues. You know that as well as I do."

Chase leaned on the oar and turned them a bit more northerly, staring off at the lighthouse. He roared with laughter. "Jesse, them Boston folk smack their lips over three-day boiled cabbage and corn beef, flaked cod that would turn a hog's stomach, and fin and haddy so hard it would break a shark's jaw. Hell's delight, they wouldn't even *notice* a nice hot little blue laying in a nest of parsley, new potatoes, and melted butter."

They rowed on and on toward the light, and the men turned now and then to stare at the pinpoint, so bright and yet so tiny against the black swirl of wind. When they turned back to where the *Kirkham* had been, they saw answering bright and tiny spots in Walter Chase's eye somehow reflecting and focusing Sankaty.

By ten that night the wind was blowing a three-quarter gale, and the current was rotating to the north-east. They could not go against it, and Walter Chase ordered the anchor down again. Now the wind, filled with a fitful snow, was bitter, and the men slumped against each other, their sweat drying coldly under their clothes, their heads nodding. Chase continually worked the steering oar, roused the men as they drifted off into frozen sleep, ordered the bow crewmen to watch the chafing of the line, and continually rotated his head seeking the great seas moving in the dark. They suddenly appeared as dim, faintly phosphorescent mountains that dashed out of and into the dark at terrifying speeds.

In the intense and shouting dark, the seas loomed huge and unsuspected. There was a wildness about them, a wholly random cruelty. The storm had blown for two days and unusual current motions had been set going. Walter Chase's head swiveled back and forth. He sensed the movement, the surge and back-flow. The chill ate at his bones but his own cold resolve was more arctic still.

Chase Five examined the lumpy and stationary sea. He then examined the rate of change of the water profiles. This was a deadly business! The circulation due to wind stress had rotated the current further than usual to the east. This set up a possible amplification with the flow between Bass Rip and McBlair's Shoal. There was a statistical possibility of one or more resonant occurrences that night! Yet, they were still relatively unlikely. No! Chase Five clamped the time flow even tighter and increased the gradient. Within minutes a resonance would actually occur! The wave would build at the north end of Rose and Crown, receiving energy from the cross flow and a sudden wind gust stress. It would break in a mile-long line just north of them and reach them cresting at eighteen feet. The chance of their staying upright was one in three. The chance of their not swamping was . . . nil!

Chase Five, within the theoretical bounds set by entropy flow requirements, stopped time utterly. The continuum waited as Chase Five's neural interconnections achieved a higher level of synthesis. He saw a single possibility. If this resonant wave was unlikely enough . . . yes . . . that was it! Extreme value probability theory could be modified within the time domain, providing that no significantly less likely event was occurring at that instant in the energy continuum. He could lower the expectation and make the wave more unlikely without interaction within the energy domain. Furthermore, it was not just the wave itself that was unlikely, but the wave interpreted by Chase Five, himself a most unlikely event.

That was it! He changed the probabilities, and the wave, instead of building towards its terrifying height, received its new energies at slightly different times and . . . No!

The wave was suddenly building again! Chase Five sensed some other manipulation. Staggered, he clamped tightly on the time flow and asked his first question: "Who?"

When Keeper Chase modified the laws of extreme value probability within the continuum, he forced us time-using observers to become participants in his struggle with the storm. While highly unlikely events occur infrequently, they exercise a hugely disproportionate effect on the evolution of the continuum. Just as a coastline on Keeper Chase's world will lie unchanged for a hundred years, to be altered drastically by a single unlikely storm lasting a few hours, so the improbable but possible events in the evolution of stellar and information systems often determine the long-term character of huge volumes of energy and temporal space. We could not, then, allow such essential probabilities to be manipulated at the whim of energy storms and energy-users. Thus we intervened and canceled the change. Keeper Chase detected us at once and asked his first question. We decided to answer him . . . almost totally.

Chase Five received the full brunt of the information dump. Like the sky falling in from every angle, the answer to his question flowed faster than thought into his mind. It was an implosion of data, a total, sudden awareness of the continuum, of time and energy and information and their interactions. Of worlds and stars, creatures and spaces, hidden truths and intricate insights.

Chase Five was staggered. He clamped on the time flow and tried to organize it all. Like a swimmer, thrown deeply into the dark blue of the deep ocean, he fought and rose toward the light of day, moving through a boundless mass of data. Yet, what was happening? Why was he so deeply involved with these others? How did the *Kirkham,* one in ten thousand among such schooners, and these men, a few among millions, come to be at the center of all this? Chase Five assimilated the focal points of the continuum, but he did not yet understand himself or the nature of his adversaries. Clamping and clamping on the time stream, he desperately asked his second question:

"God?"

Irony, in the sense understood by those in Keeper Chase's world group, is not a normal component of time-using organizations and duties. Yet Keeper Chase's second question to us achieved the exact essence of that special quality. For if there was a single conscious entity within the entire continuum at the moment who qualified as "God," in the sense of Keeper Chase's question, it was Keeper Chase himself. We could not determine how large an information excess Keeper Chase could tolerate, but his confusion seemed to offer us an opportunity. We responded with the remaining information that we had withheld the first time: we showed Keeper Chase how the continuum was organized within its various aspects and, finally, the nature of consciousness within this organization and its relationship with the information, time, and energy aspects of the whole.

The second dump of information was not as extensive, but far more staggering. For Chase Five finally saw himself within the total continuum. He saw the circularity and hermetic nature of his activity at the *Kirkham,* the unlikely, really senseless character of the rescue and how unimportant, really meaningless were the men now barely alive in the wet and pitching boat. Good Lord, what was the point anyway? His control wavered and time began to slip. The wind moved back towards its own natural pace. The seas became more independent. . . .

Now wait! Chase Five, in his puzzlement and despair, still processed data. And suddenly he saw the fallacy, the problem with their attacks against him. He steadied and clamped time. Yes! Yes, of course! He was stronger! The circularity didn't matter! What mattered was *only* the event! Everything led to that. And the more *unlikely* it was, the more *essential* it became. Yes! He, Walter Chase, Keeper of the Coskata Life Saving Station, was exactly and completely his own justification. And now Chase Five struck back at them. Masterful in his total control of information, gigantic astride the interlaced worlds of energy and time, he stated his third and final question. But because he completely dominated the continuum in all its aspects, he no longer asked. For he knew with complete certainty that none of them could deny what he stated.

"I am central to the evolution of the continuum. My control and my improbability are proof of that!"

At once the growing wave received its various inputs in harmless and likely sequences and passed under the Coskata boat as a huge but almost unnoticed roller. And with that, the storm on the Nantucket South Shoals began to die. For it, like all storms, had to obey the laws of probabilities, and after two harsh days, it was moving off and softening as it went.

Walter Chase, the steering oar now inboard as the wind slackened, saw that dawn and the new tide were coming together. "All right, boys! This time we'll get there!" he shouted. In came the anchor and off they went, the great seas cresting no longer, the wind lessening, and the temperature rising as snow squalls came and went, grey against a dull dawn.

On and on they rowed, and Walter Chase now became aware that Perkins looked odd. His eyes were shining, liquid and bright, and his cheeks were much too red and also shining strangely. The boy rowed as strongly as any, but Chase watched him with more and more concern.

"Perkins," shouted Walter Chase, "see if that mate from the *Kirkham* can relieve you for a while."

But Perkins was thinking of Abby on the beach. She would probably be there when they came in, for her brother was in the Surfside crew and he would have told her that they were out. "I'm OK, Skipper," he said in a voice that Chase could barely hear. Chase peered through the snow at the rowers. Perkins was very sick. Perkins must ...

Chase Six realized that Perkins was dying. The boy's level of consciousness integration had slipped drastically. Desperate, Chase Six plummeted down Perkins' time line seeking solutions everywhere. But the lessening of the storm had sapped his abilities. He could no longer clamp on time or integrate his hard-won information to tasks like this. Yet his very agony gave him the control to achieve the data that crushed, and crushed again, his hopes. How tenuous and marvelous self-awareness was in the continuum! How delicate, beyond yet imbedded within the energy system, linked with loops of information, operating within and yet outside of time. Perkins had driven himself, and been driven by Chase, beyond reintegration. And yet, Perkins was filled with joy! Within himself, Chase Six finally wept. And as he did, his powers fled away in an unending stream like the fog of a harsh night evaporating as the morning sun pierced through and through it.

Keeper Chase's great time-based powers failed as the emergency abated. Unable to maintain the temporal gradient without the urgency of the storm, he could no longer retrieve or even sustain his vast information resource in any practical sense. Yet he had defeated us and dominated the continuum at almost every moment of his adventure. Staggered after his second question and the implications of our answers, he went on to his final and greatest feat. He dared us to prove that he was not an essential evolutionary force within the continuum. Since such a determination would require understanding of other continuums, if such exist, and that necessary understanding would involve an information entropy gradient so vast that it could not even be theoretically sustained, he effectively blocked all further intervention.

But in the end he could not save his youngest crewman. He learned that conscious self-awareness is the most improbable and delicate balance of all within the continuum. Even his great strengths could not bring Surfman Perkins back from the temporal disintegration towards which he had slipped. If the energy-users of Keeper Chase's world group understood how novel and tenuous such consciousness actually is, they would surely behave far differently than they do.

The actual effects of his alterations within the continuum will only become evident in distant times and through much statistical activity on our part. But his greatest effect was the introduction of his third question, to which we may never have a complete or satisfactory answer. Of course, the so-called "heroes" of Keeper Chase's world group always have this as their primary purpose; that is, the introduction of central and intractable questions.

At a little after nine in the morning of the twenty-first of January, the Coskata boat was sighted through the fading snow from the bluffs of Siasconset, eight miles south of the shore they had left the day before. Soon the entire community was out on the beach, silently watching the surfboat moving toward them, steered by Walter Chase standing at the stern.

The 'Sconset school teacher, a young, thin man who had spent two years reading literature at Harvard College, ran up the bluff, a dozen children behind him. As he topped the rise, the thin sun suddenly pierced the damp air and illuminated the tiny boat and its huge captain, looming black even a half mile out.

"Godfreys mighty!" exclaimed the young man to no

one in particular. "It's Captain Ahab, himself!" for he believed that literature and life were contiguous.

"Naw tain't," said Widow Tilton. "Hit's Skipper Chase and the Coskata surfboat." She turned to stare at the young man and laughed. "Hit's the only red surfboat around. Skipper painted it red after the Muskeget boat was almost lost in the ice last December, 'cause no one could see it. They wrote from Boston. Said it was nonregulation. Skipper Chase, he wrote back. Don't remember all he wrote, but there was something in his letter about them desk navigators whose experience with ice amounted to sucking it out of their whiskey and sodas at lunch."

The school teacher had been only half listening, but now he turned and grinned at Widow Tilton. "He said that to them, did he?" The young man stared again at the approaching boat and then ran down the sand hill. "Come on, boys!" he shouted back at his class. "Let's help get this boat up!"

The Coskata boat grounded silently in a long swell, and a huge crowd waded into the backwash and pulled her up the slick sand. Everyone tried to help the men get out, yet still no one cheered. Instead, soft and kind words flew everywhere, and joy and comfort seemed to warm the very beach.

Walter Chase boomed at the Macy boys to get their oxen and haul the boat up to the dunes. Then he turned and saw Perkins helped and held by Abby Coffin. The boy could no longer speak. Chase smiled at the girl. "Abby, don't take him home. Get him to your sister-in-law's house here in 'Sconset and put him to bed. Get him warm, quick as you can!"

But Abby knew. She could see the emptiness in Roland Perkins' eyes, his fevered cheeks. She wept, so full of grief and pride and love that she could not speak either. But always afterwards she remembered how sharp and yet sad Skipper Chase's eyes had been when he spoke to her and how completely he dominated the beach in those moments at the end of the rescue.

"Isaiah!" shouted Walter Chase. The youngster dashed up, beaming all over his face, so proud that Skipper Chase had picked him out of the great crowd.

"Yessir, Skipper!" he grinned.

"How's that hoss of yours, Isaiah?" said Walter Chase, and now he grinned too.

"Fastest hoss on Nantucket, Skipper," replied the boy promptly. "She'll win at the summer fair for sure!"

"Well, you climb aboard that nag and hustle for town. Find my wife and tell her we got back safe. Then find the rest of them. You know where the crew's folks live?"

The boy nodded and dashed off. Everyone was now moving up the beach toward the village. Each crewman of the *Kirkham* or man of Coskata was surrounded by residents helping them along, throwing coats or blankets over their shoulders, talking at them about the impossible miracle of the rescue.

Captain McCloud of the *Kirkham* staggered along between his huge black crewman and the Widow Tilton, herself well over six feet and two hundred and fifty pounds. Suddenly the old man pitched forward on his knees, pulling the weakened Negro down with him. "Dear God!" he shouted. "Thank Thee for this deliverance! Thank Thee for sparing thy humble servants. Thank Thee . . ."

Widow Tilton pulled the old man to his feet and, looking back, saw Walter Chase, huge against the dull sun, his tiny eyes like daytime stars. "You better not worry about thanking God, Mister," she suddenly said loudly. "It was Skipper Chase got you back here, and don't ever forget that!"

"Walter." It was his uncle beside him. "When they said you was coming in, I put on a gallon of coffee. Come on. Why, man, you're shaking like a leaf!"

Indeed, Walter Chase suddenly was shaking. He could not stop it and he let his uncle lead him over the dune and down to the little house with its roaring drift-wood-filled fire and the huge blackened pot of power-ful coffee.

"Uncle," said Walter Chase as he sipped from a huge mug, "I'm shaking so damn much I've got to drink this outside."

He opened the door and stepped back into the nar-row, rutted 'Sconset street just as Joe Remsen, sharp in his blue uniform and issue cap, driving the dapper black and gold-trimmed buggy of the Light House Service, pulled by a smart, high-stepping bay, whirled around the corner and pulled up short in a cloud of dust.

"God in Heaven, Walter!" shouted Joe Remsen. "You all did get back!"

Walter Chase, his huge hands still shaking contin-uously in the thin, cold morning, looked smiling up at his old friend. "Joe, that's just the handsomest one-hoss outfit on the island," he said simply.

"Walter, they say she came apart less than an hour after you got them off! I saw her masts go down at noon yesterday from the tower!"

Walter Chase stretched suddenly and stared, quite piercingly, back at Joe Remsen. "Well," he said, "we didn't need her after the crew got off, did we, Joe?"

At the time his old friend thought Walter Chase was joking, and he laughed out loud. But thinking back on that moment in later years, he realized that Walter Chase had meant what he said. The *Kirkham* had been allowed to collapse because she somehow wasn't *needed* any more. Yet he never asked about it again but only wondered.

Joe Remsen climbed down from the buggy and shook his head. "We figured you were goners. That damn tug went as far as Great Point and then turned back last night. Too blamed rough, they said, the rotten cowards! By God, Walter, there won't never be another rescue like this one! You better believe that! They're going to build that canal one of these days. Them gasoline engines'll get better and they'll put them in the surfboats. God Almighty, you took seven of them off. Not one lost. Twenty-six hours out in that smother! It's a miracle! Why, man, you moved heaven and earth . . ."

The hot coffee drained its warmth through Walter Chase and suddenly he felt drowsy. "Joe, we never did try a drail for squeteague out there. Just too blamed busy the whole time. . . ."

And the two old friends grinned and chuckled at each other in the winter sunlight on a 'Sconset street.

Three Days
at the
End of the World

The First Day

The research vessel *William Scoresby* lies at the main dock of the ocean campus on a falling tide. On this sunny October morning the wind blows gently from the north, and the bay and sky are brilliant, transparent with that dark blue of the New England fall. At night the bay and coast will wink with lights and pinpoint colors in the sharp, dry air. Leaning on the rail of the well deck, I am tensely awaiting the completion of repairs on the big profiler, that essential acoustic searchlight that prints with tiny sparks the nature of the sediments and water miles beneath the keel.

I feel . . . hard to describe my almost unbearable anticipation, the tight knot of impatience, and some fear, I confess, yet an exaltation too. Feelings seldom met in my profession, yet not completely unfamiliar. I have felt this heightened sense before . . . here, two years past on that last, angry night when my wife left, forever, to her teaching job in Michigan . . . a few times, not quite the same perhaps, when I overdid on grass. (My heedless, careless children have dealt with me so casually, but they did turn me on and occasionally will deign to buy me a little.) I find that occasionally a strong grass trip will produce a kind of artificial anticipation, a sense of impending . . . something . . . and I feel, like today, overcome with a formless restlessness.

Yet I am certainly an appropriate person to preside over one of the ends of our world. A Distinguished Professor of Oceanography, winner of the Humboldt Medal, discoverer of the Franklin Projection, a method of extrapolating synoptic data to predict future trends . . . and named for me. (Next month I will be made a Fellow of the American Meteorological Society.)

Out beyond Long Island, well offshore beyond the shelf where the water plunges to black and quiet ooze, there lies a source of infection, a deadly place of death and . . . yes . . . sin. That is certainly what we seek in our small vessel, the legacy of an act of sin. When my wife left me, shouting on that final bitter night, she surely saw me as a great sinner. "Your only love is for things of death!" she had grated at me, her teeth a hard line, her eyes bright and full of hatred. Perhaps she had a point. I was born too late to make the great discoveries, the exciting leaps of intuition and intellect that Scoresby and Humboldt and the others made with their slow and dangerous ships and their crude devices fashioned of wood and bone. And, yet, that isn't quite right. They are as much a part of what is happening as I am. All our works lead to this point in the history of the North Atlantic Basin. How could we have prevented it? Once humans gained the ability to influence the total activity of the earth, our eventual sin was inevitable. My casual children would dismiss this voyage as only another death trip.

Listen! I have had a fine education! I was forced to take courses to prepare me for the end of the world. They were mainly in the Department of English Literature at a small and rich liberal arts college in southern Vermont. For though I majored in physics there, we were not expected to regard ourselves as professionals. That all came later, in the law, medical, and scientific schools where facts flooded the academic day. At Wilston College we were to become full men, men who could apply the humanities to the difficult job of running the world. It's easy to see now that those few decent professors in the humanities courses were shoveling shit against the tide. The Wilston system was too chancy, too casual. America is governed by graduates of Wilston, their humanities seminars long forgotten or ignored. The CIA chiefs, the slumlords, the robber barons of oil and profits, the cynical politicians, all too many from the Wilstons of America.

Me too. I must stop trying to escape from this guilt, large and terrible as it is. I could have spoken two years ago and I did not. I certainly could have spoken last spring, after the second cruise, but I did not have the strength of the source. I *had* to have another set of points. My professional cleverness has always been in the interpretation of data. I had to get more solid facts, cold and terrible to flog them with, all those noted and important Wilston grads. And we are, after all, old boys together. I have friends in the Office of the Oceanographer of the Navy, at Scrips and Woods Hole, where weapons and environmental research go hand in hand, where manipulation of the seas is the goal and where life and death are so intermixed that no full professor can tell them apart. I hated my wife when she tore at me with her half-baked, rad-lib crap, but there is some truth in her people's anger. If only they weren't so weak and doctrinaire and uninformed.

I took a course in modern poetry at Wilston. (Part of my "humanities distribution" requirement. This university still has such things today.) It was the best course I've ever taken. The professor was a cheerful, red-faced drunk, given to reading poems in a resonant, slightly hoarse voice. He was the only undergraduate teacher I ever had who treated me exactly as an equal human being of exactly equal worth and with ideas of exactly the same importance as his own. I was an honor student, clever, articulate, hating the humanities as vague, stupid and disorganized. Looking back, I see that he really loved us all, and especially the thorny, noisy, clever ones. Did he really believe that we would behave better in the Pentagon or the Department of State because he had read us poetry?

My undergraduate days came after World War II, a time when the world's end was a lively topic. On one remarkable day, Professor Feingold was plowing cheerfully through T.S. Eliot and had spent some minutes comparing Eliot's end-of-the-world ("not with a bang but a whimper") with that of Robert Frost ("fire and ice").

I hated Eliot. I thought him exactly the kind of poet Wilston professors would like; effete, delicate, upper class, gently antisemitic. "I think the bang and whimper poem is the most self-indulgent baloney in the book." I spoke firmly. Feingold grinned. He loved to argue.

"Yes, you certainly don't take to old T.S., Mr. Franklin. You find him faggy, I suppose?" That was a pretty tough start. We were, after all, upper-middle-class sophisticates and supposedly above making value judgments on a man's sexual preferences. But he was only cooling me off.

"Not that," I said more slowly. "I just find the idea that the world is coming to an end because a girl screws before she's married and some Jews own property instead of people in the Church of England . . . well, it's all just ridiculous!" A murmur of assent swept over the class. I was winning!

Feingold didn't seem to know it. "Ah," he said briskly. "Eliot is talking about individual moral decay with, I confess, some unattractive examples thrown in. Do you think that moral decay is an inadequate image to project the end of the world?"

"It *is* inadequate. The Greeks collapsed after the Peloponnesian Wars and the moral decay those caused, and the Romans faded after four hundred years of all kinds of moral decay. The world still hasn't ended in either place."

"Let me give you two thoughts." Feingold shook his fingers at the class. "In our world, the world of atomic bombs, moral decay might actually lead to a real end of the world. That is, a real, scientifically possible end of the world. Secondly, the world ends for each man when he dies. I'm assuming you don't believe in ghosts or reincarnation. What Eliot may be saying is that when a man dies in a state of moral corruption, his death is a whimper rather than a bang. You mention Greece and Rome. I think they both rather prove my point. They did, both of them, end with rather a whimper. Greece providing the tutors and hired brains of imperial Rome, which, if I remember correctly, sort of faded away four hundred years later when the barbarians wandered in from the woods."

"All right," I said. "I'll grant that the physical destruction of life on earth might be regarded as an act of moral decay. . . ."

"Might!" shouted Feingold, his voice steady and powerful. *"Might* be regarded as an act of moral decay! Why, don't you see that the suicide of the race is the final, the ultimate culmination of all our moral collapses; the endless butchery of serfs and soldiers, the Flanders trenches, the death camps, Hiroshima. That would be the final and greatest act of evil ever consummated, the total triumph of hate and death!" He grinned again. "Sorry to interrupt. You say you grant my first point. Fine. Let's go on to the second."

I never got sore with Feingold, but I didn't want to let him get away with all that vague and emotional hokum. "I *don't* grant your first point, as a matter of fact. A nuclear war is one thing, an accident is another. Suppose our excessive use of combustion changes the climate so that we can no longer exist. That would be stupid as Hell, but I don't see it as an act of complete depravity."

Feingold made an elaborate shrug to the class and held his hands palms up. *"Exactly* Eliot's point. Stupid. Chicks giving it away to anyone. Slumlords gouging. Little guys dying in meaningless campaigns in odd corners of the world. Stupid people doing stupid things. Driving their cars to nowheres to pass empty days of boredom and polluting the air as they go. How much of a whimper do you want?" The class snickered. He had dragged me one hundred and eighty degrees around to some kind of acceptance of the poem's ideas.

I never won with Feingold, but I actually liked the way he pulled his switcheroos and swamped you in a mud bath of rhetoric. "Let's get to the second idea," I doggedly plugged ahead. "The idea of individual death as the end of the world. I might actually participate in the end of the physical world and yet find it a moral and heroic experience."

Feingold peered at me in a very alert way. And as

I look back on that class now, what he said next seems very wonderful and prophetic. He said, "Yes, you might. I doubt that I'll participate in the end of the world." (He didn't. He died of liver failure in 1967.) "But you may be there. And . . . yes, you might even stage-manage some of the proceedings. And if you do, remember Eliot's ideas of style. Give the rest of us a classy end. And a dignified end. Elegant, with lectures and slides." Now he was kidding me again, but I could deal with that OK.

"I should think you'd be a fan of rage and struggle." And, raising my hand, I intoned a line from my favorite poet in that course, Dylan Thomas. "Rage against the falling of the night."

Feingold was delighted. He beamed. "Ah . . . of course! But that is a poet's reaction, not a scientist's. You probably think the great idea wars today are between the sciences and the humanities. Not so. You people are only the handmaidens of the historians and economists, the people who think in aggregates, in statistical processes. The technicians are only resident wizards, employees of social scientists. Veblen understood this. You are children with magical hands. The great ideological wars of the future will be between poets and historians. The one talking only of individuals, the other only of large groups and large policies. Wilfred Owen versus General Haig. Well, we all know who will win, don't we? But the fight is worth making anyhow. That's all Thomas said. Acting, fighting, is the core of life even if the end is not attainable."

So that was how classes went in English Lit 456 (Modern Poetry: 1900 to the present). Not much preparation for our voyage on R/V *William Scoresby,* but something to be grateful for, I suppose. I wish Professor Feingold were here now with his glib tricks and his moon face. With him watching, I think I might do it better. I would not, in any case, be lonely. Anyway, he was my friend. I wish I had told him that sometime. I hope he knew.

Marty Balder, leading ocean tech, is at my elbow. "Sparker's working again. I think it'll be OK. Anyway, Jill is going along and she can hack whatever might come up." I nod. Jill is a steady, capable tech, one of the spin-offs of equal-opportunity hiring. "Marty, are the Van Dorns OK? And the oxygen sensors?"

"All checked," he says briskly. "Have a good trip."

We have lost two hours and will not be on station until almost midnight. I walk rapidly forward to the wet lab on the well deck where the nearest intercom is located.

"Bridge? Wet lab."

The chief mate answers. "Bridge, aye."

"We're ready to steam, Jim."

"Aye, aye, Perfesser Franklin," and a moment later the air whistle shrieks over the quiet campus. On shore, a group of my undergraduates hastily take leave of two girls fetchingly dressed for tide-pool specimen collecting and chase, shouting, up the gangway. The campus cops muster to handle the lines and gangway, the engines rev, and in moments we are backing off from the pier, a few persons waving as our flags snap briskly in the wind. I am so tense! I will check the Van Dorns myself. I will calibrate the oxygen equipment. I will prepare the clamshell dredge and specimen bottles. I have many hours of steaming to fill with work.

The *Scoresby* is the smaller of the two ocean-going vessels operated by the university. She is one hundred and eighty feet long and began life as a Navy coastal freighter working the Japan-Korea run during that long-ago war. The director of the lab named her for a Scottish whaling captain and amateur oceanographer, Fellow of the Royal Society, and Doctor of Divinity.

The director's main interests are cetology and fish acoustics, and Scoresby was a big student of whales. I approved of the naming because Scoresby was also an apt experimentalist and owed to no man in his ability to draw general conclusions from specific observations. My thing too.

My last run on *Scoresby* was in the spring, another two-day outing beyond the shelf, well east of Long Island. Normally I don't make offshore cruises in the fall with the undergrads, but after looking at the spring data, I knew we could not wait another year. So I went to the ship committee and fought for these two days to be taken out of a one-week refit period and, in the end, with the director backing my phoney, academic reasons, got the time over the dead body of the marine superintendent. There are advantages to being the star in the director's crown, but of course I will pay the next time ship or government-surplus favors are handed out. Funny how I keep assuming things will be the same when we return. How will the director deal with all of this? I cannot foresee it.

We are plowing a straight course a little south of east. The sea is brilliant and the day so bright your eyes ache from looking at the horizon. The wind is dropping and we will have a perfect night. None of my undergraduates is seasick, an unusual situation. They loll chatting about the deck sucking on soft drinks from the machine in the wardroom. I should take a nap in my cabin but know that would be hopeless. I have had the Van Dorn water samplers modified so that we can get dissolved oxygen without draining them first. I ask Jill and Harry Harvey, my assistant and doctoral student, to help me check each one with surface water. I am brusque, professional, fatherly. Do they know that things are amiss, that I am wound as tight as tangled B/T wire? Probably Harry does. He has known me two years. Also, he is as smart as I am and has the added quickness of the young.

Finally the loudspeakers announce dinner and we straggle below. An oceanographic vessel shares at least one characteristic with all tourist ships, the essential need for large amounts of good food served often. One is either sick or ravenous on these cruises, and the undergrads, crowding into the tiny dining room, grin cheerfully at the huge platters of fried chicken on the galley stove. My students, our tech, and some of the crew share tiny four- and six-person tables, but at the corner table only two of us may sit in slightly more comfortable chairs emblazoned with *Captain* and *Chief Scientist* on their backs. This is an essential arrangement. If the captain and chief scientist are not forced to deal socially with each other several times a day, the voyage may turn to feuds and duels from which flow only missed stations and lost gear.

I sit alone, waiting with some anticipation the appearance of my table mate, another and certainly our ultimate example of equal opportunity: Olga Petersen, master.

A child in Sweden, she came with relatives to the U.S., where she grew up and married a young ship's officer. Rather than sit home waiting for him, she studied and passed her third-mate's exams, and they then sought assignments to the same ship. Her last berth before this one was as first on an oil-field supply vessel out of Perth, Scotland. Her husband was master. They were out in the January smother of the North Sea trying to resupply a rig when the big wave came, one of those freaks that appear now and then. It caught the vessel maneuvering at the edge of the landing platform. Petersen saw it coming and went hard astern and he was backing well but the monster just picked up the ship and surfed it into the landing stage

and rig struts. The pilot house was sliced off with
Petersen inside while his wife and the docking party
were creamed up against the deck house when the ship
decelerated and all the water came aboard. They sank
in moments. Olga Petersen was the only survivor. She
already had masters papers, and so when this job was
advertised, in she came. A tough broad, I thought,
when *that* story went around.

The first cruise she captained for us was the director's annual pilgrimage north to fuss with the whales
at the edge of the pack. The weather blew all to hell
and *Scoresby* took a tremendous flogging. At the
storm's height the director broke his ankle in a fall
down a ladder, and *Scoresby* wound up rescuing a research vessel from the U of Miami. Anyway, I was
having lunch with the director soon after his return,
he surrounded by his crutches and his big white foot
up on a stool for, I thought to myself, people to kiss.
Up came our publicist in his plaid trews and large grin
to slap the director's shoulder. "Bad luck about your
foot. The whole thing sounds terrible. What happened?
Was the captain having her period?"

The director's eyes narrowed. "Bill, Captain Petersen is the ablest officer this school has ever had. She
has rough-water ability I couldn't believe. And she
saved our asses up there. She's tough. She'd boil your
balls for breakfast, Bill!"

This was the director's macho or he-man side, seen
mainly with admirals and the humanities faculty. He
spoke loudly to make his point, and I never heard
another crack about our lady captain after that. But
I couldn't bear letting the director, no fan of women's
lib, get off quite so easy. "Sounds like you're ready to
lobby for the equal rights amendment?" I tried not to
smile.

The director refused this bait. "Perhaps I am for it,"

he muttered. "That woman saved my life. She steered through hell and we weren't hurt. And when we came up on that Miami boat! What a mess! A-frame over the side and slamming on every roll, a thud you could hear for miles. Mast and booms down, a twenty-degree list. We would have looked like that or worse if she hadn't piloted."

"Too bad she wasn't steering when the big wave hit in the North Sea."

The director shook his head. "When that big one comes, there's no fighting it. Maybe in the open with room to maneuver, but that close to a rig they had no chance."

"Good evening, Dr. Franklin."

I look up. She is just sitting down, a woman less bulky than I had imagined but tall and sturdy, dressed in neat khakis with her shirt neck open. Her sleeves are rolled to elbows and I see muscled, sunburned arms. Yet the wrists are womanly, small, the hands quite graceful. Her smile is wide and pleasant.

"Hello, Captain." I rise halfway and then sit, wondering if I should have risen at all. Captain Petersen nods cheerfully to acknowledge my courtesy with the friendliest of looks.

"What fine weather for your cruise," she says. "We're making wonderful time. I think we may reach your first station a little after twenty-hundred hours."

"Terrific!" She certainly can crowd this old bucket. "I was sorry to miss you Saturday." (Yesterday I had given my station list and research plan to the chief mate, the captain being off the ship.)

"Yes, I had to see the yard boss about our refit," she replies. I wonder if this is a slight needle about my stealing two days from the lay-up period. I look at her face closely but see only the most cheerful and open expression. Her sharp blue eyes are softened by her blond, short hair and light but full eyebrows. But at the corners are the spiderweb lines from long work on the bridges of ships, the brown tightness of the sea person. She seems very professional, a capable skipper. She looks like the person who did what the director said. Except she is not . . . tough. Rather, controlled, I think. In charge of events. Tough does not connote the smartness I see.

"I hope these two days are not messing up your yard business."

She smiles so warmly! "Dr. Franklin, the yard has ample time to complete its work, starting Tuesday. I told the ship committee that when they asked."

Our masses of fried chicken, French fries, fried tomatoes, and fried zucchini arrive and we begin to eat. The food is greasy and delicious. A quiet falls on the dining room. "Is this a particularly interesting area we're going to?" she asks. "You've been here before?"

I look up, startled. "Well . . . yes . . . it has some interest. How did you know I was out here before?"

She laughs in a most open way. She is certainly as cheerful a captain as I have ever met. "I'm a snooper when it comes to chief scientists," she says. "I consult the logs of past cruises. Then I know what to expect. I read about the director's past cruises into the pack ice. That helped me to understand the director. And that helped me to help him."

Now I laugh. "And you discovered that the director is as mean as a treed wolverine, as cussed as a Model T in the rain, and as unpredictable as a rattler under the bed?"

Off she goes laughing again. She is so jolly! "The director is a bold and resourceful man," she says finally. "And I know you and he are old associates. You are the only one he sees as an equal, and I think you may regard him so as well."

That is certainly both an astute and a gracious thing to say. "I think I can run a better experiment than the director," I reply, "but I could never match his style. He's one of the top two or three bigshots in ocean-science administration in the world, and he's up there playing old Bill Scoresby in the pack ice, risking his neck and having the time of his life. I can just imagine his satisfaction when you took that Miami wreck in tow."

She shakes her hair back and laughs again. "His first signal was, 'This will cost you guys four martinis at the next acoustics bash.' We had to tie him into a chair on the bridge, the swells were still heavy."

But a new idea strikes me. "And what did you discover from the logs of my cruises?" Suddenly, I wonder very much what she will say.

She smiles only a little. "Well, you are kindly but perhaps impatient. You improvise beautifully. You are not known to ever make a mistake."

I am shaken. "Captain Petersen, the night my wife left me, she said that same thing. When you just said it, it sounded like a blessing. When my wife said it, it became a curse." That is a scene I don't like to recall. The tenseness had flowed away, talking to this handsome woman, but remembering that evening, I feel my stomach tight and knotted once more.

She nods. "Never making mistakes can be a curse. It seems to affront those who do. It is an affront that grows with time."

I must be looking very woebegone, for she suddenly rises and half takes, half shakes my hand. "Thank you for an interesting dinner, Dr. Franklin. And don't worry about being too capable. We professionals must stick together, you and the director, me, a few others. We are a precious few, Dr. Franklin, a band of brothers."

That seems to me a very warm and generous parting and I suddenly feel better. I think about her and her husband, backing down on that great wave, and I can see none of that terrible agony in her round and open face. But she is a very controlled person. A very private person. I like our captain. I want us to be friends.

At twenty twenty-three we slow and stop, rolling only slightly on a calm and moonlit sea. I decide to pull a Van Dorn string first. The profiler shows a good gooey bottom, but I want to establish our location within the affected zone before we get a chunk of sediment. I leave Harry Harvey and the undergrads with the winch and samplers on deck while Jill and I watch the descent on the big profiler in the below-decks electronics lab. I always use an acoustic target end-weight when sampling in water this deep so that I can track the end of the string in relation to the bottom. Down goes the echo, the sparks running along the paper and smelling like old streetcars in the rain. As the string descends, we see the echo pause as they splice on new sampling bottles every few hundred feet. "Pretty close," says Jill finally, turning to look at me.

I punch the intercom button. "Ah . . . well deck, this is profiler." I squint at the papermarks. "We only have two hundred feet of clearance left. Don't put this last sampler deeper than fifty feet and then shoot the works."

I leave Jill to watch the retrieval on the sparker and climb to the well deck. The first messenger weight has gone down and, hopefully, is shutting the top bottle and setting free the next messenger which will close the second unit, and so on down the string. On the first sampler I have added a spring-deployed acoustic target which will tell us if the entire closure sequence is complete. We wait, imagining the lead messengers hurtling down the line into the dark. "Bottom sampler closed," says Jill over the speaker. "A perfect run!"

I think: We don't have them back yet, sweetie. But the line is running onto the winch, and the first sampler comes up the side of the ship and over the rail. Harry Harvey and an undergrad open the little door I have added and pop in the oxygen sensor. There must be no chance of contamination with surface oxygen. Harry sets the meter and peers at the dial. There is a pause.

"Shit!" he says suddenly. "Something's wrong. Less than two parts per million." Suddenly the deck is very quiet. Everybody has turned and is looking at me. Everybody knows that this is about half the expected surface value out here. Everybody now knows that the old data freak, the "ocean fox" (yes, they called me that when they gave me the Humboldt medal), is onto something heavy. Harry is blinking nervously at me.

I think: Relax, kids, it's only the fucking end of the world. I had planned this station to be just outside the infected region, and instead we are deep within it. Either the spreading rate is much greater than I predicted, or . . . and this "or" is much scarier . . . the source strength is so great, so overwhelming, that the gradient from the center is an order of magnitude more than I found last spring. I must change the entire plan, estimate new stations. I was going to work inward along a radius line; now I must work outwards. I must plan new intervals, but I cannot project until we get another station. My thoughts begin to unravel a little. We only have twelve or so hours for this. Jesus Christ! They are all standing around me, the moon bright, the water soft and calm. The stars are sharp points over the great bowl of water of which we are the center. I must go to the bridge with a new station. I must get my special chart, the chart only I have seen that shows the source location and the oxygen isopleths from the other cruises.

"For Christ's sake!" I suddenly shout at them. "Get the rest of the string aboard! Get off your asses! We've got much more to do than I thought! Move!" Guiltily they start from their reverie and the deck work begins again. I duck into the forward chart room off the wet lab and lean over the big drafting table, staring at my map. I suddenly think: Perhaps we have a position error. Even if we were ten miles south of where we thought, that would make quite a difference. I call the bridge. Captain Petersen answers immediately.

"Could you give me a present position, Captain?"

"Just a moment," and then she is back reading off the numbers. My mind is in something of a turmoil. I find it difficult to concentrate on a plot of the position. But when I do, I see we are right at the desired location.

"Listen . . . ah . . . Captain. Can you estimate a position error for me? We've run into something . . . ah, odd. I need to be sure. . . ."

She interrupts my maunderings. "The circle of confusion is five yards, Dr. Franklin." Clear, impersonal.

I shake my head. I've got to control myself. "Listen, you mean to tell me you can get to within *five yards* with Loran B?" I am shouting. I must not be so abusive!

"We're locked on the satellites, Dr. Franklin. And we're getting confirming triangulation from the Montauk-Bar Harbor-Bermuda range on the long-wave, slave-master system."

I am flabbergasted. "You . . . you mean our satellite system is finally, actually working? I didn't know that."

Even over the scratchy intercom her laughter is pleasant. "I felt we had to have it for the director's arctic cruise. The Loran crossings are very oblique up there."

God, this woman is a marvel! Four years and two captains had passed, and nobody had been able to get sensible data from our satellite navigation system. And in a month or so, she . . . "Is this the correct position, Professor, the one you wanted?"

"Yes, yes," I say. "Look, I'll be right up. We've got to change the station plan. Everything is changed . . ." and I stare at my chart and wonder how to select the next station. Best to steam out on a radius, but how far? Make a guess? Extrapolation projection? Screw it! I decide to guess. To try twenty miles and see. I mark my chart, roll it up, and leave the chart room. On the well deck they now have six of the eight samplers back aboard. I look over Harry Harvey's shoulder at the data sheet. No mistake on that first one. At depth the oxgyen is down to almost nothing. Bad! Bad! God, that source is strong! Unbelievable!

"When you get the string back," I say, "we'll grab a bottom sample, just one. Right here. And then secure the big winch. We don't have time for any more on this cruise. Now, Harry, when you pack the goo into the baggies, be sure everybody wears rubber gloves. I don't want anyone touching the sediment with bare hands. Sluice the deck and the grabber at once after you get enough samples out of the claws."

Harry says nothing, but a big rangy Southerner, an older undergrad who came to us from a N.O.A.A. tech job, shrugs. "Ah sure never heard of that," he says. "You claimin' the dirt is poison or somethin?"

"God damn it!" I shout. "I don't want any stupid arguments. Either do what is told or get the shit off the deck! And let's speed this up. You people must think this is some kind of moonlight cruise."

Well, they hop to after that. Boy, I'm not doing this

very well! Professor Feingold would not be impressed. Why should I crap on these kids? They didn't put it down there.

I climb the bridge ladder and find Captain Petersen on the port wing pensively sipping coffee and staring out at the moon's brilliant track. "Ah, Professor Franklin, can I give you some coffee?"

Can she? "God, you bet!" She has heard me cursing at the students. I sigh. I suck on the cup she hands me. We are in the navigation space at the back of the wheelhouse. "Well," I say quietly, "we'll have to scrap the station list I gave the chief mate. I want to make the selection station by station. Our next stop will then be *here*," and I unroll my chart and indicate the guessed location. She leans over the chart next to me and writes down the coordinates on a pad. She must see my lines of constant oxygen and the location of the source, but she says nothing.

I return to the deck as the grab sampler is lifting over the side, back from its trip to the bottom, its jaw spewing mud and water in a swinging arc. "Looks like a good catch," says Harry as the grabber clunks down on deck. Carefully, in rubber gloves, they scoop the mud and detritus into plastic bags. I should have grabbed a sample last spring but the gear was on the other vessel. We will refrigerate this dirt and give it to the soil chemists later. I watch them hose down afterwards. Whatever is in the sediment is potent. It might kill people as well as diatoms.

We steam north and drop the Van Dorns again. Oxygen higher, but we're still inside the infected zone. I make a quick projection, and at three in the morning we get surface oxygen about where it should be, forty-five miles further out on the radius line than I expected. I send Harry and some of the undergrads to bed. Jill and the tall Southern boy are working the Van Dorns like machines. I chase between the profiler and winch man. The sample bottles, filled with water from the Van Dorns, are crowding one shelf of the fridge. I decide at four to run a two-hour circumferential track and then come south on another radius. "Our next station won't be until after six," I tell my silent crew. "Why don't you all catch a few winks?" As they turn to go, I cock my head at the Southern boy. "Ah, son, sorry about that temper tantrum. Your question was reasonable. My response wasn't."

He stops and grins back in the dim lights of the well deck. "Hell, Perfesser, say any damn thing you want. Damn, you've led us onto something. I can see that. I don't care if you cuss me steady for a day. You've put us in the middle of something big. And on a shit-ass undergraduate cruise too. Weeooo," and he shakes his head. "Why, it's like drawing three cards into the middle of a straight flush."

Why should people be nice to me when I treat them badly? Why am I keeping this all so secret? Grandstanding? And, yet, I must be sure! "Look," I say finally, "this *is* pretty big. You're right. We're dealing with oxygen death on a tremendous scale."

He nods. "The North Atlantic? All of it?"

"I don't know. Perhaps."

He goes on. "Worse than that? All the oceans?"

I can't think about that yet. "I don't know," I say. "Please go to bed. I have calculations to make before the next stations."

"Jesus!" he says softly. "Jesus H. Cheerist!"

The Second Day

At six forty, a gorgeous bright morning with the wind a little brisker, we are making our first station on the new radius line. All the students are up and working, eyes bright, faces tense. I know the Southern boy has passed on what I told him, for they are sober and do not joke any more. They are thinking, each to himself: We are the most important people in the world doing the most important thing in the world.

And I am the most exhausted oceanographer in the world. I have spent the past two hours estimating stations, using my projection method to space our data properly as we cruise south again. Dealing with the day ahead seems impossible. And in the midst of putting down the sampler string, the chief mate announces breakfast. Shit! I tell the students and winch man to continue and walk into the wet lab. "Jim, my gang will have to go to second sitting. And you'll have to leave us a winch man too."

"Gee, Dr. Franklin, cookie won't like that. I can hold this station for you until your bunch gets fed. No problem."

Something pops in my skull. "Look, Mr. Mate, we're fucking well not wasting an hour at this station to please the cook! You can damn well get some off-duty people to go in and eat now! We'll be in when we get these samples up and not before!"

Well, that tears it all right. Why didn't I send Harry in to pass a message? I'm really unglued. Terrible to act like that with the mate . . . and to let the crew hear it too. The loudspeaker is silent, reproaching me. Then her voice comes on the box. "Professor Franklin, work your station. We'll fit around you on the meals." How gently and graciously she says that. And how much worse I feel when she does.

"Sorry, Captain," I mumble. "Long night. I'm slipping my marbles. . . ."

And an hour later I sit, sodden with fatigue and guilt, at my tiny table under the sullen gaze of the steward and the cook. But then she is there, daintily unfolding her napkin and smiling as pleasantly as though we were lunching at the faculty club. I try to smile back and poke at my mass of eggs and the accompanying rasher of bacon, itself sloppy with syrup from a gigantic mass of flapjacks. I feel sick.

"Please, Dr. Franklin," and she still looks at me in a very friendly way. "The mate should not have said that. The idea, after all, is to get your data."

I stare at the huge platter of food. "What I said was worse than what the mate said," I mutter.

Very naturally and warmly she takes my hand again. "Dr. Franklin, I think you should try to rest, for a few hours anyway. Harry Harvey is a very capable young man and he can. . . . "

I stare at her. My eyes must be completely red. "I don't think I could sleep. . . ."

"Of course you can sleep. You're exhausted," and she briskly turns to the kitchen. "Steward, take away Dr. Franklin's coffee and get him some weak cocoa." She turns back to me, speaking in a low voice. "Whatever is happening, Dr. Franklin, you should let Harry be a part of it. He is very proud of being your student, and the reason he became your student is because he knows that you are at the center of important events."

I am too zonked for this. Tears start to my eyes. "Captain," and I am whispering so that my voice won't break, "we are finding the oxygen death of the North Atlantic, perhaps of the world oceans. I simply can't . . . entrust. . . ."

She is looking at me closely, shaking her head. "No . . . no . . . all the more reason to let the human things have priority. Give Harry his morning. Let him be in charge." She is looking at me intently. "Tomorrow all this must come out. You . . . you and the director will have to deal with it then. You *must* be ready. You *must* sleep!"

How does she know all this? She is saying what old Feingold would have said, about the human things, about behaving with style. "Yes, you're right." I turn and see Harry watching me from across the room. I beckon him over.

"Harry, I'm going to sack in till noon. I've projected the next group of stations on a chart in the forward chart room. Plug ahead. Try to do as many as you can. Be quick. Be sure to wake me at noon, or before if the readings are looking really different from the other group. OK?"

Harry sticks up his thumb. "You bet! We'll go like the wind."

I cannot eat my breakfast. I rise unsteadily. "Thanks, Captain Petersen," I croak. I wonder blearily what the crew is thinking about all this. But, who cares? They will know soon enough.

The chief scientist's cabin is a small but private place. The students sleep in four- and eight-bed cabins, but the chief scientist has a tiny nest. I close the light-tight shade, roll onto the narrow bunk and, as she predicted, am gone in moments. And I dream.

At first it is pleasant. I am with my wife again. We are young and on a great beach that stretches as far as the eye can see in either direction. We are both looking for a private place to make love, and though we don't speak, I know she is thinking of this just as I am thinking of it. But the beach is open dunes. There is no grass or shade and no private place. The dunes are hot and we are becoming tired and thirsty. And now the beach smells badly, and my wife, her breasts visible and desirable under a tiny bikini top, scowls at me. We walk in the backwash of the waves to keep cool, but the water is hot and does not seem as wet as it should be. It is almost like a sandy fluid burning our feet, and now there are things turning over and over in the hot surf, and I see they are rotted things. I am hot and my wife has turned on me and her face contorts and her lower lip juts. She spits spittle at me with words I cannot hear but the words are "Death! Death!" Then I turn to the sea and the waves are huge and hot, moving so languidly, now filled with shocking shapes and pieces of creatures. I try to run back from these lazy, terrible waves and the corrupt things that lump out of their smooth forms but the water drags on the feet and the heat is unbearable! My wife spits "Death! Death!" The great filthy seas are rolling in, stinking of corruption, and I cannot move back now. I raise my hands and try to scream but it is all soundless! Yes I must . . . get . . . back . . . or—

I throw myself upright in my bunk, soaking with sweat, a shriek in my throat, and Harry is gently rapping at my cabin door. "Noon, Professor, noon . . ." he is calling . . . calling.

"Thanks, Harry, I'll be right out." I am drenched and disoriented. If only I weren't so lonely. I am undone. And I suddenly think: I am the messenger of defeat. They will destroy me! I put my head under the sink faucet and the water runs. And as that cooling sense spreads, I suddenly stand up straight. "Shit," I say aloud. "I'm whimpering! Fuck T. S. Eliot!" And I am again myself, some sort of living testimonial to a liberal arts education.

Harry has done beautifully while I nightmared away the morning. Two stations complete and the third in progress. I am still shaken but try to be pleasant with all the people I have dumped on. The Van Dorns are coming up, and Harry catches my eye and cocks his head toward the forward chart room. "Want to come look at the chart, Prof?" he says. We go into the little room off the wet lab, and now there are two charts on the big tilted board. My chart has some additions, but next to it is a larger sheet, a North Atlantic Basin sketch map. And on this I see much activity, what look to be isopleths all the way to the Arctic Circle. I point to the most northward line.

"What's that?"

Harry grins. "Two parts per million D.O. line." He points to the number 11.4 written next to it. "Eleven point four years to reach that point."

"From when?"

Harry looks sideways at me. "From the start of the spread."

"How did you find that point in time?"

He points to a much smaller oval. "Back projection. Here we are today." The number on this line is 2.4. "According to what you've got so far, this spread started two point four years ago."

"Very good. Perfect. You're right on the button."

He looks sharply at me now. "You know when this started, then?"

"Yes."

Harry is quiet for a moment. I point again at the farthest north line. "Will it actually depress to this D.O. level?" I ask him, holding my breath.

He shrugs. "I don't know the source strength. That two-dimensional Franklin projection," and he grins as he says my name, "is only based on the time series. It assumes an infinite source strength."

"Harry," I say tensely, "you can get the strength in terms of the rate, the derivative. Remember Corollary Three in my second paper?"

Harry jerks his head down sharply. "Shit! I was trying to think of a way . . . of course that's it. God damn! I thought I really knew your stuff backwards and forwards." He seems so disappointed that I suddenly put my arm around his shoulders.

"Hey, buddy. You've done about five times as much as I could have if I did nothing but this all morning. Let's get that strength now, together. We may need to prop each other up when we see what comes out."

Harry picks up his portable computer and strokes the keys. He seems cheered up in an instant. "OK, OK. Let me look at this program sheet again." And soon he is poking and writing and poking keys again. I let him work. His nerves are better than mine. It would take me six tries on that electronic toy to get the same answer twice at this point.

Suddenly he puts down the machine and sits back, staring at me, his eyes wide. "Professor Franklin, the source *is* infinite . . . or as close as I can tell. There's absolutely no sign of decay. That coefficient has three zeros behind the decimal. The depletion coefficient is even smaller." He stares at the sheets, the charts, at me again. "Holy shit. . . ." his eyes are wide and he seems to be seeing me for the first time. "This is . . ." he runs his hands through his hair. "Why . . . why . . . this is the worst disaster to ever . . . and you predicted it!" He stops and grabs my arm. "We were at the Atlantic Basin conference last winter in New York. Not a mention of this. Nobody knew. Good God! How did . . . how could . . . ?" His eyes are staring and he grips my arm tighter.

If Harry were an undergraduate, this would not bother him so much. He would regard me as just one more wizard-professor pulling one more analytic rabbit out of the advanced math hat. But Harry *knows* what is possible with projection and sampling. And he also knows that I have come three times exactly to this spot, starting within one year of the actual beginning of the infection. And those two knowings are not compatible . . . unless I am a true wizard using methods not known to other scientists . . . or else the luckiest station picker in the history of oceanography. And, in fact, I *have* been drawing on methods outside of science, but not magical ones. Nothing more complicated than good old shop gossip.

"Harry . . . Harry, close the door and I'll tell you all." Actually I do not tell him quite all. I do not tell, for instance, that Fred Kenyon and I were zapped on some super hash in a hospitality suite at that All-Oceans conference in Miami, when he told me this story.

Harry sits down again, pushes the door closed and then pulls down a dog to hold it. "This is what Professor Fred Kenyon told me at a Miami conference two years ago," I begin. "Do you remember the spring that South Vietnam was defeated?" Harry nods, staring at me. "Well, you may remember also that the government was desperate to keep this war going over there a few more months, to forestall the collapse with new money and aid from Congress. At that time I thought, most people thought, that the President and the Pentagon were simply nuts to make such a big deal over pumping money to a totally defeated country which obviously had no chance to come back militarily. But they knew something we didn't. They had a new weapon. They had started developing it, I suppose, at Dietrich or some other germ-chemical weapons lab because the military herbicides didn't really work to strip out the foliage. Remember the "orange" that they sprayed on the trees to open up the jungle to the helio gunships? Well, according to Fred Kenyon, they finally hit on something really wild, a herbicide that could recreate itself in the plants it was poisoning. Fred, he was a biological type, you know, gave me a lot of jazz about virus imprinting and molecular simulation of other chemical forms. The point was, here was a herbicide that turned plants into more herbicide. You had no decay of poison strength because the more the stuff got into the ecosystem, the more of it there was."

Harry nods. "The infinite source," he says slowly.

"Yes . . . the infinite source." A quiet lies between us for a long moment. I continue. "They got this thing and tested it. When Vietnam began to fall apart, they cranked up to produce it. Apparently in those last days the government had a ship loaded to go to Vietnam, filled with the goodie and the systems to disperse it."

"We were going in with aircraft again?"

"No need. The South Vietnamese had plenty of planes. We would just show them how to spread the shit. They would fly the missions. Well, anyway, the President and DOD couldn't hold the thing together over there long enough. The vessel actually sailed the day before we began evacuation. At that point, they made a slight mistake. . . ." Harry's cheekbones are white. "Somebody, or some think-tank, decided this stuff might be handy to stockpile in Europe."

"To spray on the oil sheiks' deserts?" asks Harry, his voice twisted with anger and contempt.

"Kenyon claimed that this stuff had created a real fuss with the war gamers. He referred to it as a 'humane deterrent.' Claimed it has no effect on humans. Apparently they saw this as some kind of intermediate weapon between conventional shoot-'em-up stuff and the big nukes. I suppose they thought it would be a potent threat if Egypt jumped into Israel again."

"And how the fuck were they going to get it out of the Nile, out of the ecosystem after they got it in?" Harry is suddenly shouting in my face.

I put up my hand. "Hey, buddy, hold on! Jesus, don't you think I said the same things to Fred Kenyon?"

"Sorry, Prof."

"Well, you can guess the rest. They diverted the

vessel. There was a storm and the ship was run down by her consort, a guided missile cruiser. She lies, not too far away . . . there." And I put my finger on the center of Frank's nest of isopleths. "The stuff must be converting the plankton to poison and using oxygen as it goes. Of course there's no renewal, and the normal diffusion processes shift it around. I don't know how high it attacks on the food chain, but of course the fish can't hack it in the low oxygen, and even if they could, their food is dead and sinking into the abysmal depths."

"Contemptibly stupid assholes!" grits Harry.

"Fred Kenyon assured me that he only found out about this after it happened. But they knew he was a good and solid friend of DOD and the Pentagon. So they hired him as a consultant to work over the biological activity of the stuff and make predictions about what was happening at the wreck site. They got the data and samples and Fred did the lab stuff. But old Fred had guilt. He was scared of seeing how it acted in his lab tanks, and I suppose he had to tell somebody outside. I think he picked me because he knew I cruised out here now and then, although he never asked me to do this. Just told me the story and gave me the wreck position. You know the rest of it. I came out here first a year ago last spring, and it was obvious that things were going on in the water column. But the D.O. was only down a part or so, even over the wreck; so I figured the ocean was tougher then Fred's lab tanks. Then last spring things looked worse. More water involved and higher activity. I knew I had to make this fall trip then."

I do not tell Harry other things about my night with Fred Kenyon. How he whimpered in his hash high about guilt and disaster. How I returned to my hotel room and my wife, awake and stiff in her twin bed, the room freezing from the air conditioner blast. Me, excited from the secret and horny from the hash. My wife, hating me, wanting to hurt me for her wasted years, her subservience to my work and reputation. "You may be a great ocean scientist," she spat at me, "but you're a rotten fuck. You hurt and you rush and you're rough. I always hated it!"

I wept then, sitting facing away from her on my own bed. Because there had been a time, when we were younger on Cape Cod, when she had turned softly to me in passion, when we had joy in each other no matter how clumsily we both expressed it. She needed to remake history, to convince herself that those days had never happened. That I had possessed and ruined her and used up her life out of egoism and carelessness. And of course one doubts one's own memories. There is so much wounding today between men and women.

"Isn't Kenyon the one that died in that Caribbean accident?"

I jerk out of my reverie and nod. "Yes, the summer after our talk."

"Do you think they killed him?" Harry's voice is cold and twisted.

Funny, that never occurred to me. I suppose I'm really a very establishment figure at heart, the legacy of Wilston College. "Well, I don't see how. That was a real hurricane, after all. I mean, if the CIA can pull off a hurricane at will, we're way beyond paranoia."

Harry stretches and yawns. "Do you think the stuff is harmless to people? You had us use the rubber gloves."

"After what I've told you, do you want to shove your naked pinkies into that black goo?"

Now Harry grins again. "No way!" and a sudden knock comes at the door. "The string must be up. Shall we move to a last station?"

I nod. "You've done great. We have plenty of time for one more, and we'll be in by midnight, making the marine super the happiest man in the world."

As we undog the door, Harry puts his hand on my arm once more. "Professor Franklin, how much of the world's oxygen is generated by the oceans?"

We are silent. Finally I say, "You won't believe this, but I've never looked that up. It's in every basic ocean text. Go to the library room on the second deck."

"No," says Harry. "Let's look that up tomorrow. After we get in. And . . . Prof."

I nod.

"The kooks, the eco-freaks, they were right all along, weren't they?"

"Yes," I nod again. "But they will win a bitter victory."

By fourteen hundred we have pulled our last water sampler, and the ship is turned for home. The undergraduates organize the zillion sample bottles, secure the gear, and recalibrate the instruments. Harry and I are closeted in the chartroom looking for mistakes in the various Franklin projections, but by suppertime I am convinced that none exists. The worst of all possible news is in, and we are running on rails toward the TV studios.

At my tiny table that evening all seems to be forgiven. The cookie, far from lounging in his doorway staring daggers at me, presents me with the finest steak in the fridge, done rare and seared perfectly. I am relaxed and savoring the food. My solo part is, in one sense, over, and the next parts will involve the director, the news people, and whatever. But now it is Captain Petersen who is in a state of modest agitation. As soon as we are served and the steward has busied himself at other tables, she leans across and whispers, "Do

you know that we are under surveillance by an un-
marked aircraft?"

"No. Who?"

"Well," says Captain Petersen, looking at me with
raised eyebrows, "I suppose the Navy or the CIA. I've
seen these planes before but they are usually shadowing
Russian ships."

"Where is it now? I haven't heard an engine."

"They made a flypast after breakfast this morning
but we were under way then. They came by again in
midmorning when your gang was pulling samplers.
That probably satisfied them. I watched in the big
glasses and they were photographing. I followed them
for half an hour. They went out about ten miles, began
to climb, and look now to be at over twenty thousand
feet and maybe twenty miles to our northeast. Obviously they've been tracking us and getting the position
of our stations."

"And they're following us home?"

She nods. "Professor Franklin, can you tell me what
is going to happen? Is there a nasty little surprise waiting over the horizon? Are we going to be stopped and
boarded?"

"Not a chance," I say firmly, grinning. "The director
would *never* allow such a thing!"

She bursts out with a gush of laughter. "Between you
and the director, this is turning into quite a job!"

"Look, seriously, I don't know at this point what it
all means. But to properly answer your question, yes
. . . I think they might try to stop us." I lower my
voice. "The cause of the low oxygen is a secret wreck
containing a cargo of a very deadly military herbicide.
They must be very worried at the Pentagon. This is
going to make Watergate look like a shoplifting caper."

"Professor Franklin, would it be practical to transmit your findings to the lab now . . . by radio? I assume they're monitoring our traffic, and such a message would remove their incentive to have a little piracy scene at sea."

I think about that for a moment. "We could . . . but I'd rather not. Once this gets into the hands of a radio man ashore . . . and who is to say he will copy it exactly right . . . we lose control of the thing. It will dribble out through the night by rumor and hearsay, and . . ." I look at my watch. "All the bigshots at the lab will be somewhere else now. God knows if we could get through to the director before the news people show up."

She nods. "Then I'll proceed on my plan two. If we see a vessel on the search radar heading in our direction, I will alter course, force him to chase us. If they do that and get within ten minutes of us, perhaps then we should think about using the radio?"

She has conceived the exactly correct response. "Perfect," I say, and we eat a heaping strawberry shortcake in silence. "Why," she says finally, "have we . . . we Americans . . . done so badly with our leaders? They are so cruel and yet so incompetent at the same time. What is happening to us?"

"Ask the poets," I answer, and we finish in total silence.

At twenty hundred hours the intercoms rasp out: "Professor Franklin to the bridge, please." I race up the ladders three steps at a time and burst into the wheelhouse. Captain Petersen is hunched over the plan-position radar viewer.

"Captain Kidd closing with us?" I say.

"Take a look," she answers, turning away from the indicator and speaking to the helmsman. "Alter course to forty degrees." Then she lifts the flap on the engine-room speaking tube. "Engineer, we need maximum revs. At once."

I press my face to the soft rubber shade, and there in brilliant green is the echo, off to port, blipping intensely each time the sweep circles over it.

Captain Petersen returns to the viewer and glues herself to the eyeshade. The wheelhouse is silent while *Scoresby* vibrates along at flank speed. "The bearing is opening. Range is increasing." she says.

Five minutes later she stretches and smiles at me. "So much for our delusions. That poor fisherman, or whatever he was, will never know how we feared him. Helm, alter course back to two-eighty-three."

"It's probably a BMRT," I suggest. She looks puzzled. "Big Mother Russian Trawler," I explain. "They're all over the place out here. Actually, Captain, I think Washington may not fool with us. They may be desperate, but they don't really know how much we know, and to intervene out here with guns would boomerang, if, for example, the director already knew what we were looking for."

"They are evil," says Captain Petersen with surprising intensity. "Power and death, that is what they seek."

At twenty-three forty, R/V *William Scoresby* is abreast of the main dock of the lab campus. The monkey's fists are flying across the narrow strip of water, and the campus cops are wrestling the big lines onto the iron bollards. The dock is brightly lit for our arrival, and several girls are waving enthusiastically at us while several boys wave back. Harry Harvey and I are leaning on the rail watching the bustle.

"Well, Prof, see you tomorrow," says Harry as his wife drives up in an orange bug. "Anything I should be doing?"

"Catch me between nine and ten A.M.," I answer. "We'll get some transparencies made of these charts with maybe a couple of colored overlays to show the spread. OK?"

"You bet," and Harry is off down the gangway, swinging his overnight bag and waving cheerily at his cutie wife.

I am now alone and the lights ashore begin to wink off. On this trip back I have tried not to think about this time, but it is finally here. When I was a young assistant professor, I thought the most terrible thing was to be stupid. When I watched a weak student struggling with ideas that I could grasp in a moment, I felt pity but also gratitude that such a terrible frustration would never seize me in that manner. Now I know that was a childish and foolish view. The moments when they give you the medal are fine, all right, but there are great blocks of time in between those moments. Loneliness is far worse than stupidity. And smart people, having fewer like themselves to choose from, are often lonely. At this moment I would . . . almost . . . give up all my career, my medal, my papers, my students . . . if only a woman was standing by a car on that pier. My great old house is empty, filled with things my wife selected over the years, filled with my books, an echoing cavern of many rooms that was built a hundred years ago for a large and lively family.

My depression grows as the pier lights go off. Three years since my wife moved to another room in our rambling place. And more years before that of acid arguments. But I have a tiny plan for which only the most forlorn hopes can be entertained. Do I dare? Why am I so shy, so weak? I climb, slowly this time, step by step, to the bridge. If only she has not left.

"Ah, Professor Franklin."

Hurray! She is in the wheelhouse. Now I *must* speak my piece.

"Well, ah, Captain. Our fearful trip is done. I wanted to . . . ah . . . say thanks and to apologize again for . . ."

She shakes her head, smiling. "You've handled your mighty secret well, Dr. Franklin. This has been a very professional cruise."

So now I must launch my tiny ploy, my wretched, sorry effort which only my aching loneliness would possibly bring forth. "I . . . wonder if I might . . . take you over to Zabo's place for a quick drink to celebrate our safe arrival?" Zabo's is the nearest pizza and beer roadhouse, where clots of the oceanography staff can often be found. What will she say? I am as tense as when we left the pier two days ago.

She takes my hand, smiling. "Professor Franklin, at Zabo's right now are numbers of my crew getting bored and soused and numbers of your students getting excited and soused. We would be involved in shop talk and agitation. I think we would not have much opportunity to talk about . . . things."

My heart sinks like a stone in the deep ocean. "Oh . . . OK . . . well, some other time, then . . ." What my face must show I can only imagine, for she hurries on. "I have another proposal," and now her voice is softer, less assured. "We could go to my little house on the beach and have our drink there. And you can tell me about the end of the world, your own special end of the world."

How my heart leaps now! How stupid to have hesitated! "Oh, yes . . . how nice of you to ask me. I think, Captain, ah . . . Olga. Well, my first name is Bernard, Bernie."

She laughs so merrily at that, completely herself. "Bernie and Olga. How dull we sound!"

The Third Day

I am thinking, on this bright and brisk morning, that even uptight, distinguished-professor bigshots are totally, effortlessly overmatched by the gift of love. Our petty academic empires and specialties, our cruel elitism, our contempt for the uneducated; all . . . all submerged and torn away by a mouth parted in a sigh, a lowered eyelid fluttering as passion gusts like a silent storm of bells. Olga's hair smells faintly of earthy sweetness. My heart is ringing.

"Dear Bernie." We are in her little kitchen sitting at the breakfast bar, side by side, our heads together, our hands touching on the table.

"Listen!" I whisper. "Tonight, let's meet at my house. I have thousands of rooms, bathtubs, showers, beds. We can run through them all. . . ."

But horny old professors should not confuse personal passions with a proper ending of the world. Practical Olga draws back and looks at me from warm eyes. "Bernie, sweet. Tonight you may be on the TV, God knows for how long. Your house will be besieged with media people; your phone probably tapped and certainly ringing. If you do get away tonight, the only sensible place is here where nobody can find you."

I nod and I sigh. Captains must act like captains. "I'll get here. Count on it."

And now she is all business. "Bernie, I've got to move *Scoresby* by noon if we go in for refit. Do you think the Director will want that, after he talks to you?"

"No, I think he'll want an immediate return to the yesterday station."

Captain Olga thinks about that. "Look," I say. "It's about eight o'clock. I'll get going to my office and hack the data into some kind of order. You get on the phone and try to locate the director at home. Tell him I told you that I found pollution so serious and critical that I believed he would not want *Scoresby* out of action this week. He'll probably come chasing over to the lab campus to find me. If you can't reach him by nine or so, give me a call, and I'll get that feather-headed secretary, Minda, looking for him."

"All right. I won't do anything about shifting *Scoresby* until after eleven. You two should be together by then ... Bernie?"

"Yeah."

"They may have already been in touch with the director. Do you think he might try to suppress this?"

I, of course (fink that I am), always assume professional and responsible behavior from everyone. Yet ... she might be right. The director and I have been friendly associates for a long time, but ... not friends ... not really. I suddenly realize that I don't know quite how Director John McGinn will deal with, as Olga called it, my mighty secret.

"I hope that won't happen. I believe it won't. Not just because John is an honorable person, but because too many people know ..." and suddenly I look at her. "I think," I end lamely.

Olga's house is ten minutes by car from the campus, and I soon pull into the ocean physics building lot, still mostly empty and quiet in the sunny, windy morning. My mind is dashing about, sorting the data and its development into groups and pieces, dealing with the director in several different scenarios, facing hostile and frightened questions from still-unknown adversaries. But that is all just dust-dry exercises dealing with the end of the world. Underneath it all is a core of lust and wonder. Olga's breath against my ear. Her softness under the khaki uniform.

"Professor Franklin?" I did not notice or even

imagine them. Yet I know them in their conservative
suits, their short hair, and their distant smiles. Not
exactly robots. The shorter one is almost fat, and there
is a suggestion of redness, of a booze problem, about
his face. And I think, in surprise: Human?—while
they extend their open wallets with the badges and
cards inside.

"If you're here about a student, I don't give verbal
comments or answer verbal questions. You must write
me asking . . ." But I know they are not here about
a student. There would only be one, then, and he
would not be in a parking lot at eight fifteen in the
morning.

"We'd like to talk to you about your cruise the past
two days," says the tall one in his flat Midwestern
voice. "The material involved at that site is covered
by secrecy orders and . . ."

Now my mind is really racing. They have two cars!
I suddenly realize, the second one lurking on the other
side of the lot with two men inside quietly smoking.
How stupid to have not forseen this! I should have
arranged with Olga . . . "I'm afraid you'll have to see
Dr. McGinn if you have questions. He's the director of the lab. . . ."

They stare at me coldly. Many have tried to say
our intelligence services are little more than Ivy League
buffoons playing spy. But Americans have never lacked
the will to hurt and kill their own people. We are no
different than any society. It's really only a matter
of selecting the kind of people you need.

"We don't think the director does know about your
research, Professor. You're evidently playing some sort
of lone hand in this. Governments have to protect
themselves too, Professor Franklin." And with that
menacing platitude, they put their wallets back in their
coats, and I hear a car door open across the lot. I

must act this instant! Either run around the corner and shout for the campus cops . . . and how will they react even if they hear me? Or get back in my car and lock the doors. But these persons are experts at things of which I have no understanding. My tenseness shows and the tall one holds up his hand. "Don't do something foolish. This isn't a game, Professor."

"Bernie! Just the guy I want to see!"

What a wave of relief floods over me! The director himself is walking briskly toward us from the bioscience complex. How events have reversed themselves! Now fear and anger is in their faces, especially the tall one. How much does he know? Do they think I can bring down the government? The party? The system itself? Just how desperate are these men?

"John," I say and my voice is quavery, terrified. "We've got to talk now. A terrible emergency . . ."

"So I gathered," says the director, barely looking at the two spooks. "Your student . . . ah . . . Harrison Harvey gave me a call. At midnight, for Christ's sake! Said the world was ending. Oxygen gone or going in the North Atlantic. Said I should call you but you weren't home. No answer. Tried you this morning. Gone again! What in hell is going on, Bernie?"

So Harry called the director. On his own, never a word to me. There are wheels within wheels. Others can act independently, surprisingly. Yet Harry doing this has . . . saved me? Even saved my life? Suddenly I realizes that, if I had been the student, I would probably have done the same thing. In his independence, his assurance of self, he chooses to grasp events, to not be a spectator. "We must talk inside, John," and I indicate the rolled-up maps and papers under my arm.

The big goon has turned to the director and, automatonlike, has his wallet once again in his left hand.

"Dr. McGinn, I'm afraid we must hear this discussion too. The Department of Defense is deeply involved. . . ."

McGinn looks sharply at them for the first time. "You boys are up early," he says, and now his voice is like ice, stiff and about to crack in anger. "But you have no claims here. Dr. Franklin is not an employee of the government, holds no clearance, and is working on private research. If you want to talk to me about this, you'll have to make an appointment. Unfortunately, I'm quite busy this week. Please call my secretary and tell her what you want. Perhaps she can fit you in."

The spook takes a step toward McGinn and, his final mistake, puts a hand on the director's arm. "This really is too important to wait. . . ."

But the director, moving only his head, has turned to look at me. "Bernie, will you walk over to the guard shack and ask them to come over here. Tell them we have some people making nuisances of themselves, and I want them removed from the university property."

The tall one steps back. "Now just a minute here . . ." but they are no competition for the director. Once he and I are separated, any plans of seizure are ruined, while the possibility of bringing along the director with me must seem impossible with him standing there, his voice a stabbing icicle. His control and confidence is a wall against that initial bit of violence, that first lawless step. The car doors slam and, suddenly, we are alone in the parking lot and the director is looking at me grinning.

"Were they here to take you away, Bernie?"

"I think they were. I think you may have just saved my life." The director's eyebrows shoot up at that, but he says nothing.

The drafting table next to my bookcase is covered with books and minor paraphernalia, but I sweep it all onto the floor and spread out the two maps, holding the corners with little lead whale paperweights that one of my children gave me years ago at Christmas.

"John, before we look at the data and the projections, let me tell you how this all got started," and McGinn nods soberly and sits in the chair beside my desk. As I did on *Scoresby* yesterday morning (God! Only yesterday!), I tell the story of Fred Kenyon and the herbicide that recreates itself and the three trips to the site. "You know we need three good stations to make decent projections, and we finished the third yesterday afternoon. I'm sure the computations are OK."

John McGinn stands up and stares at the North Atlantic Basin sketch map and the isopleths of dissolved oxygen. "You're saying that Atlantic surface D.O. will depress to less than two parts even beyond the Arctic Circle?"

I nod. "And over the cap too, John. I can't see right now what will stop it." How silent the building is! The stillness between us is like wool.

But suddenly an extraordinary sound intrudes. John McGinn, hard-nosed administrator, driving chief scientist, member of commissions and committees, advisor to the Congress, utters a deep sob.

Startled, I look up and see that John's cheeks are wet and tears are running down wind-creased cheeks. "Bernie! My God! The krill can't live in that! The whole food chain will disappear! The whales . . . The whales! We'll never save them. Everything we've ever done . . . Meaningless . . . Utter disaster!"

Now my cheeks are wet too. I put my arm around John's shoulders. We stand together, staring blindly down at the map. John walks to the window and looks out. I wait. Finally he turns and smiles. "Bernie, I have a lot of public images and crybaby isn't one of them. If we could keep this little scene between the two of us, I would be most grateful."

And now I smile back. "Only Olga will know. I must tell her everything. But the tears do you no discredit. There really is no other proper response."

Old John changes like the New England wind. His grin is broad, boyish now. "Olga? Captain Petersen? You and Olga Petersen? Why . . . of course, Bernie! How perfect! How wonderful! Why, she's *more* than a match for you."

"Well, John," I say, "I'm not competing with her. My first wife and I were into that. I . . . I need a captain. That's sort of been my problem."

"If you decide to get married and I'm not the best man, you're fired. Tenure and the AAUP will never save you, Bernie. . . ." John McGinn runs on, but the chart still lies on the table, and we must turn to it again.

"Bernie," says John McGinn, "we're going to find out how to reverse this! We *must* believe there is an answer," and in moments he is on the phone to gorgeous, dopey Minda.

"Now, Minda, get your pad," says McGinn. "Write everything down because you won't remember. Ready? First, there will be a general emergency meeting of the entire school, students and faculty, at eleven this morning. All classes are canceled. Attendance is compulsory. Call the department secretaries and get them going on rounding up the staff and students. We'll meet in the main lecture hall in the *Challenger* building. Second. Cable the following message to Captain Malo, R/V *Ocean Tracker*. They're off West Africa. Cancel all research programs at once. Urgent you return here as soon as possible, starting no later than twenty-four hundred hours this date. Wire confirmation. Details to follow. Signed, McGinn." The director turns to me, covering the phone with his hand. "Malo and *Ocean Tracker* can act as your relief and consort out there as soon as they get back, Bernie. Decide today who you want as chief scientist on board. Minda, read that back." Then come calls to the publicity office, the marine super, the chairman of chemical oceanography, the . . .

Harry Harvey knocks on the door at nine thirty, and I leave the now-shouting McGinn, scoop up my papers, and step into the quiet hall. Harry smiles at me. "Sounds like the director is going to save his whales, no matter what," says Harry. "I . . . I called him about this last night."

"Thanks, Harry, for doing that," and I tell him my little story of the parking-lot kidnaping caper and my rescue by John McGinn.

Harry is silent a moment, then: "I didn't guess about that, Prof. Who would? I called McGinn because I thought it would help you if he realized other people were in on this and stirred up about it. I knew you wouldn't cop out. I guess I needn't have worried about McGinn either. But this spook thing. . . ."

I nod. How warm and proud I feel with Harry. "Harry, we're together in this until it's resolved . . . one way or another."

"Then I'd better get some overhead projector slides of the stuff. I heard about McGinn's eleven o'clock meeting from the physics secretary. I'll use contrasting colors on the isopleth overlays, OK?" And off he dashes with our charts and data.

When I reenter my office, John McGinn is talking with my Olga. "Captain, restock *Scoresby* for water and grab sampling plus possible current drifter deployments. Food for crew and full staff for a week. Dr.

Franklin as chief, and we may have consorts. I have
a request into Maryland right now. The university's
big one, R/V *States Pride,* is at her dock, and the lab
director there is in with the university provost now
about this. Oh . . . ah . . . Bernie just came back in.
Here he is, Captain." And McGinn hands me the
phone.

"Hi, Bernie."

I find I cannot speak for a moment. Her voice has
released a flood of joy. I finally manage, "Hi. Hey,
they almost got me in the parking lot, four agents in
two cars. John McGinn came by and saved me like
the Seventh Cavalry."

Now she is briefly silent. "Bernie, please stay with
the director until your meeting. Promise?"

"Absolutely. All is well. Will you be at the meeting?"

"Of course. Oh, Bernie! Think! Tomorrow we'll be
together in my little cabin on *Scoresby!* How I love
you!"

And that astounding vision, so far beyond any possible concupiscent dream as to be entirely outside the
normal reality, has instantly reduced me to a foolish
babble of "My beloved . . . my beloved . . ." until
a beaming John McGinn retrieves my phone and fin-
ishes off his instructions to the captain of my soul.

To have started the campus-wide meeting by eleven
in the morning required a greater miracle than even
John McGinn could work. But by eleven twenty the
auditorium is choked with people, standing, sitting on
the floor, pushing in at the doors, and all quiet, waiting
patiently for doomsday to begin. Harry is ready at the
projector with our slides. I am ready with my notes.
And now McGinn stands up and stares out at the great
throng, the TV and newspaper people, the university
president and his entourage of deans, people from the

legislature and the governor's office, the crew of *Scores-by,* dear Olga, my friends and my enemies.

"Let's get this meeting going," shouts McGinn. "This is going to be a busy day for all of us." The auditorium is still as death.

"This is Professor Bernie Franklin's show," says McGinn and his voice is hard and cold again. He looks scornfully at the media people and the politicians, then darkly at the president of the university, who came to us from the Department of Defense. "As you listen to Bernie's story and findings, I suggest you think about what has happened to this country. I suggest you consider how we can make our leadership, both political and military, responsive once again to sane and proper goals. We stand on a knife edge of disaster! Think about whether you want to leave the solutions up to incompetent, faceless . . ."

I am astounded. The end of the world has radicalized John McGinn. The establishment has made a formidable enemy. By the six P.M. news, what may he be saying? I suddenly think: I would not wish to be wearing a military uniform in America tomorrow . . . . But McGinn is as brief as he is vituperative, and suddenly he turns and smiles at me. "You all, or most, know Bernie. They, our elected and democratic government, tried to kidnap him this morning in the physics parking lot. To silence him. To silence us. While the Atlantic Ocean dies!"

A gasp. Surely the most effective introduction I have ever heard. I stand up and look out to sweet Olga and I am calm and steady. With a practiced hand I spin the main dimmer knob around, and the room goes smoothly dark. Harry snaps on the projector, and I, like the thoroughly educated Professor H. M. Wogglebug, am silhouetted, pinned by light against a corner of the huge screen. But it is not my nerves that now spread like webs on the glowing rectangle, but the fate of the world. For we have confounded Christ and Darwin together. By the merest shrug, the most casual, unthinking gesture we destroy not only ourselves, but, grossest, most disgusting evil of all, we will kill the fish and birds and beasts. All innocent, blameless, possessing neither sin nor understanding. Who or what permitted us to be stewards of this earth?

Outside, the sunflash on the sharp whitecaps glitters like silver coins against the cooling, dark sea. Gulls wheel and cry, and late-season sailors tack over the choppy waves, their cheeks wet with joyous spray. But in the auditorium all is dim and quiet. My voice spins out, telling of the ruin of our hopes, the end of our fitful days. And before this day has ended, other strong men will weep, and many more will curse. Dreams and ideals will fail, and hate and fear will loom and spin like the great banked clouds of a hurricane. But Olga and I will rage against the falling of this night . . . together.

I am content.

Buoyant Ascent

The phone rang steadily in the dark bedroom and Molly Kaplan blearily brought her wristwatch dial close to a sticky eye. "Jesus, three-thirty!" She waited, knowing it was a wrong number. Yet the damn thing kept going. "Shit!" She fumbled for the receiver in the dark, got it, reversed it twice, and finally managed a "Yeh?"

"Doctor Israel Kaplan, please. Commander B. J. Smith calling, U.S. Navy."

Molly could hardly believe it. "Listen, Buster, it's three-fucking-thirty in the morning!" she shouted in the general direction of the receiver.

A pause. "I understand that . . . is it Mrs. Kaplan . . . ? but we have a very urgent emergency. I certainly wouldn't call you at this time for any other reason."

Molly, her temper thinning steadily, leaned over and flicked on the bedside light. A soft yet handsome woman in her late forties, she managed to squeeze her bowed, full lips into a fearsomely thin line as she stared at the silent form of her husband.

Izzy Kaplan was not, in fact, asleep, but he had convinced himself that a position of utter passivity coupled with an absolute minimum of respiratory activity would see him through whatever was stirring up his wife.

"Izzy!" shouted Molly, now running at full volume. up to, Izzy?" she said more quietly but far more ominously. "You swore you'd never take another dime now? What's going on?!"

Kaplan abandoned his fake sleep plan and gently lifted his head. "Tell them I don't make house calls," he croaked.

His wife was now sitting up on her side of the large bed, her breasts jutting out the Providence Medical College T-shirt she wore as a nightie. "What are you up to, Izzy?" she said more quietly but far more ominously. "You swore you'd never take another dime from those bastards! And after the way they went for you . . . What *is* your price, anyway, Izzy?"

There was no bypassing this, Izzy Kaplan finally realized. He would have to sit up, deal with his wife, deal with the navy, deal with a fatigue so great that he wished he could simply faint. He rolled over and pushed back the covers, a small, naked, wiry man, almost sixty but trim and muscular. His large face was that of a hawk; a beaky nose, deep, inset eyes that peered brightly . . . not now, but most of the time, and thin white hair that grew more bushy as you went back. "Molly," he said softly, "I haven't had a professional word with a navy person for two years."

Molly looked at her husband with total suspicion. "Right! And they just happened to pick your name out of the phone book as a hyperbaric specialist, I

suppose? By God, if I find you're making a laughing
stock of me by sneaking around doing dirty navy business . . . I'll . . ."

Kaplan, who a few moments ago could only imagine
sinking into total blankness, found himself suddenly
energized by these totally unjustified accusations.
"Yes!" he snarled, sitting up and facing Molly. "You'd
just love to go and bitch with those bull-dykes in your
group about Izzy Kaplan's latest sell-out!"

"You can't call my friends that, Izzy!" shouted his
wife in a sudden rage. "By God, you'd fuck any one of
them, you goat, and you know damn well you would!"

"Not likely!" shouted Izzy right back. "Before I'd
screw one of those cows, I'd cut it off!"

His wife pulled off her T-shirt in a single motion
and cupped her actually quite lovely breasts in two
hands. "Moooo . . ." she said in a cold and ominous
voice.

Kaplan, realizing he was at some sort of abyss,
smiled lopsidedly at Molly. "Hey, Mol, I didn't mean
that. If you want me to screw your buddies, why I'll
just oblige any old time."

Molly softened a bit but her lips were still tight
against her teeth. She looked downward, away from
Izzy's face. "Yes," she said with some sarcasm. "I
imagine you could. Look at you. You're as big as a
house now!"

That final accusation almost broke Kaplan's spirit.
He spread his palms in a hopeless gesture. "Hey, Mol
. . . I got to pee. . . ."

"Agggh!" Molly lobbed the phone receiver at Izzy's
head but he managed to catch it and put it under his
chin.

"Yeah? Doc Kaplan here."

Commander Smith, who had heard most of this
quite clearly, found himself once again, briefly, without

words. "Ah . . . Well . . . Ah . . . Sorry to get you up, Doctor. It's just that . . . Ah, well . . . we've got a bottomed submarine, an SSN-47 class, in about nine-hundred-and-forty feet. We've talking with them now. They lost thirty of the crew in the accident, apparently a valve jam, some flooding, plus interlock and warning circuit failures. There are seventy-one people left, and they have access to most of the boat." Commander Smith's flat, young, midwestern voice paused, waiting for some response.

Izzy Kaplan thought about the depth and shook his head. "New London is down the road, Commander," he said stiffly. "Why me?"

Commander Smith, driven by a ringing sense of the passage of time, forgot the bullshit advice fed him by the public-relations people and spoke quietly, "Doctor Kaplan, obviously we wouldn't call you on this if we could possibly help it. You know that. I know that. I'm not going to argue about what you said two years ago or what you think of us now. The situation is simply this: The captain was killed in the accident. Command has devolved to the exec, a Commander Jason Ferguson, one of your students in the Environmental Medical Program at Providence Medical. Ferguson forwarded to Washington a year ago a complete emergency plan for conserving life support on a bottomed SSN-47 class, a plan he had done as a project in your course. That plan is now under implementation on the boat."

Izzy Kaplan stared at the phone. His student, Jase Ferguson, in command of this? He spoke again into the receiver. "What do you want from me, Commander?"

"According to Ferguson, they project a little over six days before they have to put on the emergency breathing apparatus and ramp the boat pressure. Getting them at that point is probably not possible. Our catamaran mother-vessel, USS *Tringa,* was off Norfolk and she's already on the site putting down anchors. The DSRV team in San Diego is loading up to come east. Frankly, Doctor Kaplan, what we want you for is to keep track of the life-support optimization with Ferguson, following his plan. Admiral Kincaid feels that you'll understand each other better since you worked on the plan together in your course."

Kaplan sighed. Kincaid was an old enemy indeed. "If I come, Commander," said Kaplan firmly, "I'm not just coming to OK Ferguson's calculations from the sub. I'm part of the rescue operation and I'm to be included in all discussion of operations, decisions, and input to and from the sub."

Now it was Smith who sighed. "Doctor, there are seventy-one of them. Jesus, you wrote the book! You interviewed the *S-4* people, the rescue sailors, the old congressmen. You know what losing these folks would mean. If you have a way of getting them up . . . hell, believe me . . . Admiral Kincaid is going to listen!"

But Izzy Kaplan had lived shrewdly almost sixty years and this passionate plea in the face of a dangerous and unknown future only proved that a thirsting man will say anything for a drink. "I accept your assurances, Commander Smith, with the understanding that if I'm not fully taken into the operation, I won't participate."

"Of course, of course," said Smith hurriedly. "Now, we're staging part of the operation out of Quonset. If you could get there by six this morning, we'll have a Coast Guard copter going out. The *Eadie* lies on the lower edge of the continental shelf, east of Long Island."

"The *Eadie,* that's the sub's name?"

"The *Thomas Eadie*. You know, that navy diver who got the Congressional Medal . . ."

Izzy nodded. "For saving Fred Michels when they tried to get air into the *S-4* off Provincetown in 1928 . . . well, Commander, it really is all coming together with this one, isn't it?"

As it turned out, Molly decided not to waste Izzy's awakened condition on a bathroom trip so that it was some twenty hot, active, disheveled minutes before he managed to dress and get started for his office at Providence Medical.

A November wind carried fits of rain across the black, empty streets, but there was little strength in it. The Physiology Building was mostly dark as he fumbled his keys into various doors that led to his sanctum. In the midst of this mass of books, reprints, instruments, and things having no evident use whatsoever, sat Peter Sledjewski, one of his engineering students. The boy's feet were comfortably up on Izzy's messy desk and he pensively lipped a beer can, staring at a small black and white TV.

Peter looked around as Izzy unlocked the door, grinned widely at his professor, and said in a singsong voice, "I know where you're going."

"It's on the news then?" asked Izzy.

"Is it? They've been showing cuts of the *S-4* and the *Squalus* for an hour. They even woke up one of the future widows for an interview." As he spoke, a still photograph of Thomas Eadie, posed formally in his chief's uniform, his medal hanging about his neck, stared sternly and unblinkingly out of the TV at them, dissolving to a movie of the launch of the *Eadie* at Groton, five years back.

Izzy shrugged and pulled open a bulging file drawer. "My student, Jase Ferguson, is in command of this mess," said Izzy quickly. "Got to find that paper he wrote on life-support extension in his sub." As his fingers closed on the thick document, filed under the heading of 'Navy Fuck-ups,' Peter Sledjewski spoke in a serious voice.

"Prof. They must be really desperate to call you up, don't you think?"

Izzy turned. "Jason is my student, after all, and he did write the air conservation drill in my course."

"Prof, how long do you think they have?"

"The boy scout on the phone said six days. They want me to fine-tune it with Jason to maximize everything."

Peter Sledjewski looked directly at Izzy. "The most you could squeeze out of that is a few hours, one way or another, right?"

Izzy shrugged again. "Probably not that. With their usual dumb luck, they've got the best man in the fleet in charge. I doubt that I can show Jase a thing."

"So," said Peter. "They've got a problem. It's tight. So tight that they called you up, so tight they're willing to give you a piece of the thing in spite of everything that's gone before."

Izzy, Jason's paper in his hand, sat down in the student chair across from his desk. He ran a hand roughly over his broad, wrinkled forehead. "You know, Peter, if you weren't so hog lazy, you'd be one hell of a student."

Peter looked over his shoe tops at Izzy. "You're thinking the same thing about the DSRV that I am, right, Prof?"

Izzy nodded, his eyes hooded. "The *Eadie* bottomed on an angle. The rescue sub can't mate up with her trunk."

Peter nodded and popped a new can. "Prof, four years ago after the blizzard they had C5-A's and Starlifters coming into Green Airport, no sweat. You know

goddamned well that if the exercise was routine, they'd
have a DSRV into Green by now. Hell, they've got
two of them out in San Diego."

Izzy kept nodding. He was partly talking to himself. "Sure they would! But at a high angle, they
wouldn't dare bring one east until they tried it out on
a sister ship at Diego, in the harbor. What are they
saying on the TV?"

Peter shrugged and took a long pull on his beer.
"The usual nothing-shit. The deep submergence rescue
vehicle is preparing for its daring mission. Crews are
assembling. Just PR crap. Prof?" Izzy nodded. "Could
they make buoyant ascents . . . with the Seibe-Gorman
suits?"

Izzy shook his head. "Not from over nine hundred
feet. That system is redlined at six hundred."

"They wouldn't just sit there and smother, Prof.
Jason would try it, you know he would!"

"Jason loves the navy and the flag, Peter. He might
wait too long. And what if the first ones don't make
it? He couldn't keep sending them up. Jesus Christ!"
Izzy rubbed his cheeks. "I'm going out there to watch
a fucking disaster! I mean the S-4 was fifty years back
when I wrote it up. Forty to the Squalus. But to live
through one of these . . ."

The TV played music quietly and they sat listening
for a moment to the patter of rain on the windows.
Kaplan stood up and shoved the report into his overnight bag with his mini-calculator. "Are you a janitor
or a night watchman?" he said to Peter suddenly.

"Both," said Peter, "can't you tell?"

"Then why in hell don't you get those dust balls
that are rolling around and sticking to my pants?" said
Izzy, pointing at his filthy floor.

"Prof," said Peter, winking, "If you get those guys

up, I'll sweep up the dust balls. I'll even shelve your journals!"

Driving south down the interstate, Izzy Kaplan could now think of nothing but a high-speed ascent in the water column; the head back in the suit, the gas gushing up the throat, the continuous surge and snap and ripple of the fabric from the tremendous velocity drag. But the throat was the key. Form a tube. Think of forming a tube! The rain pattered steadily on the windows and the slick, black road curved smoothly, almost empty in the glare of the street lights.

Turning east for Quonset, Izzy considered the exit circle of error on the sea surface. How large would the arrival-location uncertainty be? Nine-hundred-and-forty-feet times what angle? If they had to draw the rescue vessel back too far, an embolized escapee might die before they got him out of the water and into a decompression chamber. That data must exist, thought Izzy, at least for some six-hundred-footers. We can extrapolate it.

The venerable Quonset Air Station had long since been abandoned by the navy, a victim of the old-Nixon-southern-strategy plus a liking by admirals for sun-belt locations. Indeed, one of the least-offensive comments Izzy had made on his still-unforgotten TV, prime-time talk-show appearance had been a suggestion that in any fleet actions, the citizen would be safest on a U.S. vessel. "For," Izzy had said, "the Soviets are clearly spending their efforts on Arctic warfare and with our ships mainly off San Juan and the Virgin Islands, there's no way they could even find each other, much less fight."

The empty buildings of Quonset passed on either side as Izzy headed for the water, but there was light and activity ahead and as he turned past the black, bulky cube of a jet-test cell, he suddenly came upon two flood-lit SeaCrane helicopters loading pallets into their capacious innards. Izzy parked his car out of the way and jogged through showers to a hangar door where a rain-coated officer stood with his clip board and lists.

"Hi. I'm Doctor Kaplan. Commander Smith said I could get transportation here to *Tringa*."

The officer nodded. "The Coast Guard is doing our passenger shuttle. They're due back in about a half hour. Doctor, why don't you get some coffee in the hangar while you wait?"

Izzy was glad to do that at five-thirty in the morning and he managed to get down three cups of the hot, sweet stuff before a big, twin-rotor machine settled down into the flood-lit area and disgorged two officers who immediately whirled away in a staff car.

The officer now stood at the open side door of the machine and shouted against the engine noise into the red-lit interior. "We've only got one passenger on this trip, a Doctor Kaplan." The white-coveralled figure inside, his face unseen behind a full-protection mask, handed down another flying suit.

"It's cold as a witch's tit in this thing. Tell the doctor to put on a suit."

Kaplan pulled the bulky, padded garment over his overcoat, then awkwardly climbed the ladder into the copter's cabin. The crew moved like white slugs in the chill, red glow, hoisting aboard and storing small packages and bags. Izzy took one of the eight seats in the center of the fuselage and stared out a small, oval window. A SeaCrane was lifting off ponderously, the officer waving in the nasty dawn. Now their rotors began to hiss and up they went, the lighted patch of Quonset growing smaller as the rain beat against the machine. Then they were clear up through the clouds and the rain was gone. A thin, November sun spread its faintest warmth through a high, cirrus layer, and beneath them lay an unbroken cloud cover out over the Atlantic. Izzy suddenly wondered about the weather forecasts. What sea state could they come up into? Nobody knew that; it depended on the surface operation. At that velocity, it shouldn't matter until they tried to get them out of the water.

The machine bored steadily eastward out over the shelf, then finally began a descent, striking the cloud layer again at about two thousand feet. They went down through it rapidly, the rain again beating on the windows, and now Izzy looked out and saw the fleet of vessels that clustered together in this patch of ocean. Dominating it all was *USS Tringa,* the gigantic, catamaran mother-vessel. Amost seven-hundred-feet long and half as wide, *Tringa* lay to a double moor, rolling sullenly in the long swells.

As they came in over her stern, Izzy could see a nuclear boat nestled between the huge hulls, only a needle-thin stern showing. This would be a sister vessel to the *Eadie,* on hand to answer questions of method and fit and trial that arose on *Eadie* as the rescue progressed. In the dawn semi-darkness, the stern landing pad on *Tringa* was starkly lit by floodlights. But the true center of the stage was almost empty, a huge circle of water, fitfully searchlighted by three destroyers and another, small mother-vessel. At its exact center a day-glo-orange buoy rose and fell on the long, dark seas. Izzy stared at that tiny, bobbing speck of color and again imagined a bulky, suited figure surging upward, faster and faster. Izzy put his head back and opened his mouth. He imagined his throat was a steel pipe, rock-solid, as the air whooshed out. He exhaled with a gasping shriek, pushing as hard as he could just as the copter touched down like a feather on *Tringa*'s deck.

Fits of rain blew across the deck, for the wind was stronger out here. Still, the long roll of the huge catamaran was easy enough and Izzy, shrugging out of his coverall and handing it back up into the red inferno of the copter, looked around for an exit off the deck. Two figures came up and waved, lifting their rain hats briefly so that Izzy could recognize them. "Captain Gold . . . Mary. Nice to see you both," said Izzy as they approached.

Immanuel Gold, a careerist M.D. in charge of the minuscule Hyperbaric Medicine branch of the navy, was no great friend of Izzy, but the short, fat man knew there was too much on the line at this point to worry about grudges. "Doctor Kaplan, we're delighted to have you on the team. Let's go get some breakfast."

But as he spoke a seaman appeared at his elbow and spoke in his ear. "Oh, sorry, folks," said Dr. Gold. "We're bringing out two extra decompression chambers and there's some problem with the specs. Look, Mary, you take Doctor Kaplan to breakfast and we'll meet at the briefing."

As Gold dashed off, Izzy turned to the tall, angular woman whose broad, horsy smile and almost hidden behind a watch cap. "Well, Mary, this is quite a gathering of the clan!"

They pushed into a warm, lighted companionway, doffed their raincoats and stepped along the dry corridor. Surgeon-Commander Mary Jackson strode purposefully ahead, her broad shoulders turning slightly to pass through the oval doorways. After much walking forward they turned into officer's country, set off by a curtain of royal green, and then further to the senior officers' dining room, an amenity that *Tringa* was amply large enough to justify.

Seated at a pleasant, polished-maple table and ordering from a menu, they smiled at each other while the young waiter took their orders. As he left, Izzy cocked an eye. "So how are they doing down there, Mary?"

Mary nodded. "So far they seem to be right on target as far as life-support usage. Energy is up but they're really working on that. Apparently it takes quite a while just to shut everything off."

"And how do those seventy-one guys feel about it?"

Mary smiled. "Well, Izzy, there are actually sixty-seven guys and four women."

Izzy put down his fork and stared. "So? Four girls? That's why you're here, Mary? I didn't know they took women on patrol."

Mary laughed a single bark. "You don't read the newspapers, Izzy. Really! They've been trying it on three boats for the last six months. But you're right. I'm here because there isn't a single, top-rank female in hyperbarics in the U.S."

Izzy sighed. "Perhaps we can buy one from Canada?"

"If you did," said Mary icily, "then Canada would have nobody."

Izzy chewed on a crispy fried egg. "So they must be thinking of a buoyant ascent, Mary?"

Mary shrugged her large shoulders and folded her Norwegian-sweatered arms across a wide, flat chest. "They claim to think of all the contingencies, Izzy, but they like the DSRV better."

Izzy leaned forward and spoke in a lower voice. "The *Eadie* is leaning over, isn't it, Mary?"

She nodded. "About fifty degrees, and ten down by the bow." She paused, then, "They're apparently building a trunk to adapt DSRV to the *Eadie's* exit. They've inclined a sister ship in San Diego and they're going to try a hook-up."

"When?"

Mary shook her head. "I don't know, Izzy. It's very hard for us to find out about DSRV. I'm here on the buoyant ascent contingency. They've . . . well, they obviously have a problem because the press output on DSRV has been tremendously vague . . ."

"Mary, have they made any start on testing the Seibe-Gorman escape suits at nine-hundred-and-forty feet?"

"Not that I know of. But in all fairness, Izzy, they only got this tub anchored three hours ago. Also, there's a team coming with the *CURV IV* vehicle which they claim can lead an air and power line to the *Eadie* and hook it in."

Izzy shook his head violently. "Jesus, Mary! What happens if the weather deteriorates? They couldn't possibly remain on station pumping air into the boat. It'll be another *S-4!* The navy runs for Provincetown while seventy-one of them smother. Furthermore, they can't keep power-scrubbing forever down there without renewing the bath by heating. Can they send that kind of juice down?"

Mary shrugged again. "That's all in the future, Izzy."

Izzy dropped his voice another notch. "Mary, Kincaid is not very smart and he's a bastard besides. The DSRV cost over a billion dollars plus unlimited overruns in the research phase and the Navy Department is desperate to use it. Kincaid knows damn well that if the suit ascent is proven safe, public pressure will be wound tight to bring them up. Instead of waiting around while the engineers diddle with DSRV and CURV to gimmick the impossible, the crew will be ashore and riding down Fifth Avenue in a parade that will make Lindbergh's thing a third-rate Bar Mitzvah. And the DSRV establishment gets an investigation instead of medals!" Izzy's voice grew fierce and Mary looked at him evenly.

"Izzy," she said carefully. "Shouting and abuse are not going to get these people up."

Izzy sat back shaking his head. "You're dead wrong, Mary! Shouting is the only thing that *will* get them up! I can feel it."

But as they walked aft to the main wardroom, Izzy's assurance began to fade. "You know, Mary, I don't know a goddamn thing about the respiration physiology of women. Like, how does their airway resistance compare? And lung structure? Do they have a greater or lesser propensity for blebs and weak alveoli? How about their soft palate and tongue? Jesus . . ."

Mary turned and grinned at her shorter companion. "Chauvinist pig!" she said as brightly and cheerfully as she could.

But her attempt at humor failed to restore Izzy and she heard him mumbling to himself as they stepped into the big wardroom, "I knew this was going to be a guilt and inadequacy trip."

The main wardroom of *Tringa* stretched spaciously between the bows of her twin hulls. Half the compartment was now segregated by chairs and divans into a seminar area, with large screens and blackboards up front and various projectors and computer terminals at the back. As Izzy and Mary found seats, the room slowly filled with important-looking older men, about half of them in uniform.

"Look!" hissed Izzy. "There's that fool Spurling from Duke. Too bad he didn't bring one of his dogs. We could use the mutt to try out an escape suit!"

Izzy nudged Mary again. "They really are digging deep! Here comes Doctor-professor Reinhart, chief shrink from Menninger, and his entourage. Talk about the blind leading the seers! What'll you bet we get a lecture on the *Eadie* as a primordial womb in the belly of Mother Sea . . ."

"Hush, Izzy!" whispered Mary sharply. "You'll be making enemies soon enough. At least do it in an organized way!"

Admiral Kincaid and several officers finally strode into the wardroom and the conversations died away. Kincaid was a tall, white-haired man, distinguished in his waspy way, his face a mask of cold reserve. But Izzy, watching him closely, saw this stone face was brittle at best. Kincaid was grinding his molars. He was further out of his depth in this than the rest of them, what with the political problems added on to the simple requirements of rescue. However cleverly he worked it out, losing all or a major part of the *Eadie*'s crew would total his career, whereas failure to use the DSRV could have the same effect. For the briefest of moments, Izzy had a sense of his old enemy's inner state.

Now they sat staring at an enlisted man chalking data on a blackboard while Admiral Kincaid explained the present life-support situation on the *Eadie*.

Izzy Kaplan inserted a card in his programmable computer and punched in the numbers from the blackboard, hit several more instructions and read the glowing result. Kincaid had about finished when Izzy put up his hand. "Admiral, the data shows an exponential CO_2 rise instead of a ramp. Shouldn't we get Jason on the phone about this?"

A civilian in front nodded vigorously, looking at a similar display on a similar machine. "He's right, Admiral. That last data set projects exponential with only five chances in a hundred doubt."

"Thank you, Doctor Kaplan," said Kincaid stiffly. "We'll call the *Eadie*," and he nodded at the chief communications specialist at a portable switchboard panel. Two quiet minutes later they heard:

"Commander Ferguson here."

Izzy suddenly jumped up and stepped quickly to the panel, squatting next to the mike. "Jase, it's Doc Kaplan. How are you doing, old buddy?"

"Prof! Hey, great to hear you!"

The metallic voice, borne from the depths on a twenty-thousand Hertz carrier, still expressed delight. Mary watched Admiral Kincaid's patrician, old face turn sour with distaste. How they hated Izzy, and how they hated to have him here.

"Listen, Jase, your last data set shows an exponential on the carbon dioxide."

"I noticed that, Prof. We're drawing samples from several parts of the boat and with everyone in bed, we've got some local anomalies. I just finished a volume-average of our spaces and we're still on a ramp."

"Now what about the power drain, Jase? What's it going to do to the scrubbing?"

A pause. "Prof, we've got to have some damaged cells, and the high angle may be a problem with the batteries too. There's no other explanation. You know, following the plan I doped a year ago, we should wait for four-point-two percent CO-two before starting the scrubber, but now I've rederived the diff equations to include a non-linear battery loss term. Instead of a single, big scrub, like we worked out in my report, I figure to turn the bad cells on at two-point-four percent and use them completely up, then ramp again and see how we're doing with the other battery bank. Of course, if our high angle causes problems there, we'll have to reanalyze."

The wardroom was very quiet. Izzy turned in wonder. "Did you hear that, Mary? He's deriving and solving differential equations down there!" He turned back to the mike. "Keep your notes, Jase, we'll work this up into a dissertation when you get up. Jase, did you factor in the higher crew CO_2 output with increased percent?"

"Sure, Prof. That just makes it all the more essential to go scrubbing soon. I just wish we had better scrubber-efficiency curves at high CO_2. I put that in the report but they never got around to running the tests."

Izzy looked around the wardroom again and wrinkled his nose. The room remained very still. "Jase, I just don't know about your women in case of a buoyant ascent. Have you got somebody up here thinking about their throat and lung parameters?"

Commander Ferguson laughed suddenly. "Prof, I've been reading about them in the NASA bioastronautics book. It's got a whole new section on women's physiology. Actually, they're much better than we are, Prof. Smaller, soft palates and tongues. Since their lungs are slightly smaller and weigh the same, they probably have better web strength. Furthermore," the voice went on, "they have a more favorable airway L-over-D and a slightly higher peak exhale pressure."

"Right!" said Izzy loudly. "That's how come they can scream so loud."

Dr. Mary Jackson noticed with disgust that even Kincaid smiled at this crack. She got up from her chair and walked over to the panel, bracing instinctively as Tringa took an especially deep roll to port.

"Well," said Ferguson, undeterred, "if we go to buoyant ascents, I'm planning to send a woman first, Jo Ann Spinolto, our first-class yeoman. She fits the NASA specs to a T and she's a scuba nut with an instructor's rating."

But Izzy got no chance for comment for now Mary Jackson leaned over the mike and spoke in a firm, clear voice. "Commander Ferguson, you've made a correct choice. This is Commander Mary Jackson of the Canadian Navy. It's well-established that women can withstand most diving stress better than men. Don't let Izzy joke you out of it."

Jason Ferguson's reply was prompt and firm. "I've got seventy volunteers for the first slot, Commander Jackson. The decision is entirely mine. Prof? Any more thoughts about us right now?"

Izzy shrugged. "You're way ahead of me, Jase. Play it the way you're going, thinking it through at each step."

"Okay. Let me talk to Captain Stroudley, if he's there. I want his ideas on our battery problems."

Stroudley, the hard-faced young skipper of the *Eadie*'s sister ship now nestled between *Tringa*'s hulls, took a chair at the panel and slipped on a headphone set, entering immediately into a quiet, tense and prolonged discussion with Jason Ferguson.

I don't like it, thought Izzy. Got to do it now. Can't wait a second. "Admiral," he said loudly. "If the buoyant ascent option is needed, we have to know how the escape suits work from the greater depth. I request permission to arrange with Henri Bettencourt of CISMAR to try the suit on an ascent dummy at their Scottish facility."

Kincaid stared across the room at Izzy. "There are several contingencies we intend to try before that desperate measure, Doctor Kaplan," he said coolly.

"I'm not suggesting we bring them up that way now, Admiral. I'm urging that we discover at once if that route is feasible. Time is critical. Even Henri may take two days or more to set the test up. We must . . ."

Kincaid lost his temper. "Look, mister. You're not here to tell us about ascents! I'll decide that question.

There are plenty of problems for you just keeping them alive!"

Izzy stood up and strode for the door. "Nuts, Admiral! Jason will keep them alive longer than I can . . . or you can. You people will live through a public shit-storm if Jason has to make outside ascents without proper preparations. I'll be damned if I want any association with that kind of decision, especially when there's still time to find out!"

He stalked out of the wardroom, then stepped out of their sight in the corridor to take some deep breaths. He let his anger cool a bit, although not too much. Kincaid would eventually have to come to Izzy's position, but there was no time to wait for that. Something about the way Jason spoke of the energy problems on the *Eadie* disturbed Izzy. Time was unrolling steadily and choice narrowed with each passing second.

"Ah, excuse me, son?"

The white hat stopped at attention in front of Izzy. "Yessir?"

"Where can I make a long-distance phone call to Rhode Island?"

The sailor led Izzy over tortuous paths through *Tringa*'s innards to the main communication spaces. There, Izzy identified a lieutenant in charge and introduced himself. "Got away at three-thirty this morning, Lieutenant. Wonder if I could make a phone call to my wife?"

The lieutenant winked. "You bet, Doctor. Kind of left her in a rush, huh?"

He showed Izzy to a small booth, took the number and in a minute the phone rang. Izzy picked it up. "Hello."

"Senator Briggs's office. Miss Marley speaking."

"This is Izzy Kaplan, Miss Marley. Is my wife there?"

"Just a moment, Doctor Kaplan, . . . Sir? She's on another phone. She wonders if you could call back?"

"Tell my wife," said Izzy, his voice going up a notch in both volume and frequency, "that I'm calling from a naval vessel anchored over the *Eadie* and that there's nothing she is doing more important than what I have to tell her."

A minute passed, then he heard Molly's low, hard voice. "Yeah, Izzy?"

Izzy wondered if anyone else was listening. He leaned forward. "Turn on your tape machine, Molly, so there's no misunderstandings later. Now, the *Eadie* is leaning over and that means . . ." Quickly he explained the technical and political problems. ". . . so I want you to get the senator. Now. At once! Tell him that he's got to call Kincaid and ask why they haven't started tests on the escape suits at the greater depth. We may not have six days, Mol."

Molly snorted. "You mean those bastards are risking their own people's lives so they can justify the DSRV, Izzy?"

"Well, sort of, Mol. Kincaid will come to testing suits, but maybe not for a day or two. I'm worried about . . ."

"So why in hell should you or I or the senator save these bastards from their own stupidity?"

"You bitch!" said Izzy suddenly. Then more quietly again, "forget the fucking politics and peace shit. There's seventy-one of them. For God's sake, Molly . . ."

"Why should the senator get involved in this anyway, Izzy?" Molly's cold voice bored in. "It sounds like Kincaid and his friends may wind up buried in crap no matter what. Thad Briggs would never get mousetrapped into this kind of meddling. Who knows which way it will cut?"

Izzy paused and blinked. "Molly," he said grimly, "they have four women on the boat. Jason figures to send one of them up first. Think about what that means for your damned ERA!"

"Bullshit, Izzy. By that reasoning, they ought to make an AMA diver the prime minister of Japan."

"You fucking cunt!" Izzy cried out in sudden help-lessness, and at the top of his lungs. So loudly, in fact, that all speech in *Tringa*'s big central radio room sud-denly stopped and two dozen faces swiveled to peer at the small booth in the corner.

"Now listen carefully, Molly, because this is all authentic stuff." Izzy's voice was now far colder and more acidic than his wife's. "You call ole buddy Thad Briggs as soon as I hang up and you tell him to get Kincaid on the horn and give him the message I gave you. Otherwise, you tell ole Thaddeus that I, Doctor Israel Kaplan, will name him as an adulterer and a fornicator of my wife, a man who pumps and plows his Executive Assistant . . . who also happens to be a director of the National Rights for Women Commit-tee . . . in his office, in the cars he rides in, probably in the senate subway, and anywhere else that ole Thad's ole pecker gets perky. Is that all coming in clearly, Mol?"

A pause. Then in a surprisingly mild, almost soft voice, Molly answered. "We agreed not to talk about that, Izzy."

Izzy clenched his teeth. "That was before the *Eadie* bottomed, you whore!"

"I'll call him," said Molly in an even voice. "Good-bye, Izzy."

Izzy Kaplan sat slumped and rubbed his eyes for a while, thinking of other ways he might have done that, feeling nauseated and sick from the violence he had used on his wife.

Izzy opened the door to his booth and found the entire communications watch of *Tringa* staring at him. The young lieutenant walked over grinning from ear to ear.

"Doctor," he said, "I surely admire a man who can talk to his wife like that. Why . . ." He shook his head. "If I ever . . ."

Suddenly, Izzy grinned back. "My wife can throw a phone a hell of a distance, Lieutenant, but not from Rhode Island to out here."

The young man shook his head. "Yeah, but you got to face the music sometime. Oooeee! My wife doesn't even let me use words like that anymore. Says they degrade women and sex. All that stuff . . ."

"Ah, well," said Izzy briskly, "just tell her that old couplet about sticks and stones. Look, Lieutenant, I've got a more complicated call to make. To Henri Bettencourt, Compagnie Internationale Sousmarin, in Scotland. Their number is Lochstrom 624. I've got to find out the status of their ascent dummies in case Admiral Kincaid decides to test the buoyant-ascent escape suits."

The Chief Communications Specialist stared at Izzy, then at the lieutenant. "Lochstrom 624 is a phone number?" he asked in disbelief.

Izzy nodded. "That's the UK number. Actually there are probably fifteen digits but you'll have to call London Information to get the dialing code."

Izzy looked at his watch. Henri should be getting ready to leave his lab. He would just have to work through the night to move this along.

In a few minutes the chief gave a sharp whistle from across the room and when Izzy looked up he grinned and pointed to the booth. Izzy sat down and lifted the receiver.

"Henri? Henri Bettencourt?"

"Izzy, my friend! How fine to hear your voice! And from the submarine tender. How is it going with the *Eadie,* Izzy?"

"Okay, okay, Henri, but there are problems with the Seibe-Gorman suits. . . . " And Izzy quickly explained the need for tests. "So, Henri, do you have an ascent dummy we could use for a field trial? I know you can manage that depth at Lochstrom."

"Absolutely, Izzy," said Henri Bettencourt. "Jacques, our best one, is fully instrumented now. We can get you lung pressures, suit pressures, velocity, acceleration, gas flows, all sorts of things, Izzy."

"Super, Henri. Listen, could you kind of get going on this from your end? Communication from here is complicated. You should call Captain Ben Virsig at ONR-London first and tell him to get moving with Seibe-Gorman to obtain identical suits to those on the *Eadie.* These are Mark II's, but there may have been small changes within the Mark. They'll have all the serial numbers down in Somerset. Then you or Virsig can get going to find suits for testing. Maybe a sub at Holy Loch could help. Hey, haven't you got some buddies at Holy Loch, Henri?"

"A few, Izzy, said Henri. "We can hold the dummy on a platform for launch, Izzy, but do you think we should try to mount a trunk and launch from inside?"

"Well, if you can get a trunk and get it mounted, sure. But that sounds complicated. I don't think we should delay for it."

"As you said," answered Henri, "I do have a few friends at the submarine base and I would think obtaining a few welders for this task should not be difficult."

"Wonderful, Henri. Anything else?"

"Izzy," Henri coughed discreetly. "We will, eventually, I assume, get some sort of authorization, purchase

order, or at least communication from the more . . . ah
. . . official naval sources on this matter?"

Izzy looked at his watch and considered. "Within
two hours, Henri, unless I've completely screwed this
up," he said.

Izzy felt better after his talk with Henri Bettencourt
and he chatted with the lieutenant and several other
radio staff about buoyant ascents and the problem of
getting the expanding air out of the lungs fast enough.
He explained how the dummy would measure the
inner and outer pressures and tell them if a danger
of a lung blow-out, or embolism, would occur.

"But aren't people different?" asked the officer immediately.

Izzy lifted his eyebrows. "Jacques, the dummy, has
adjustments so he can simulate various throat or lung
situations, like a too-big or swollen tongue, for instance."

"Kin you put tits on it?" said a very young sailor
brightly.

Everyone turned to stare in disgust at the perpetrator
of this mindless question, but Izzy only grinned at the
boy. "You mean because there are four women on the
Eadie?"

"Sure!" said the youngster, not a bit chastened.
"They got to come up too. God, you couldn't leave
them down there, Doc!"

"Everything suggests they'll have an easier time
than the men. Women have generally greater respiratory toughness," said Izzy. "So if Jacques says it's
okay, we'll figure we can pop Jacqueline up too.

The lieutenant shook his head. "Damn. Wait till
my wife hears that! The thing is, Doctor, if the women
are so damned wonderful and smart, why aren't they
rich?"

"They are," said Izzy quietly. "Who do you think holds all the stocks, disposes of all the trusts . . . ?"

At that point a young ensign appeared, as if by magic, at Izzy's elbow. "Excuse me, Doctor Kaplan, but Admiral Kincaid would like to see you."

Izzy looked at his watch. Molly had pulled it all together in twenty-six minutes.

In the privacy of his office, deep in officers' country, Kincaid was coldly furious. "There's a real problem finding anyone to work with you, Doctor Kaplan, considering your hostility to the navy. However, since Senator Briggs is a senior member of Armed Services, we are constrained to cooperate with him on the matter, and that means with you as well. I might say I bitterly resent your . . ."

"Admiral, let's agree that we both want them up safe and let the rest of the bullshit lie." Izzy looked at Captain Gold who stood in embarrassed silence next to the admiral. "Will Manny set things up at ONR-London and Lochstrom, Admiral?"

Kincaid nodded grimly. "Captain Gold has instructions to offer you every assistance."

"Let's go to your place, Manny," said Izzy, and they left Kincaid at once.

"I don't mind working with you, Izzy," said Gold softly, hurrying along after the short, half-jogging Izzy.

"Listen, Manny," said Izzy. "Henri and I will get you the biggest medal they give to desk types. Even Kincaid might wind up with a good-conduct stripe."

They turned into Gold's more spartan office and Izzy began rattling off orders. "You verify direct to ONR-London about finding duplicate suits. I've started that. I need transportation to Lochstrom. Some kind of courier flight, the faster the better. Henri needs an open purchase order and the Holy Loch O-in-C needs to be unleashed. Although I don't think you could stop them at this point. Now, Manny . . ."

At sixteen hundred hours, that very same day, Izzy Kaplan stood in a companionway waiting for transport back to Quonset. Throughout the naval establishments in the United Kingdom a series of spasms and pulsations were developing that might eventually turn up escape suits and a way of testing them at nine-hundred-and-forty feet. Only Mary Jackson had come to see Izzy off into the wet, dark, blustery afternoon. Indeed, his tenure on *Tringa* had been so brief that he was hardly missed at the senior officers' dining room that night where various distinguished physiologists and hyperbaric specialists discussed the day's events.

"Mary, if Jason starts them up before I get back, you'll go into the tank with the first girl?"

Mary Jackson nodded. "That's why I came, Izzy."

Izzy shook his head thoughtfully. "I don't have anything to suggest, Mary. You've done it all plenty of times, ice, oxygen, the electric toys, the thumper. They've got every kind of life-starting widget the mind of man can conceive."

Mary Jackson's eyes narrowed. "Izzy, the first one is the worst. That's the one who shows the rest that it's possible. If he sends up a woman . . . and she lives . . . they can't deny us then, Izzy. Those macho bastards!"

"Hey," said Izzy, with a wan smile. "You're a Canadian, Mary. Texas is two thousand miles south."

Mary looked at him with a curled lip. "You think it's different up there, Izzy? With the famous Mounties and the lumberjacks and all that other male crap? Why do you think Quebec wants to secede, Izzy? Because those sexist, bourgois French bastards are scared to death we'll show their wives how to live outside of slavery!"

But Izzy was shaking his head harder and harder. "Mary, Mary, we're doctors! Jesus, we took that crappy oath, Mary! Don't load all that politics on her when you get her in the tank. She's . . . she's just going to be scared as hell. Like us, Mary! Hold her hand. Tell her how great she looks . . . how the blue of the medal ribbon will set off her eyes. Just keep telling her she's super, Mary!"

Mary suddenly gave Izzy a huge hug, enfolding his head between strong, sweatered arms and a large and slightly-undulating breast. "It's going to work, Izzy," she said, her voice cracking, and Izzy, retrieving his head, stood on his toes and gave the tall woman a kiss on the lips as the rhythmic chatter of the descending helicopter echoed flatly off the deck.

Quonset seemed almost back in its palmy days as Izzy's copter slid down through the clouds and popped over the airfield under a five-hundred-foot ceiling. Now there were many SeaCranes and other rotor machines parked in front of several hangars, along with truck-trailers and mounds of gear. An entire complex of pressure tanks, cable drums, and boxed equipment represented the CURV device, an unmanned, remote and cable-controlled submarine that could carry cables into the depths. Several white decompression chambers with their cluster of support devices sat on pallets, evidence of the growing possibility of buoyant ascents by seventy-one persons. But still, Izzy noted, no sign of DSRV, the small and expensive rescue sub designed to take men out of bottomed military submarines.

The same officer still mustered his lists and nodded curtly when Izzy came up and introduced himself again. "Your courier pilot will be right here, Doctor

Kaplan. Why don't you get some coffee while you wait?"

This time Izzy carried his cup back out of the hanger and stood in the drizzle beside the busy lieutenant. When the man looked up from his lists, Izzy pointed across the field to a nearby hangar. "Did I actually see a McCann Bell and kit over there, Lieutenant?"

The man whirled on him, cursing. "Isn't that the goddamn stupidest thing, Doctor! That fucking bell should be in the Smithsonian! I didn't know we had any left. And now it turns up in the middle of this . . . with fucking people who can actually run it!"

"It worked beautifully with the *Squalus*," said Izzy mildly.

The officer eyed him narrowly, then grinned. "Yeh, Doctor, in 1938 for Jesus' sake! There's no way that hatch seal would work at this depth! And besides . . ." But at this moment a flyer with marine insignia turned around the corner and walked up to them.

"Hi. I'm Major Pangborn, your courier pilot, Doctor Kaplan. We're ready to head for London when you are."

Izzy shook the extended hand. "Now!" he said simply and they walked along the hangar line until they reached a large, two-cockpit jet aircraft parked just off the old Quonset runway turnaround. Major Pangborn showed Izzy how to get into his suit and chute pack, how to use the oxygen, and how to piss in the bag. "It's only two hours, Doctor, so if you need to crap, do it now," said the major practically.

The acceleration at take-off was impressive and as they drove skyward at about a sixty degree angle, Major Pangborn in the forward cockpit babbled along at Izzy. "You'll have to brief me on the next leg, Doctor. As I understand it, we pick up some of these escape suits at Heathrow and then head for Scotland. I'll have to find a field close to Lochstrom . . ."

But the jet howled up through the thickening clouds and suddenly broke into the clear upper air where the sun still shone and the trails of great airliners criss-crossed the brilliant blue above them. Up they went inexorably and Izzy could only blow his breath out completely in a gasp as the hot sun broke blindingly into his cockpit and the acceleration fell away. They rode up over the rim of silence and set off for England.

"Mach two plus, Doctor," said the pilot cheerfully.

But all Izzy said was, "It's completely beautiful . . . so blue! So immense!"

"Less cramped than submarines," answered Major Pangborn. "Of course, things happen faster up here."

Yet it seemed to Izzy that nothing could happen as rapidly in this huge and peaceful space as the sudden, ugly emergencies that always waited hidden in corners of the dark bottoms of the seas.

They came down like a bullet along an RAF runway at Heathrow, over the slick, black asphalt, turning rapidly into a huge, almost empty hangar and then suddenly sitting still as the engine whine fell away.

Like Rhode Island, it was dark and blustering rain at Heathrow, and Izzy peered out of the hangar wondering who to phone when lights popped out of the rainy blackness and a Land Rover with naval seals on the windshield pulled in. Izzy's old ex-friend, Captain Ben Virsig, USN, jumped out and grabbed Izzy's hand. "The suits are coming, Izzy," said Virsig, an aging, blond, overweight man in black rain gear. "Believe it or not, there were ten to go to the *Eadie* that they replaced, for some reason, and never sent. We found them in a warehouse at Southampton and I've got my best driver bringing some up. You wanted four?"

Izzy nodded. "The numbers all check, Ben?"

The big man nodded back vigorously. "These four are right out of the middle of the group on the *Eadie*. They should be identical. Come on. I'll take you to dinner in a terminal while we wait for my folks to get here with the suits."

Major Pangborn decided to stay with his plane so Ben and Izzy drove off to the big domestic terminal and an indifferent meal plus several drinks.

Captain Virsig puffed on a cigarette and looked at Izzy across the table. "Well, Izzy," he said a bit awkwardly. "It's great to be working with you again, especially on something like this. Something this important . . ."

Izzy nodded. "I know we disagree on things, Ben," he said, "but getting Jason and the rest up is the whole show right now."

Virsig leaned forward, his flushed, heavy face puzzled and frowning. "Izzy, why did you say all those things? Why, Izzy? What was to be gained by all that old stuff? All that business about Vietnam and the flyers being yellow and dumping their bombs anywhere? That business about the lack of casualties in the underwater teams . . . ? Jesus, Izzy, you called us all fucking cowards. . . ."

Izzy looked steadily at his old friend. "No. I never called *you* a coward, Ben. God knows, not you or Jason, not the good ones. Now listen, Ben! I've already completely fucked-up my marriage because that spineless shit, whose ass you have to kiss every day, that Kincaid, didn't have the simple guts to tell Washington, 'Fuck off with the DSRV! I'll get the crew up my way and as fast as possible.' So don't give me any bleeding shit about how great you people are and how bravely you killed Dinks. I'll wreck my life to get Jason up, Ben, but I don't have to listen to your whining about the rotten navy."

Ben Virsig puffed harder on his cigarette, took a drink, and looked Izzy in the eye. "Bullshit, Izzy. You've got your alter ego in Jason on the sub and you're going to do the thing expected of famous and Pulitzer Prize historians, namely pull off the next historic rescue yourself, completely and totally, and naturally write it up."

Izzy sat back and grinned. "I figured Henri would say that, Ben, but I'm glad it was you. Now think about it. Is that what's happening? I'm too close into it, Ben. If DSRV or CURV can do it safely, then Jesus, that's got to be the way."

Captain Virsig signaled for another round of drinks and drummed thoughtfully on the table. "No, Izzy, we hate to say it, but you're probably right. The battery drain is getting worse on the *Eadie* as it gets colder inside. The weather's blowing up and CURV has a sea-state limitation. There's still a stability problem with DSRV carrying the trunk, plus a half-knot current in that area down near the bottom that they just discovered."

Virsig puffed harder and harder, then stamped out the butt. "No . . . you were right to call Senator Briggs, Izzy. The faster we test, the better! But let me say this, Izzy. There are as many shits out of the navy as in. You know Briggs, Izzy, and the crowd he runs with. You say you aren't kissing Briggs's . . . or someone else's ass, Izzy? I say you're a liar. And who do you think pays the bills for your beloved Henri Bettencourt? Exxon, BP, Mobil Offshore, and various lovely Arabs who still behead people. Great lovers of freedom, sweetie! You're better off in a sub, especially now that we give you women along with the great chow."

Izzy shook his head and spoke seriously. "Ben, how do you think I'd do as a commune doctor in Israel?"

Captain Virsig grinned. "You mean with khaki short-shorts, hairy legs, and followed by a flock of midwives . . ."

"And a Sten gun in my black bag," said Izzy quickly.

Virsig shook his head. "They don't use Stens anymore. I don't know if you could get an AK-16 into a black, doctor's bag."

"The hell with it, then," said Izzy. "Ben, is somebody thinking about plucking them out of the water after the ascent . . . in, say, sea state eight or nine?"

"You bet somebodies are thinking about it, Izzy," said Virsig. "Look, that's the kind of dumb systems thing we're good at. You and Henri do the suit bit, the single human bit, and we'll do the getting-them-out-of-the-water bit."

Captain Virsig sat back and rubbed his flushed face. "I don't know why I talk like that, Izzy. None of those things are bits. None! Good people are going to be hurt, maybe killed trying to do them. They're not little or bit-sized things at all."

"Oh, they'll seem small enough by the time our society gets through with them, Ben," said Izzy sourly. "In the end, you have to look at it professionally . . ." but Izzy remembered with a wrench that he had called his wife a whore over this professional matter, and he fell silent.

The Land Rover from Southampton had arrived and a chief was showing Major Pangborn one of the suits as Ben and Izzy arrived back from dinner. Izzy stared at the huge, day-glo-orange suit with its small face-window and various fitments, then shook his head. "One size fits all, Ben. That girl will disappear in the folds of that thing."

"She probably outweighs you, Izzy," said Virsig. "How are we doing, Major? Found a field?"

"A good one," said Pangborn. "Forty miles from

Lochstrom. I called Holy Loch and they'll have a couple of Land Rovers waiting for us. Might as well get into our suits again, Doctor Kaplan."

As he pulled on the coveralls, Izzy looked at Ben Virsig. "Ben, can you work out the transmission to the *Eadie* so we can tell them direct what we're finding?"

Virsig nodded. "There's a Commander Finch at Holy Loch. He's at Lochstrom now with a mobile microwave shooter. He'll aim directly at USS *Baleen* at Holy Loch who will transmit via our secret and absolutely reliable means, namely satellites, to *Tringa* and thence to the *Eadie*. We'll all be waiting, Izzy."

At that moment, around the corner of the hangar ran a mob of perhaps twenty young people in long hair, unisex jeans, hefting gyro-stabilized minicams and tiny, intense spotlights that sent wild shadows flickering inside the hangar. They instantly surrounded Izzy and Virsig and began firing questions.

"Clear out, you bastards!" screamed Izzy. "I'm flying to Scotland! There's no time for this!"

"Doctor Kaplan!" shouted the tallest, leather-jacketed camera-hefter. "Why are these tests necessary? Shouldn't the sailors be coming up now before the weather gets worse?"

Izzy whirled on him and the next morning, all over the Western world, people watched a small Jew, half-dressed in a bulky flying suit, shake his fist at them from the screen. "You bleeping bleeps!" they saw him shout. "Do you know what bleeping nine-hundred feet of pressure is like? Do you? When those people get in that chamber, they're going to be taken to that bleeping depth in less than thirty seconds! It's like a bleeping hammer stroke . . . you understand . . . a hammer stroke! Everything has to absolutely bleeping work, you bleeping . . ."

Men looked at their wives that morning and said in

wonder, "Didja hear that? Like a hammer stroke he said. . . ." But by evening, of course, there would be still newer wonders to catch their interest.

At the hangar, a group of hard-running shore patrolmen and bobbies cleared out the TV crews and soon they were off the runway and climbing up into the blue air again. Izzy drowsed on the brief trip to Scotland, but woke up as Major Pangborn felt his way down into a pitch-black, raining, Scottish night, worse than Rhode Island or London, and careened along a short, lumpy runway with a terrifying scream of full reversed thrust.

By the time Izzy arrived at Lochstrom in a bumping Land Rover, it was three A.M. Scottish time and just about nineteen hours since the phone had rung in his Providence bedroom. Suave, tall, mustachioed Henri Bettencourt, Managing Director of Compagnie Internationale Sousmarin, met them in the steady downpour, took one look at Izzy's face and hustled him into a small bedroom off his lab space. "Izzy, we have some hours yet preparing Jacques for his first ascent. Do you want food or just sleep?"

"Sleep, Henri," said Izzy softly, pulling off his coat and kicking off his shoes. He fell onto the bed and Henri Bettencourt stood looking down at Izzy as the small, older man pulled the blanket up to his chin and mumbled, "It's getting cold on the *Eadie,* Henri. We must bring them up soon . . ." He was asleep in a moment.

Through some statistical miracle of weather, Scotland, early that November morning, was gorgeous. The storm had left interesting clouds that the still-hidden sun caught and tinted pink over the low, dark-green hills around the stark, shadowed blue of the deep loch. The low, concrete buildings of CISMAR unobtrusively hugged one corner of Lochstrom's shore, but much of the research establishment was underwater, staged at various depths down into the deepest regions of the loch. In these underwater labs trained the famous eight-hundred-meter teams of CISMAR, the only commercial firm in the world to work regularly below this depth in the open ocean with non-armored divers. Within a huge, low, heated shed lay the rows of chambers in which trainee or medically-treated divers spent days returning from the high pressures of the Loch bottom. Or even some continental shelf, for CISMAR, using their own Starlifter, often brought decompressing divers back to Scotland for observation or further training while they waited out their time in the tank. This was saturation diving carried to its final conclusion, in which groups of men moved about the world doing their work but living in a totally alien, pressurized environment, completely apart from their fellows.

Izzy looked around at the beautiful morning, took a deep breath of cold, totally-fresh Scottish air, and shook his head admiringly. "Henri," he said, "you're loaded with more goodies than ever. You must be coining money!"

Henri smiled down at Izzy. "When they come to us, Izzy, they have tried everything else. Like your oil-fire man, Red Adair, we are cheap even though their lawyers scream at us. Saturation below eight hundred meters, with no work or danger bonus, costs eighteen hundred dollars a day, per saturated man, plus about the same again in support wages. It adds up rapidly, Izzy."

"You must have a nice overhead pack, Henri. You sure didn't buy this with green stamps!" said Izzy while Henri smiled.

Trucks, large and small, were parked down by the main pier and suddenly one of them gave a series of sharp honks. "Ah. They are ready to dress Jacques and submerge the trunk. We will have an ascent within the hour, Izzy."

"Less than a day to this, Henri," Izzy sighed. "No wonder you guys are rich. I could never organize anything like this."

Henri put his arm around Izzy's shoulders. "Each does his own part. You fly around the world shouting at people and I sit here like a mother hen on my white decompressing eggs."

CISMAR had a classy, water-jet maneuverable pier, shaped like a huge, plastic, articulated snake. Henri expertly steered this out into the loch with Izzy gripping the rail until they reached the main test platform. On this steel bed, and dwarfed by it, was a horizontal cylinder, just large enough for a man to stand inside at its center, and sticking out of its top was a second, thinner cylinder about ten feet high with axis about fifty degrees off the vertical.

"We welded a spare escape chamber from Holy Loch into a standard transfer tank," said Henri, pointing upward. "I decided to match the angle of the *Eadie,* so everything would be as correct as possible."

"How did you get this done so fast, Henri?" asked Izzy in astonishment.

"Ah, before and while you slept, Izzy, every first class welder from Holy Loch and Lochstrom managed to fit into the job. My only problem was finding things for everyone to do."

A young French engineer, ducking his head, came out of the horizontal chamber's exit and waved at Izzy. "Doctor Kaplan. Hello! Any choice on which of the four suits, sir?"

"You pick," said Izzy cheerfully, "while I pray."

Jacques, the dummy, lay on his back next to the chambers. He was dressed in proper U.S. Navy blue dungarees and had bare feet. On his dark, high, quite-distinguished forehead some sailor had scrawled in chalk, "I want a raise!"

Henri smiled at that. "We will give Jacques a medal instead, Izzy. But we mustn't pin it on him or we'll puncture the nylon."

The three men unfolded an orange suit and then gently lifted Jacques, who was only slightly floppy, into the wide, zippered opening. As soon as the suit was sealed they handed bulky Jacques into the lower cylinder exit hatch to a technician waiting inside. The young engineer followed the dummy in and waved back at them. "We will put him in the trunk down there, Henri, after we are sure there are no leaks. Doctor Kaplan, should this first exit pressurization be a thirty-second cycle?"

"Absolutely," said Izzy quickly. "Let's make it as typical as possible. Henri, is Jacques all . . . wound up inside? Ready to go?"

"Jacques is recording right now. The data is going into a tape machine in his stomach, Izzy." Henri turned to shore as the chamber hatch bolts turned shut and made an emphatic downward gesture with his thumbs. Then he led Izzy back on the movable pier and steered them to a small, moored submersible as the test platform rapidly submerged with hardly a ripple.

"My newest toy, Izzy," said Henri, beaming and winking. "A practical diving saucer. We will watch Jacques' great effort and photograph it, although we will not be able to match his upward velocity."

There were two seats in the saucer and a perspex top that dropped over them. As soon as they were settled, Henri turned some switches and the saucer began to sink. "My dear colleagues," said Henri into a microphone fitted near his head, "we begin test one, buoyant ascent, Seibe-Gorman Mark II escape suit. Lights, please."

Instantly the entire water mass of that section of the loch was brilliantly illuminated. The water was clear and green and Izzy could easily see the descending test platform at least a hundred feet below them, but Henri increased their sinkage rate and they soon caught up to it. "Acoustics?" said Henri.

"Here, Henri," came a voice out of a small speaker.

"We will profile the ascent at maximum resolution."

They sank down and down into the green alongside the test platform. Finally they slowed and stopped, the platform showing only the smallest sway as it tugged on the ends of the four thick cables that held it to the bottom.

"Trunk?" said Henri.

"We are putting Jacques in," came the voice. "I have set his head attitude at position B-three; rapid-ascent, optimum-angle. He is set on mean values in all respiratory parameters. We are ready to start."

Henri backed the saucer off the platform that now bulked alone in the green mass. "Commence the exit cycle," said Henri.

"We are counting, Henri. Ten to air start. Nine. Eight . . ."

They waited tensely. "Two . . . one . . . air on!" Now the engineer read the escape chamber pressures . . . "Four hundred . . . five . . . six . . . seven . . . eight . . . nine . . . equalization!"

Izzy, intently watching the top of the slanted, vertical cylinder, saw its hatch slam back and a huge, inflated, orange figure fly out, momentarily encased in a giant, silver gas bubble. Jacques tore through the top of this bubble which shattered to a million small ones as Henri sent the saucer in a sudden upward rush. But Jacques flew far faster ahead of them, an orange giant, his suit rippling in waves of fabric, his limbs trailing aimlessly, buffeted by the fluid drag forces.

"Dummy on the surface," came a voice.

"Was that a minute and a half?" said Izzy. "My God, it seemed like nothing! It's so fast, Henri!"

The saucer popped up next to Jacques, now floating comfortably on his back, and Henri lassoed the dummy's foot and slowly towed him to the pier. As they got Jacques up on the pier, Henri and Izzy saw there was now a large crowd of navy officers and enlisted men standing silent on the shore of Lochstrom watching them. Several men stepped forward to help load Jacques into an electric truck. "We must read Jacques' memory out onto a monitor, gentlemen. We will keep you informed," said Henri briskly.

Henri, with Izzy sitting beside him, drove the silent truck into a low cavernous building and then directly into a small room filled with electronic and video racks. Together they carefully unzipped and removed the suit, leaving Jacques on his back in the truck. Pulling up the dungaree shirt, Henri revealed a neat, multi-pronged female jack where Jacques' belly button might otherwise have been. Henri unwrapped a cable connected to a tall rack with a typewriter input, dials, switches and a big TV screen, and plugged Jacques in.

Izzy felt his throat constrict. Oh, God. Please make it right, he thought. Oh God . . .

The TV screen flashed green and two perpendicular lines of numbers appeared forming a graph. "Jacques thinks in the metric system, Izzy, but I'm showing both," said Henri.

Now a red line moved rapidly from the bottom of the screen upward. It bulged to the right, suddenly shot well out, quivered, and finally slid back toward zero as it neared the top of the screen.

"That is lung delta-P," said Henri, his voice low and completely even.

But Izzy barely heard. He was swallowing as quickly as he could to keep from being sick, blind with sudden nausea and panic. "There's a fucking pressure spike, Henri!" he finally managed, his voice a whisper.

Henri pressed some buttons on the keyboard below the monitor and a slightly-curving green line showed from top to bottom on the screen, lying much closer to zero along the pressure axis than the tip of the lung-pressure spike. "That is fifty percent embolism, based on a normal, infinite population of escapees."

Izzy, suddenly faint, sat down on the floor and put his head back against the cool concrete wall. "What are the chances of losing all of the first three, Henri?" he said softly.

A table now appeared on the TV screen at Henri's touch. "Over fifty percent, Izzy."

Neither spoke for a long minute and to Henri, Izzy seemed to become smaller as he crouched against the wall, drawing up his knees, his hands rubbing and rubbing his large, white face. "Henri! I can't tell Jason . . . oh, Lord, what will I do, Henri? Oh . . . oh . . ."

But Henri only stared firmly at his friend. "It would be most stupid to tell anything to anyone until we discover the cause. Pull yourself together, Izzy! As your most-excellent President Truman said years ago, if you wish to make a soufflé, you must be ready for the heat of the stove!" Henri turned back and entered more keyed instructions. The lung-delta-P graph reappeared, but superimposed over it were two new curves in blue and yellow. "Now, Izzy, blue is suit pressure and the yellow is lung pressure, with their difference in red. Do you see how the spike in the lung-difference occurs as the suit pressure falls most steeply? Now I will obtain curves of the rate-of-fall of pressure,

Izzy," and Henri's fingers danced over the keyboard as Izzy took his hands away from his face and got slowly to his feet.

"Ahhh!" said Henri excitedly. "You see, Izzy! The first derivative of the suit-pressure maximizes at the same depth as the delta-P spike! Now . . . we will see what the suit gas outflow looks like." And the fingers again flew over the keys. "Voilà, Izzy! The flow actually decreases at about two hundred meters then . . . then you see, Izzy! It also spikes and suit pressure falls precipitously! Now, we will isolate the cause. . . . I will enlarge the grid. . . . Izzy, look! That portion is only five meters full-scale and we note a ripple in the flow . . . and the pressure! The air release flapper valves are oscillating and blocking at the high density!"

And to Izzy's complete astonishment, Henri suddenly flung himself out of his chair and onto the orange suit lying rumpled next to the small truck. For a moment, Izzy thought his friend had funked even worse than himself and was about to pound his head on the floor. Instead, Henri attacked the black, plastic gas-relief valve on one shoulder of the Seibe-Gorman suit. He unscrewed the valve assembly and pulled out a four-leaved rubber flapper valve and a floppy spring. Throwing these two items into a basket, Henri looked impatiently at Izzy.

"Come, Izzy, we will take out these flappers. They are causing difficulty and they are only there to keep water out of the suit on the surface in case of a delay in rescue."

Izzy dropped without a word onto his knees and removed the valve parts from the two ankle units while Henri busily disassembled the remaining torso exhaust valves.

Hurriedly they unplugged and dressed Jacques again

and, in minutes, were trundling him down in the truck to the water's edge.

The group of navy people had grown, and standing at their front, his eyes squinting against the bright sunflash off the waters of the loch, stood Vice-Admiral Polder, COMSUBARCTIC, "Pole-Axe" Polder, generally considered the meanest bastard in the service. His heavy, beetle brows were drawn together and his craggy face had the temporary passivity of an approaching line squall.

"Henri, I want to watch Jacques pop out. I'll brief the admiral," said Izzy quietly.

Henri mustered several enlisted men and explained that Jacques should be taken from the loch quickly to prevent the water from entering the suit and then his mouth. "For," said Henri, smiling, "Jacques can drown just as you or I."

As they watched the platform and diving saucer submerge, Izzy explained to Admiral Polder about the pressure spike in the dummy's lung and the suspect flapper valves. Polder barely nodded, his eyes fixed on the loch.

Once again Henri announced the test and then they heard on the P.A. system the steps of the air-start and chamber pressurization cycle. "Eight hundred . . . nine . . . Equalization!"

Izzy looked at his watch, waited until almost ninety seconds had passed and looked up. A moment later Jacques popped into the sun, a nosegay of suspended spray about his head, only his legs below the knees still in the water. As he hung for a moment, a tiny rainbow segment appeared in the air behind him and then he fell gently backward to bob on the placid waters of Lochstrom. The sailors, hot-rodding Henri's pier quickly to the spot, lifted the dummy out of the water and held him upright to let any water drain to his feet. A moment later the diving saucer appeared and they were soon driving Jacques back to the analysis room, now with Admiral Polder grimly riding on the truck bed next to the dummy.

Izzy rubbed and rubbed his cheeks, thinking . . . please . . . please . . . please . . . as they again undressed and plugged in Jacques. The room was silent as Henri typed on the console. The coordinates appeared on the screen and the red line again moved swiftly upward, but now it was smooth and always-decreasing with no spikes or anomalies of any sort.

Izzy gave a great shout of triumph and as Henri turned to grin at him, his twirled mustachios bristling, his straight teeth shining in the soft light from the TV screen, Izzy seized his old friend under both arms, lifted him from his chair and hugged Henri as hard as Mary Jackson had hugged him on *Tringa*.

"Oh, thank you, dear Henri! Oh my dear, dear Henri!" cried Izzy, kissing his friend, first on one cheek, then on the other, crying and laughing, hugging and kissing, until even "Pole-Axe" Polder took off his hat and stared, blinking, at the label inside, and had to clear his throat several times.

"Doctor Kaplan," rumbled the admiral, "shouldn't we be in touch with the *Eadie* on this?"

"Absolutely," said Izzy, suddenly dropping Henri back into his chair. "Henri, let's try the other three suits, flappers out, one ascent each, to make sure this one isn't a weirdo!" cried Izzy, beaming at them. "While you do that, we'll call Jason! Come on, Admiral!"

They dashed out into the sun, almost running into Major Pangborn who was scanning the scene at the loch with much interest. "Major!" shouted Izzy. "Can we get going in your plane in ten minutes? Can we get a copter to it instead of these damn Land Rovers? Can we go direct to Quonset?" And as the major jogged along with them, dealing with these questions, they came to a parked, semi-trailer with a high, guyed mast and dish pointing north. Izzy rushed up the steps and banged open the door.

"Commander Finch! Contact the *Eadie!* Quick before they start them up!" he shouted to a short, thin officer who turned in astonishment at the sudden racket.

Soon they were linked with ONR-London, USS *Tringa* and the *Eadie.*

"Jase, Jase! Do you have an escape suit there?"

"In my hands, Prof."

"Unscrew the top of a gas-escape valve. There should be a rubber flapper and a spring inside?"

"Check."

"Throw them away. Screw the top back on and do the same to the other five valves . . ."

"Izzy, this is Ben Virsig. With the flow that much easier, there could be bigger suit-to-suit differences, just due to the way they were folded."

"Henri's testing the second suit now, Ben."

"Captain Virsig, this is Henri Bettencourt. The second suit shows an almost identical pattern of lung-delta-P. We are preparing for number three."

"Did you hear that, Jase? Second suit identical!"

"Wonderful, Prof!"

"Commander Ferguson, Mike Polder here. How are things on the *Eadie?*"

"Cold, Admiral, although lots warmer since you folks called. And our scrubber's gone. The second battery bank had worse damage than the first. We're spreading lithium hydroxide and I'm estimating thirty-three hours to five percent CO-two. But that assumes we only lose two more degrees of temperature."

"This is Ben Virsig, Commander. If you should start ascents, how rapidly can you make your exits?"

"Perhaps ten minutes at first, but we might cut it a bit. We have to close the hatch remotely and then pump her dry. It takes very little juice, but six minutes of time."

"*Tringa?* How about your surface cycle time?"

"Doctor Gold here. We are now at sea state five to six, prediction of seven or eight by tomorrow morning. We're drilling our recovery swimmers using our own dummies. We believe the *Eadie* cycle will be controlling, but we'll have to regulate the departures to insure the area is clear. Mr. Bettencourt?"

"Henri, you there?"

"Henri, a call for you. . . ."

"Sorry, Doctor Gold, Izzy. We are about to launch Jacques again."

"Mr. Bettencourt, will you give us a statistical summary of the surface exit circle size when you have completed your tests?"

"Certainly, Doctor Gold. We can test until you achieve the significance level you wish. Local currents should not be important at these velocities."

"Yes, we have the profiles anyway. One more question, Mr. Bettencourt?"

"Yes?"

"What major lung injury incidence do you project for a sample size of seventy-one?

"Two-point-seven hits, Doctor Gold. But that assumes a random normal population of healthy males. You could have only one, perhaps none."

"Prof?"

"Yeah, Jase."

"Thanks for doing this."

"Thank Henri Bettencourt, Jase. Without his toys and his mind you guys would be popping like balloons."

"Thanks from my crew and myself, Mr. Bettencourt."

"Thank you for the chance to participate, Commander. Many lives and much treasure will be justified by your escapes. May God bless you, my friend."

A few minutes later Izzy and Major Pangborn were lifting off in Admiral Polder's copter, Henri and the sailors waving beneath them. Thirty minutes later the courier jet was air borne, screaming up into the brilliant Scottish morning, the rolling green and gray hills falling away behind them.

"Kind of a short tour of the UK, Doctor Kaplan," said Major Pangborn," but interesting nonetheless."

"Major, you have a future as a tour guide," said Izzy.

"That fellow, Bettencourt," said Pangborn thoughtfully, "unusual business he runs there. Talented, well organized. I guess if I had to do that deep diving stuff, I'd want him looking after me."

"Henri is a rock, Major. Once off Surinam his chief diver suffered cardiac arrest in a transfer bell under pressure. Henri compressed to three-hundred meters in less than two minutes, opened the fellow's chest . . . Henri is an engineer, not a doctor . . . and saved him with heart massage. Of course, he had seen it done a few times. He's like ice, Major!" Izzy fell silent as they hung, seemingly stationary, under the endless dome of sky.

It was late afternoon when they came over Presque Isle and Major Pangborn began his descent to Quonset. Izzy could see below them a part of the sprawling weather system that covered the northeast coast of the U.S. and they went down into blinding rain squalls and the buffeting of cross-winds.

The long Quonset runway was more than ample for the jet, and Major Pangborn rapidly taxied his way past hangars, weaving by equipment piles and finally turning into the same hangar that Izzy had first entered less than two days ago.

The bookkeeping lieutenant, now bolstered by a desk and several yeomen, looked grimly at Izzy. "We're still flying to the *Tringa,* Doctor Kaplan, but I don't know how much longer."

"What's the forecast, Lieutenant?"

"Total, rotten shit, Doctor! One of these three-day northeasters. Thirty to fifty knots, sea state of God-knows-what!"

"They're liable to cream some of the surface swimmers in that," said Izzy thoughtfully. "Well, that's Gold's and Kincaid's problem."

The copter take-off was rough and scary, and Izzy closed his eyes. Three physician-commanders from Bethesda were also aboard. The navy was funneling uniformed doctors of every specialty out to *Tringa.*

Izzy turned to the man seated next to him. "What's happening with the press, Doctor?" he asked. "I haven't seen a TV in two days.

The man smiled faintly. "Oh, the navy can either get them up safely or commit collective hara-kiri."

"No middle way, eh?"

"None," said the officer decisively.

The storm had broadened and thickened so much that they flew offshore entirely within it, buffeted and jerked in sickening swoops. Finally they descended and the afterdeck of *Tringa* suddenly appeared. The cloud ceiling was at a couple of hundred feet and beneath it were the white caps and the wildly rolling ships. Even in the brief glimpses before they slammed down on *Tringa*'s pad, Izzy could plainly see that an ascent was about to start. The space around the orange, submarine-sunk-here buoy was empty, but at the edge of a large circle many small boats rolled and darted. Kincaid had anchored everything he could up to windward to break the wind and seas, the destroyers laying to single anchors rolling almost forty degrees in the steep waves.

But it was the oil that made the real difference. They were leaking it continuously from the windward vessels, and though great waves surged across the ascent area, they never broke and the general chop and confusion was massively damped by a method used for a thousand years or more and still not understood.

Izzy turned to his companion and grinned. "Want to bet that Kincaid gets handed a citation from the Environmental Protection Agency for dumping all that fish oil out here?"

"Fuck EPA in the ear!" said the man, his face dead white as the huge *Tringa* took a vicious, corkscrew plunge, then shook herself and came up ten feet in less than a second.

Izzy skittered across the deck, trying to keep the sheets of rain behind him. Once inside a companionway he dashed down ladder after ladder, heading astern and pausing only when an especially bad roll caught him.

Tringa's port hull had a large, water-level opening astern, in and out of which smaller boats could move. Along both sides of this open area within the hull waited dozens of men to handle the lines of any boat that might get through the gyrating entrance.

"Doctor Gold! Manny!" shouted Izzy, as he ran around the back of the space to the other side.

"Manny, have you got any up yet?"

"Ferguson is putting Yeoman Spinolto in the trunk now, Izzy," said Gold, his voice tight.

"Where's Mary Jackson?"

Gold pointed out through the hull opening as *Tringa* rose up on a wave and the escape area went down. Along with the many outboard-powered rubber boats that were hovering around and forming the circle was a larger, landing-type vessel, her front ramp partly down, her bluff stern to the seas, rolling madly. "In the transfer tank, Izzy. The swimmers will bring the escapee right up on that ramp and then we'll retrieve the tank in here. We figure less than forty seconds from exit to pressurization, if it all works."

"Captain Gold! From Ferguson! She's left the sub!"

Izzy and Gold stared at a tense officer with headphones, then looked out through the big stern opening.

"One minute!" boomed a gigantic amplified voice from *Tringa*'s stern, and the many retrieval boats, like runners at a start, pointed their bows toward a common center and began to edge inward.

Jo Ann Spinolto arrived in the glare of the searchlights looking very much like Jacques, and as she fell gracefully over backward, her arms almost horizontal, the two nearest rubber boats roared down upon her. In seconds the water around the floating, orange body was alive with black, wet-suited men. In another moment one of the boats, with the orange figure aboard, drove wildly over the humping seas, heading straight for the landing vessel. This now had dropped its bow ramp completely and, instead of slackening speed, the rubber boat leaped right up the ramp, the driver lifting his propeller at the last instant, and disappeared inside the hull as the ramp began to come up.

"Neat, Manny," said Izzy admiringly. "They should give you a big medal for setting that up!"

The driver of the landing vessel paused outside *Tringa*'s entrance, then scooted in as a wave went by. As the craft appeared between the catwalks on either side, line after line spun across and in moments the entire vessel was pinioned like a fly in a spider's web, *Tringa* roughly jerking her this way and that. While that was happening, a crane hook, ridden by a rigger, came rapidly down and in another moment, a small, swinging decompression chamber, pimpled by its own gas bottles and gear, disappeared up through a hole in the roof of the cavernous space.

"Come on, Izzy!" shouted Dr. Gold. "Let's see how she's doing!"

They dashed up one deck to *Tringa's* medical and decompression spaces, filled chock-a-block with white chambers and hurrying personnel. As they arrived, the little cylinder that had come off the landing vessel was being dollied up to, and mated with, a larger medical chamber. Izzy peered obliquely in one of the large chamber's windows and saw Mary Jackson's large back appear. She was handing in a stretcher on which lay a slim, young woman, barefooted and fetching in damp and rather open navy dungarees. Another doctor handled the rear of the stretcher and as soon as they were completely in, Izzy seized the microphone at the chamber control station.

"Mary! How is she? It's Izzy!"

Commander Jackson turned to face the window and Izzy instantly knew the answer. Her eyes were like stars of the dawn. Her smile was huge and uncontrolled. Her large, strong body was so alive with joy that Izzy could only clutch Dr. Gold's arm and whisper in delight, "You see, Virginia? There *is* a Santa Claus!"

"She's perfect," came Mary Jackson's proud voice. "The slightest nose bleed in one nostril and not another thing. Ears perfect! Lungs perfect!"

"Can Yeoman Spinolto answer questions?" asked Dr. Gold.

After a moment of interior discussion, a pert, round face appeared at Izzy's window. "Hi," said Jo Ann Spinolto. "I feel fine."

Izzy smiled warmly at her. "Sweetie, the TV is just going to love you to death."

She wrinkled her nose at him. "I yelled all the way up, Doctor Kaplan. Yelled, *not* screamed!"

"Jo Ann," said Izzy, winking, "if you want to scream at my pad, you can do it as much as you want. Or, you can yell too."

"Izzy, stop that!" said Mary Jackson, laughing. "Jo Ann, Commander Ferguson has a question."

"Yeoman Spinolto," came the crisp, metal voice from the *Eadie*. "Did you strike or catch on anything on the way out of the trunk?"

"No sir. I went out as slick as a whistle, sir. When the air came on I felt this intense band of pressure around my head, but of course I was doing my Valsalava Maneuver. Then . . . then I was just in the water with this tremendous flapping noise all around and I had my head back and I was yelling and yelling."

"Did you hear that, Jase? She felt that yelling was the best way to clear her lungs."

"Well," said the girl. "It just felt so right. I knew the most dangerous pressure-increase point was at the surface so I just tried to increase my yell all the way up."

"Anything else, Yeoman? Everyone here is listening to this."

"No. Except that they have a wonderful, speedy way of getting us out of the water. Tell them to just relax."

"Doctor Gold," came Ferguson's voice. "We will send the next man in two minutes, if you are ready, and then one each ten minutes thereafter. We will check on minute eight to be sure the exit area is clear. Is that satisfactory?"

"Chief swimmer?" said Gold.

Over the loudspeaker they heard a calm voice with

the gale screaming behind. "Ready at the exit circle,
Commander Ferguson, count us to your exit please."

"One minute fifty, one minute forty . . ."

Izzy blew a kiss at smiling Jo Ann Spinolto and
rushed off with Dr. Gold to watch the next ascent.

As they soon learned, Jo Ann's ascent had been
deceptively simple. Few of the *Eadie*'s older crew
members could withstand this pressurization rate without losing one or both eardrums. They arrived at the
surface completely disoriented, vomiting in the suit,
and in urgent risk of drowning in vomit even in the
brief time it took the swimmers to get them out of
the water. As the weather worsened and even the oil
failed to completely eliminate breaking seas in the exit
area, they attempted to vector the rubber boats more
closely, using acoustics and computer projection of the
exit point. In spite of this the eighteenth man virtually
drowned in the blood from a gigantic nosebleed when
his rescue boat was delayed by overturning in a cross-
sea. They kept him going with a breather and chest
massage until they could restart him on *Tringa* with
electricity, but his brain waves showed he was hurt.
Then came a sinus hit of unusual intensity, the sailor
screaming so loudly he was clearly audible directly
through the walls of his chamber. The desperate at-
tending doctor compressed him to two-hundred feet of
pressure, then loaded him down with morphine and
went into his nose with two distinguished specialists
peering in to offer suggestions.

Teeth exploded. Izzy came up to a chamber as an
exhausted Captain Gold peered furiously in the window. "I don't give a shit how much it hurts to drill
your teeth. If you go on patrol with a mouth like that
again, I'll court martial your ass!"

The young sailor inside, his jaw aching, sat terrified on a bunk.

"Manny," grinned Izzy fuzzily, "I don't think that's any way to treat one of the all-time heroes of the submarine service."

Dr. Gold sighed and nodded. "Henri Bettencourt was quite explicit about the embolisms, Izzy, but he didn't tell us about all the rest of this."

Incredibly, the first pressure injury due to gas bubbles was not a lung embolism but a mild case of itching skin bends that disappeared at sixty feet of recompression. But then an old and overweight chief blew his lungs and died as they tried to get him undressed. Dr. Gold looked at Izzy through droopy, defeated eyes. "We should have had Ferguson send the risky cases first, Izzy, before the seas began to slow up the recovery."

Izzy shook his head. "You couldn't have saved that one, no matter how fast you reeled him in. That was massive bubble damage. You'll find froth in his head instead of blood, Manny."

By early morning they could no longer bring the landing vessels in and out of *Tringa,* so one of them with its ramp down was tied by thick hawsers into the space and the rubber boats made the trip all the way from pick-up to *Tringa.*

At some point an officer from the *Eadie* took a spinal hit and Izzy, Dr. Gold, plus half-a-dozen other experts were involved with that as the nose bleeds, sinus pops, and eardrums continued to arrive. Sometime later that wild morning, half asleep and holding himself in a chair with both hands as the catamaran jumped and jerked with unceasing violence, Izzy opened his eyes and saw Mary Jackson in front of him.

"Izzy, Izzy! Jason Ferguson is coming up! It's almost over!"

Izzy lurched to his feet and groggily followed Mary aft to where they could look down a hatch into the stern well. The scene was now partly obscured by continual spray and green water. Tied in a nest of ropes, the landing vessel jerked and pulled like a mad dog trying to escape a net. They heard "One minute!" faintly against the howl of the wind.

Izzy never did see Jason Ferguson come out of the water. The exit area was now a screaming froth of white confusion. Rubber boats moved gingerly and jerkily on these great seas, disappearing in deep hollows, then suddenly flying upward as though on a catapult. And out of this confusion came one of them with the last member of the *Eadie*'s crew aboard, rushing in on a cresting wave, coasting a moment in the smother, then gunning up the ramp where black swimmers knee-deep in swirling water handed the orange body into the entrance of a transfer tank. The cable was hooked up and the final load, swinging like a misshapen clock pendulum, went up into the decompression space.

Izzy, already up on the medical deck, took one look in the tiny port of the transfer chamber and turned to Mary, his eyes wide. "He's hurt, Mary!" he shouted and jumped into the entrance lock of the mating medical chamber. "Tell them to bring me up!" he cried as he spun the door shut with a clang.

Izzy, compressed in moments to one-hundred-and-sixty feet of pressure, stepped into the decom chamber rubbing his ears as two doctors handed Ferguson's stretcher in through the transfer port. Jason's eyes were closed and he was breathing jerkily and shallowly. Izzy felt his pulse, made some reflex tests, and turned on the doctors. "OK! Let's get his clothes off. We'll ice him! Quick! Chamber Operator, give me ninety feet of oxygen in this mask!" He carefully put the mask over Jason Ferguson's nose and mouth and looked out through the window at Mary.

"Izzy, try to get him conscious! Go deeper!" she said tensely into the microphone.

"Operator. Take us to two hundred feet." The air hissed in sharply.

They cut away his clothes with scissors and packed ice around the white skin. "Cold water enema, Doctor! Let's get that core temperature down, man! Operator, take us to two hundred and twenty feet!"

At two hundred and eleven feet Commander Ferguson's eyes flew open and he stared at Izzy.

"Jase!" Izzy took the mask off. "How are you feeling, old buddy?"

"I can't feel a thing, Prof," said Jason in a soft slur. "I can't turn my head."

Izzy pulled a pin from his lapel and began to poke it into Commander Ferguson's arms and legs, saying tensely, "Can you feel that, Jase? . . . That? . . . That?"

To which Jason softly answered, "No . . . no . . . no."

Izzy's face showed bitter pain. "You've taken a high, bilateral spinal hit, Jase, and it's getting worse. There's bad edema . . . How's his core doing?"

"Down two degrees, Doctor Kaplan," said the navy doctor, piling more cracked ice around Ferguson's body.

"I'm very cold, Prof."

"We're making you cold, Jase. To suppress the spinal edema."

"Prof, do you have my hand? I can't feel you."

"Yes, Jase, yes!"

"My vision is going, Prof. I'm looking out of a little, dark circle." Izzy felt his hand clench.

"No, Jase, NO!" cried Izzy in sick rage.

Jason Ferguson's eyes closed and he said, as if to himself, "Think of it. Nine hundred and forty feet. My God, Prof. We did it!" and his young, wide mouth formed a gentle smile of triumph and satisfaction.

But Izzy, sitting isolated in the hard, inhuman, steel cylinder, saw their triumph turn to ashes. He tasted the bitter metallic vomit of defeat in his throat. He stared at the floor as the doctors rapidly fitted a breather and heart thumper onto Jason's body, knowing there was no return from this, no return from utter failure. "I curse you, God," said Izzy softly and with acid bitterness. "What was the point, you prick? Why would you let us get this far, you bastard! You sadistic phoney!"

All that long rocky afternoon and evening, *Tringa*, her cables slipped minutes after Jason arrived inside her hull, rolled and pitched south, out of the path of the big storm. Izzy sat quietly, his eyes closed, in the tank undergoing computer-controlled decompression. When the door finally swung open, he put Jason's ice-cold hand carefully on his breast and, stooping, tiredly stepped out.

Mary waited, and without a word, held Izzy for a while. But all Izzy could say was, "Henri. I must call Henri, Mary." He walked steadily forward, finally pushing open the door to the radio spaces. The watch officer looked up and saw his face and gently asked, "Yes, Doctor Kaplan?"

"Henri Bettencourt, Lochstrom 624," said Izzy in a voice they barely heard. He went into the booth and sat waiting some undetermined time, his mind completely blank, until the phone rang.

"Izzy?"

"Henri, we lost Jase! He took a terrible spinal hit. Massive! High! The worst I've ever seen. He came to below two hundred and ten feet but I could see him going. We iced him. Shit, Henri . . ."

Henri's voice was cool and distant. "I don't understand, Izzy, why you medical people have not solved that long ago. If you could locate the gas injury, you could certainly intervene with a tissue-shrinking drug in moments. Why haven't you studied the physics of the edema and of the gas-injured tissue in relation to norms? Perhaps acoustics could find it, Izzy? You should urge Commander Ferguson's prosector to preserve and section the injury area for physical analysis."

Izzy stared down at the phone. "Intervene? Shrink the edema? Tissue physics?" He rubbed his eyes. "You're right, Henri. Of course." Then he remembered Jason's soft, triumphant smile and he fell silent.

"Izzy . . . Izzy," and now Henri spoke more warmly. "Come back to us at Lochstrom when *Tringa* gets in. I will meet you in London. We will do those things together, Izzy. No one ever wins completely, Izzy. That never happens in this life."

Izzy was nodding mechanically. "All right. Yes. You're right, Henri. We can solve it, like all the other problems." And he was still nodding when a soft knock came on the door of the booth.

"Doctor Kaplan, your wife and Senator Briggs are waiting for you in the senior wardroom."

As he walked forward, Izzy noticed that the rolling had almost ceased and that *Tringa* was boring steadily ahead into calmer seas. "It figures they'd arrive now," said Izzy to no one in particular.

Molly, handsome and slick in a classy pants outfit, and the senator, in his turtleneck and yachty sportswear, stared at Izzy's ravaged face and hot eyes. But Izzy ignored them, turning to Kincaid. "I saved your ass, Admiral. Kiss the beads for that!" he said harshly.

"Never fear, Doctor Kaplan. You'll be rewarded," said Kincaid icily, his eyes filled with hate.

Izzy shook his head. "Don't embarrass yourself and those yellow bosses of yours in Washington by offering me a medal. I'll refuse it publicly. If you'd gotten to the buoyant ascent sooner, even a few hours sooner, we might have gotten Jase up before that fucking sea state turned to hell." Izzy drew in a long breath.

"Old sailors never die," said Molly coldly to them both. "Young ones do."

"The peace bitch speaks!" cried Izzy. "And aren't we tough-minded, we wonderful folks running this wonderful country!"

Thaddeus Briggs, looking pained, smoothed his long white hair and drew his distinguished eyebrows together. "Now, just a moment, Doctor Kaplan. I think we should realize that this operation was extraordinarily successful. . . ."

Izzy looked at them with contempt. "You can fuck my wife, Senator, but don't think you can fuck my head! The three of you aren't fit to touch the ravelings on Jason Ferguson's undershorts. How is it that somebody that fine and brave and strong must break his great heart so you assholes can fuck and drink and spend our money on any goodie or power-trip your little hearts desire? I hate your guts, all of you! Who cares about a society that has bastards like you leading it!"

Izzy turned and left, walking rapidly aft and downward until he reached the sick bay. He opened the door of a small operating theater and, suddenly brisk, strode in and picked a gown off the rack.

They were all there: Mary, Captain Gold, several other hyperbaric specialists, forming a circle around Jason Ferguson's body. They had immersed Jason in water so that the gas embolism would be readily seen during the autopsy. They all looked up and stared at Izzy.

"Izzy," said Mary quietly. "Are you sure you want to be here?"

Izzy smiled formally at her, then took the small, circular cutting saw from Dr. Gold's hand. "I'm going to do it, Mary." He nodded at Gold. "Start the tape, Manny, we'll talk our way through this."

He bent over the white body and started the saw. "I've talked with Henri Bettencourt. He urges us to locate the gas damage and edema and to freeze and section it. Then we can . . ."

There were now only three sounds in the room: Izzy's voice, the shrill, tiny whine of the saw, and the steady plop, plop, plop of Izzy's tears falling into the water bath. Yet the first cut that opened Jason's chest was as straight as if made with a steel edge.

Wave Rider

When Arthur Piver, the salesman-turned-marine-architect, was run down and lost at night off the Southern California coast in one of his own yachts, his dream of a twenty-four-hour sailing speed record died, for the time, with him. Piver was a designer of trimarans, three-hulled sailing vessels of high speed and immense stability. He believed that if one of these boats could be driven onto the crest of a great wave, one of the monsters that occasionally sweep across the South Pacific in the "Roaring Forties," he could ride it for an entire day and totally eclipse the old, clipper-ship runs. The extreme clipper, *James Baines* of Boston, had apparently achieved a twenty-four-hour average of twenty-one knots, if one believes the navigation and the log book. Piver estimated that a forty-foot Tri, on a thousand-foot-long wave, could easily double this speed, if she could be sailed continuously on the downward slope and if the wave stayed together.

Trimarans had their problems. Their stability and stiffness resulted in dismastings when gusts caught them and sheet-release mechanisms failed to act quickly enough. Running down the face of a great sea they tended to dig in one or the other outer hull and pitchpole forward. But because they rode in the upper two feet of water, being light and keel-less, they could surf: run in the continuously-downward-moving water on the front face of large waves. Under these conditions the only limitation on boat speed was the wave forward-speed itself and the larger the wave, the faster this became.

Arthur Piver's dream stayed in the heads of people to whom such matters are of interest, but there were many problems to overcome before Tri's could practically attempt such feats. The Americas Cup developments in the seventies and eighties brought in the boron alloys and internally-stressed mast structures strong enough to withstand both the shocks to which multi-hulled sailboats are prone and the wind gusts before which they refuse to lean over. Microprocessors and servo-systems were developed that sensed changes in wind, sea, attitude, and accelerations and provided the helmsman with continuous steering corrections. But Americas Cup Rules Committees continued to resist any mechanical intervention in the steering of a Twelve Meter or in the movement of its sheets, so by the late eighties interactive programmers had achieved a final development: the talking yacht. Twelve Meters spoke continuously to their helmsman and sheet captains of tiny adjustment and wheel shifts. This was entirely within the rules, for any instrument that can sense and report has been acceptable throughout the Twelve-Meter phase of the Americas Cup.

The problems in the pursuit of Arthur Piver's dream were different. A computer could not steer the big Tri's on a wave-face as well as a skilled helmsman; this had been proven by some deadly experiments along the South Forties. The feedback from the rudder and hull to the man simply could not be duplicated by any multiply-linked servos. But what the Tri captain needed was data assimilation. He had to find and vector his wave, and this took days of computation and projection, plus absolute judgment in the interception and face-riding. The talking Tri's gave helm advice to their skippers on the Twelves, but they also assimilated satellite and oceanographic weather data and projected local conditions in time.

The best of these unusual sailboats was *Wave Rider*, a forty-two-foot, titanium-hulled Tri with outer hulls as sharp as knife edges. *Wave Rider*'s structure consisted of braced tension members designed to present a minimum of area to seas breaking up between the hulls, yet to resist the worst of the torsional shocks that tend to tear Tri's apart. She was sloop-rigged with a fully-battened main and a variety of jibs and spinnakers that were set forward by *Wave Rider* herself, that is, by the computer and servos.

Wave Rider made two attempts on the twenty-four-hour sail record. In the first of these she was sailed by Joseph Spanos and his wife, Beth, herself a talented interactive programmer. Fourteen hours into the run, moving over sixty knots on a one-hundred-and-ten footer, *Wave Rider* was suddenly caught by a local side gust and rolled upward past her stability limit. The wave crest caught the tip of the sail, the yacht inverted and the mast snapped. Beth Spanos was killed instantly by a whipping stay. Her husband was saved from the inverted Tri nine hours later by a long-distance rescue copter.

One year later, in January when the easterlies really

blow high and steady in the South Forties, Spanos and *Wave Rider* made a second attempt. This is their story:

The mother ship for the effort was a chartered freighter, *Osaka Merchant,* which had the feature of a telescoping crane that could set *Wave Rider* into the water next to the ship even in considerable sea states. Funding came mainly from the TV people, they had two crews aboard, but project management was handled by the patrician sailmaker, Hillary Brent of Marblehead, whose "Brent-cut" sails appeared in the Americas Cup and other important sailing races.

But until *Wave Rider* went in, the most important, and expensive, member of the team was the project's oceanographic consultant, Professor Bob Richart, a single-handed ocean sailor himself and the best in the world in wave-state prediction.

Richart worked day and night in the *Osaka Merchant's* small chartroom, now crammed with extra electronics. The project had a direct link with the South Pacific oceanography satellite, SEASAT IV, hanging in synchronous orbit roughly over Macquarie Island. SEASAT, using interferometric instruments, provided detailed wave maps of the whole southern ocean as well as adequate wind-field data obtained from cloud motion.

Osaka Merchant had rolled and pitched south in excellent, calm weather, much to everyone's disgust, but as January arrived the trades finally began to blow south of latitude forty-five, steady at about Beaufort six, and SEASAT began to show interesting wave growths.

Joe Spanos, a short, stocky man in his early thirties, grim and withdrawn with everyone, spent almost as much time in the chartroom as the oceanographer. Now he was there continuously as the bearded Richart searched and focused the SEASAT images and made his predictive calculations.

"This is a good wind, Joe," said Richart on the third night. "See," he pointed to bright dots on the big screen, "That's a group of sixty-footers heading about due west. They're going to overrun these smaller ones and grab their energy." He pointed. "Furthermore, the way they're bunching now means they'll soon be eating each other. And when two sixty-footers add, you get big stuff. And the bigger it gets, if the wind holds, the faster they grow. I don't believe waves over a hundred feet follow the one-third-power law; the energy transfer from the wind goes up much faster. You've got that tremendous boundary-layer suppression."

Spanos peered in his expressionless way at the oceanographer, whose face and beard were lit weirdly green from the screens. "You think it's go, Doc?"

Professor Richart nodded. "If you run at your best speed about sou'west, you'll come into their zone ahead of the big ones. Of course, *Wave Rider* will be getting her SEASAT input so she can put you in a big set."

"Those guys'll have run a ways before I get there," said Spanos, "You think any might be breaking?"

Richart shook his head. "I can't see why. The wind is steady and the sea deep. Once they eat each other and get really big, they tend to be stable for long periods. I mean, what local anomaly bothers a hundred footer at fifty . . . sixty knots? Anyway, you can always climb up on the back of one and wait for the foam to die down." Richart turned and peered up at Spanos. "What you're trying may be impossible, you know," he said suddenly. "You got in fourteen good hours the last time and then a fluke. But statistically, those flukes *have to come*, Joe. It may just be impossible to get a whole day without something like that."

Spanos' thin eyes blinked once or twice. *"Wave*

Rider won't roll up this time, Doc. She can dump sail now in three seconds, if a wing goes too high. That won't happen again."

Professor Richart rubbed his beard. "The same thing never happens again, my friend. It's always different."

Tall, silver-haired Hillary Brent poked his head in the room. "From this talk, I'd say you've found a wave?"

Both men nodded, and Brent turned to Spanos. "You set to go in the water, Joe?"

The short man nodded again, but somehow the three of them did not move or act, as though not quite wanting to start what they had come for. Hillary Brent, peering in the dim light at Spanos, put his hand on the shorter man's shoulder. "We've come a long way to this, Joe," he said in his quiet, Boston voice. "You most of all."

Joe Spanos looked at one man and then the other. He was a Greek-American from Baltimore, a yacht-club boy who won the World Dragon Championships at sixteen, in between teaching rich folk's kids to sail. He had been across all the great oceans in sailboats, dismasted, overturned, ridden on the fringes of hurricanes. "I miss Beth," he said to them in a soft voice. "Once this is done, complete, maybe that can end too."

Professor Richart sighed. "Is it really so important that we sail faster than some old, stiff-collared, Boston fart of a hundred-and-fifty years ago? Sometimes I feel like we're all here just to prove you're better than any of your ancestors, Hill."

"We're here, my friends, to provide the circuses, along with the bread, to the flaccid masses of the world. Those paunchy slobs and their fatso wives will live your adventure, Joe, in their overstuffed living rooms through the eyes of the Reuters U-2 cameras." Hillary Brent wrinkled his straight, pointed nose.

Joe Spanos suddenly smiled, his lips parting for the first time. "Those fatso slobs, Hill, happen to be my folks and friends. And don't blame them. The reason we're doing this is because we're hobby nuts so obsessed with a completely useless idea that in any other society we'd have been locked up long since."

Professor Richart reached his hand up and took Joe's arm. "Joe, I'll be in continual touch with *Wave Rider* so she'll have sizes, locations, and vectors from me to confirm her direct reception from SEASAT. Once you're on a wave, *Wave Rider* will be watching local conditions while I stay on the big picture so as to let you know about approaching wave trains, wind shifts, and any other junk. Okay?"

Spanos nodded and squeezed Richart's shoulder. "Suddenly I can't wait to be up on that face," he said to no one in particular.

Wave Rider, fully rigged with sails furled and waiting, sat in the well of *Osaka Merchant.* The loudspeakers called out into the dusk, "All crew and technical personnel. We are launching *Wave Rider.* Report to the well deck."

The floodlights went on with blinding force and the cameras started. Joe Spanos, in a waterproof jumpsuit of bright orange, the letters "Brent-Cut" across his back, climbed up the port hull and crawled over the wing structure to the main-hull cockpit. There he shrugged on his buoyancy suit and umbilical safety line. This line, which allowed him to roam from one end of the Tri to the other but always remain connected in case he went overboard, had at its core the wires connecting Joe Spanos with *Wave Rider's* interactive computer system. A throat mike and ear-bone speakers let Joe and *Wave Rider* speak to each other continuously without shutting out other sounds.

After he had adjusted the bone-conduction pads,

Joe stared around, then up at the forward poop deck where the multi-eyed cameras pointed at him. "You ready, baby?"

"Systems are all go, Joe sweetie," said *Wave Rider*.

"This is a piece of cake, baby. Sea state three, if that." Spanos shoved his thumbs up, the deck crew cast off *Wave Rider's* traveling straps and the winch whined.

The big Tri, guided by three dozen hands, swung up and off over the side. They waited for a calm spot and then dropped her rapidly down into the water with a thump of stressed, titanium panels.

"Oof!" said *Wave Rider*.

"Okay, baby?" said Joe Spanos quickly.

"Fine, Joe. I'm just not used to that kind of deceleration."

Spanos ran forward and cast-off the four-point sling which was then rapidly drawn up from the Tri. *Wave Rider,* now free of the freighter, drifted rapidly away downwind.

"Put up, baby, while I get these sails hoisted," said Joe Spanos. As soon as the wind caught an edge of sail, the Tri answered to her rudder and swung up to windward. In a minute the sails were tight and pulling and *Wave Rider* was driving off in a good breeze southwest, as the men along the freighter's rail waved their caps and cheered after her.

"Baby," said Joe Spanos. "We've got a good eight hours before we hit the big stuff. I'm going to sack in. As the saying goes, call me if the wind shifts."

"Aye, aye, Cap'n," said *Wave Rider* in his ear. "And I'll keep the bleedin' mate out of the blessed rum bar'l."

Joe Spanos grinned and slid below into the thin, tiny cabin. He swung up on the narrow bunk and wondered if he would sleep. He had not slept well for a year, even at sea. He lay on his stiff bunk, his body rolling idly back and forth as *Wave Rider* drove steadily over the long, low swells in a wind that blew like a wind tunnel, without variation. Joe Spanos felt his vessel move easily under him, heard its comfortable creak and groan as it adjusted continuously to ever-different water profiles. The last thing he remembered was *Wave Rider's* "Nighty-night, Joe," whispered in his ear.

With the dawn came quite different conditions. The waves were much larger now, still long and swelly, but greatly swollen. The Tri climbed up and up on each large hill, then looked down from its eminence at the valley of considerable depth. She then coasted down the hill, scooting south across its face, turning a bit west at the bottom to run up the next large mound.

"Time for breakfast, Joe," said *Wave Rider* in a calm, but loud voice. Spanos woke with a start from a deep, heavy, resting sleep such as he could not remember. He felt the yacht skim down the face of a thirty-footer and grinned.

"That's more like it, baby," he said drowsily. "Time for me to steer?"

"I can manage these, Joe," said *Wave Rider*. "Get some food and coffee. Professor Richart figures that if we turn southeast at about eleven-hundred today, we'll run right into the northern edge of a set of monsters. We can turn south again once we get on one toward the area of maximum height. Then hang on there for the rest of the run."

"How big?" asked Joe Spanos, crouched over his swaying, gimballed stove and busily stirring eggs, bacon, sausage, and tomatoes together.

"Richart guarantees hundred-footers, Joe. But he says the wind is still picking up and they could go bigger."

"What do you think, baby?"

There was a pause. "I think we'll have the ride of our lives," said *Wave Rider*. "You scared, Joe?"

Spanos fed himself with the rapid, methodical relish of the long-distance sailor. "Tense. Light-headed. But not scared, Beth."

"Please, Joe. Don't call me that. I'm not your wife."

Spanos shrugged and gulped hot coffee. "You're what's left of her. You make her jokes, say her things. I miss you like hell, Beth."

The yacht sailed steadily, up and down, over the hills of water. "Joe, Beth made me, programmed me, designed me. But I'm not her. I can't give you what she did. I'm *Wave Rider*, Joe."

"You think I'm a nut?" muttered Spanos into his cup. "Who can make love to a Tri?" He briskly rubbed his hands together. "Okay, I won't say it, if it bothers you, *Wave Rider*. Or is it *Ms. Wave Rider?*"

"Don't be sore with me, Joe sweetie. I like 'baby' fine. We've got a big day coming, love."

Joe Spanos swung up through the narrow hatch and took the wheel. "I'm not sore, baby. I feel great! As the drunk mouse said, 'Bring on that damn cat!'" He peered southeast over the rim to where the giants scuffled and grew and began to run.

Before noon they hardened *Wave Rider's* tack and went southeast tight to windward. At fourteen-thirty *Wave Rider* spoke softly. "You should see the set to the east soon, Joe. SEASAT has us within two miles and they can see them now on the U-2 image."

Spanos put his binoculars to his eyes as the Tri topped an especially huge wave and breathed a whistle.

"Oh, wow, baby. It's the Rocky Mountains!"

The first wave of the set, even though a mile away, bulked all along the horizon and seemed to build and grow as it came at them.

"Take number three, Joe. That's Grandpa."

Wave Rider, now completely dwarfed by the hundred-footer bearing down on them, began to drive up its great slope, higher and higher, slicing upward at an angle to the wave face, the east wind flowing down the slope with a steady scream. They zoomed up over the top and before them was the next and bigger wave in the set.

"If the third is bigger than that, it's a record, baby!" shouted Spanos, for this time they climbed and climbed a slope that steepened continuously ahead of them. The downwave hull of the Trimaran dug sharply into the wave face and they ran along a contour, then worked higher and higher until they burst over the steaming wave top and faced number three.

"One-forty, Joe," said *Wave Rider.* "A damn big mother!"

"Yes sir! That's my baby!" said Spanos.

The wave completely dominated the view ahead. They could see it left and right out to the limit of vision, a huge rolling slope of gray-blue motion. It looked as hard as rock.

They approached it over the long hollow at an acute angle and began to run along the lower face.

"How far up, baby?"

"Wind steadier near the top, Joe, but it's trickier and steeper."

They worked higher, running south along the face. "We're on, baby. Tell them to start the clocks."

"I did, Joe, a minute ago. Our day has begun, love."

They sailed higher up the face, which still towered above them, now running directly south on the contour. The high wind poured from the east over the wave crest and flowed down the face, and *Wave Rider* took this on her port beam, still driving south across the wave, but moving far more rapidly west with the whole wave-set, its group velocity now at sixty-one knots.

Sometimes the peak was irregular and the wind would gust for a moment, up or down. When a lee came, Spanos turned the Tri more down the face to let gravity carry him to where the wind would be stronger on the lower, flatter water. When an upward wind gust caught them they turned up the wave front, heading for the curling, irregular top. The wind tended to be actually less on the crest since an eddy formed there as the high wind, partly entrained and driven by the waves themselves, blew up and over the sharpening wave top. This great curling eddy contained spume and spray, so the crest was constantly bathed in a smoky swirl of chill fog.

Joe Spanos steered silently, intently, feeling the Tri's motion and listening to her advice. "Port a bit, Joe. Steady. Wind gusting. We're leaning a bit far, baby. Hold her, Joe. Now run down. That's it. Watch that starboard tip, Joe . . . a bit west, love. Steady now . . ."

The wave grew steadily all that afternoon, the wind now a scream of cold air, the gray-blue face dotted here and there with foam and minor breaks. The monster was overrunning its consorts, its own velocity increasing steadily. As dusk came, *Wave Rider* spoke softly to Spanos, "It's over one-sixty, Joe. Bigger than the *Ramapo* wave."

The Tri was referring to the record wave-height measurement made years back by the U.S.S. *Ramapo*, a navy oiler, in northern seas.

Spanos grunted. "Hell, baby. The satellites have looked at plenty bigger since."

"They're in the sky, Joe. Not in the water."

As night fell, Spanos could no longer see the entire wave and he depended more and more on the Tri's special senses to tell him where they were on the face. The wave was now so large and moving so rapidly that the face wind was actually decreasing. The wave was running away from the gale that berthed it.

In the dark the phosphorescence glowed along the crest and inside the wave itself. Because the great sea was a static-electricity generator, *Wave Rider*'s rig twinkled and glowed and fingers of blue fire crackled off the crosstrees and mast. The stays lit up and the yacht hissed and sparked.

"Does that tickle, baby?" said Joe, trying to see the white crest above them.

"Just a little static, love."

The moon came up and it seemed for a while as though they were not moving at all, just rolling and pitching on an endless hillside of stationary water. To starboard, far off, was another huge, dim hillside and between a shadowed, choppy, mysterious valley. Yet the whole was moving at almost seventy miles an hour.

The wind wave was so huge that it created its own weather. The slackening, easterly wind reversed in the early morning and a whole gale now blew up the face. *Wave Rider* went over to starboard tack to maintain her southerly course, but the face water and wind were now in direct opposition and instability surges began to move up the face, like ripples in a snapped blanket. Sometimes these grew and broke, other times they tore off the upper ten feet of the wave in a huge spume of wet cloud, blowing in shreds off to the east. This continual stream of water and vapor blowing backwards was accompanied by spectacular blue sheets of Saint Elmo's fire, some of them hundreds of feet long, pouring skyward through the ripping, torn cloud stream.

The sun rose behind the wave and for a while they were in deep shadow. But Joe Spanos could see that the wave ahead had shrunk and was now no more than a foothill running in front of its gigantic consort. "Grandpa's like the Walrus and the Carpenter," said Joe. "He's eaten every one."

"Over two-hundred-feet high and two-thirds mile in length, love. Seventy-four knots. The biggest ever, Joe."

That morning they rode, rearing and bucking, over a worsening, chopping face. The instabilities grew and ten- to twenty-foot breakers, on a thirty-degree running face, charged up at them continually. And then, near noon, Joe heard *Wave Rider*'s level voice stop in mid-advice. A moment later she spoke loudly.

"Joe! Richart says we're starting to run in over the South New Zealand Shelf. Grandpa's feeling bottom already! They can detect steepening north of us."

Spanos steered them around a steep breaker and grunted. "How long till the break, baby?"

"They want you off the wave now, Joe! Brent is on. He's ordering you off. It's going to steepen and we won't be able to climb back out of it, Joe!"

Spanos stared this way and that, driving them south on the face.

"Joe, please. They want to talk, sweetie."

"If you put them on, I'll pull these bone pads off and do this completely by myself," said Spanos evenly.

"I wouldn't do that, Joe. I told them I'm talking to you."

"Then tell me how long before the curl gets here, baby. You're hooked into SEASAT and all that stuff. I know Richart won't tell us."

"I'll tell you, Joe. We might just make twenty-four hours. The break will start a hundred miles north of us and I figure the advance won't be over fifty knots, so we should finish the run."

Joe Spanos grinned at the wild, white chop around him as the reefed main and storm jib snapped in stiff bluster.

By noon the instability rollers had degenerated into

random, impossibly-steep chop so the entire face was now white breakers and *Wave Rider* pitched and rolled wildly, trying to hold her place on the wave. "The break's begun, Joe. We might still get out."

"What's the advance speed?"

"About fifty knots, Joe."

"And we only need ninety minutes, baby. We're going to prove that three million bucks and a few coo-coos can beat old Donny McKay any time, providing he gives us a hundred-and-fifty-year start."

"They're all after me, Joe! They want to talk so bad, sweetie! I've got to tell them something. Joe?"

"Tell them it's my heart's desire, Beth," said Joe in a whisper. "Oh, Beth, it's a long year, lover."

Grandpa was steepening above them and the crest was being torn more and more deeply by wind gusts. *Wave Rider* dropped lower on the face to gain some lee from the modest hill running ahead of them. Visibility was poor in the sudden sheets of spray and foam that whipped over them and the cockpit ran with continuous gouts of water. The wave towered above them, mountainous, craggy, no longer smooth and rolling as the day before but now a true grandfather giant, swollen and pocked with erupting pustules of white broken water, ragged and ripped along the top where streamers of green water tore off, spreading a cloud-cover of hundreds of square miles behind the monster.

And in the midst of the screaming, pounding seas, Joe finally heard the Tri coolly say, "The twenty-four hours are up. Mean speed, sixty-six knots. Congratulations, Captain Spanos. It's been a privilege to make this run with you."

"Thank you, faithful *Wave Rider*," said Spanos in a formal voice, grinning. "And let's not forget Grandpa while we're handing out medals."

"Joe, sweetie, we'll meet him soon enough. Grandpa's crest is over seventy degrees steep now. We can't sail up over that."

"How soon, Beth?"

"Maybe twenty minutes, Joe."

Spanos stood and put the helm hard over. "Jibe ship! Why should Grandpa have to wait?"

Wave Rider spun counterclockwise as her rig slammed over and they went on port tack, scooting up the face of the wave now heading north.

Soon they could see in the far distance ahead of them the great cloud and confusion of the wave's collapse. The curl ran steadily south along the crest and, looking up the face, Joe could see the top beginning to roll up over them. The entire wave was forming a gigantic tunnel, a hole in the water, and the wind now blew south out of that tunnel as they drove close-hauled into it. Grandpa had utterly changed in an instant, metamorphosed into a leaping, continuous, arching roof of water high over them, turning the sunlight ever-darker green. And far ahead, way down along that narrowing, collapsing, yet vast structure, Joe saw the white ruin of the wave coming at him out of steam and cloud, filling all the great space within the curl.

Joe Spanos stood, steering *Wave Rider* and steadily watching the smashed wave-face grow as the flowing, vaulting water-roof thickened and fell implacably downward.

"Okay, Beth," he said quietly. "It's coming, lover. Oh . . . Beth. Oh God, I love you, Beth!"

"It's been beautiful," said *Wave Rider*. "I love you, Joe."

The collapse-face grew, blocking all else. Joe felt the curl water catch *Wave Rider*'s masthead and begin driving her port hull downward.

"You've been patient, Grandpa," said Joe at the end. "We three are one flesh."

The TV audience, estimated at between ten and fifteen percent of all the people in the world, got their raw, red meat then. They saw *Wave Rider,* a tiny, bold insect on the gigantic, ruined face, turn and confront the running break. They saw her drive into the cavern of the curl and, for a millisecond, saw her mast poke out of the white smash of the wave, then, the tumbling glitter of her hulls. And the networks replayed it all at various speeds for some days thereafter.

Yet the designers had worked a minor miracle with *Wave Rider.* They found her later, floating awash and upright, every deck projection—mast, rails, stays, helm —ripped away. Hillary Brent rigged her again and she was the center of all eyes at the next Americas Cup match, cutting sleekly through the spectator fleet with everyone pointing at and photographing the shining yacht.

But *Wave Rider* was an expensive toy so Brent leased her to a classy, high-rise resort in the Bahamas where rich people would pay plenty for a day's outing on the fastest sailboat in the world. Eventually the Smithsonian, after prodding by some congressional yachtsmen, began to negotiate the purchase of the vessel with Brent Sails, Inc. But that next fall was a bad one for hurricanes and a violent one nicked that part of the Bahamas. Somehow *Wave Rider* got loose. They watched her from the hotel through the rain squalls, driven hard onto the outer reef and teetering there for a while. Then the wind shifted and she blew off onto the ocean side. The coral heads had punctured her hulls and she swept off to the east to sink in five thousand feet of water.

With *Wave Rider* gone, people eventually forgot about the twenty-four-hour sailing record. The Smithsonian directors had no idea where they would have put the yacht, anyway.

But always after that, among the small, specialized group who watch the big wave-sets from satellites and the decks of vessels, the Spanos Wind Wave is invoked when one wishes to compare with the greatest of them all. And when Bob Richart now and then follows a big one with a high-resolution SEASAT camera, he finds it easy to imagine a tiny *Wave Rider,* stoutly and endlessly skimming across that distant, running face.

The Battle
of the
Abaco Reefs

The fall wind blew steadily from the east, dead across Elbow Cay, and the big, vertical-axis wind machines, running synchronously in the steady breeze, gentled the island with their hushahushahusha, a giant snoozing in the lowest frequencies. Susan Peabody toyed with her coffee and half watched the tiny, jewel-like TV screen at her elbow, thinking of nothing in particular. Or, really, much in particular such as the department, and the university, and the screwing, literal and figurative, she had taken from that bastard . . . But that was already six months past, and how big a plum would it have been anyway, in a riotous, un-heated Boston? . . . . Susan, a forty-year-old, tall, thin woman, her brown hair cut short and severe, her thin lips pressed thinner still, thought to herself, hating herself as she thought it: I have a good face, high color, a straight nose and a strong chin. I have tits and my legs are long. Oh, for God's sake!

Susan focused on the TV screen, a brilliant spark of color. The eight a.m. Miami news kicked off with a fire fight between the Pennsylvania Highway Patrol and a teamster cadre after diesel fuel. In Vermont, they were shooting wood thieves at the side of the road. Then came the latest skirmish in the Arizona-California war over the water. . . . At least in Boston she would have been totally involved in her profession instead of pissing away her life here in paradise. . . .

The scene shifted to London, where Scottish nationalists wrecked two government buildings and killed a number of police. "No longer drunken soccer hooligans, the Scots were well-equipped with Mark Eleven Uzi automatics. . . ." There was a knock on the door. Susan looked down at her drab and torn dressing gown and dashed from her living-room-kitchen combo into her small bedroom to pull on a halter and jean shorts, shouting, "Coming! Coming!" Who in hell was calling at eight a.m. in Hopetown, for God's sake?

Susan smoothed her hair and pulled the door open. It was Frank Albury; well, one of the three Frank Alburys, the electronics one. "Hi, Susan," said the portly little man, "Can I talk with you a sec?" He was perhaps thirty-five, a small roll in the gut, and completely nondescript. With an even, round, bland face and thin blond hair, he ran the island C.B. operation. An electronic wizard, Jerry Ravetz had said, but all Frank had ever talked about with Susan was the discovery of Christ and scuba diving. And she shared in this second life, in his love of the water. The first time they went together to the outer reefs where the long, hot waves broke and the massive surge ebbed and flowed over the great coral heads, Susan imagined she entered the magical Lewis story of *Perelandra* and the floating islands on the great warm sea of never-Venus. Her father, a gentle classics professor, had read her all

those books, Narnia, the Langs, *Lord of the Rings,*
Oz; and as she rode the long surge of the reef looking
down on its society, she flew over fairy kingdoms and
the ride was magical.

But Albury watched the fish. Studying the fantastic
interlocking detail of their behavior and survival, he
understood absolutely that only God could make such
an intricate puzzle fit together.

"Hi, Frank. Going scuba?" asked Susan.

Albury shook his head and shrugged. "Sure would
like to, Susan, but we got some problems." He looked
at her and rubbed his chin. Then he pointed at the TV.
"You seen that fellow in Miami, that Abaco independence fellow?"

Susan didn't watch the TV much, but she had noticed
an occasional reference on the Miami public station to
such a group, one of the many splinter and terrorist
gangs looking for fun and trouble in Florida. She
smiled. "Is he coming over to run the place, Frank?"

Albury shrugged again. "Maybe. It looks like they
got some planes and ships, Susan. From Munoz, the
Florida governor. We figure Munoz has some kind of
understanding with Castro to let him go at us and Free-
town, and maybe New Providence, while the Cubans
work over the islands closest to them."

Susan laughed. "Come on, Frank! I realize the U.S.
is coming apart at the seams, but an attack on Abaco
from the state of Florida? Are they commandeering
yachts?"

Albury sat down soberly at her table. "Susan, do
you know about the satellite time-lease system?"

"Sure. The Third World rental military satellites
open to anyone who can pay the rip-off price. You
guys subscribers?"

"The Bahamian government is. We're monitoring
Florida ship movements now, at highest resolution, and

they've put a fleet to sea. All shallow-draft boats, tank-landing vessels with National Guard tanks, an old destroyer escort, some Coast Guard stuff."

"Coast Guard is federal, U.S. Treasury," said Susan.

"Susan, President Childers isn't minding the store. The governors are all going off on their own. We think Munoz is looking to set up his own Caribbean state and shut off the flow of U.S. northerners. The Abaco energy communes look awful handy."

"The Israelis would never work for Munoz."

Albury looked down at his Bermuda shorts and rubbed his chubby knees. "Munoz doesn't really understand what's going on out here. But he probably figures they'll either work or starve." He looked up. "Susan, there's a meeting of the Abaco Defense Council at ten this morning, and they asked me to come and see if you would attend."

"The WHAT?" laughed Susan. "Abaco Defense Council! Who, those dolts at the customs shed?"

"More than that," said Albury seriously. "We have a command post at Marsh Harbor out at the Wind Commune Headquarters on Eastern Shore. If you could be there at ten, we surely would appreciate it, Susan."

After Frank Albury left, Susan turned to the commercial channels and sought news of the Abaco Independence Movement, but the morning talk and game shows were in full swing. The world was breaking into tiny splinters and these fools were mesmerized by garbage . . . ! Susan shook her head angrily and watched the simpering host lead a young woman through some personal sex questions. . . . She flicked off the set and stared out at the palms and the gentle, sunny morning. Off across the brilliant blue and green Sea of Abaco the squat solar boilers centered in their mirror nests bulked behind the palms and white houses on Man-o-War Cay. The causeways and locks of the tidal-basin control system joined Elbow and Man-o-War by an incomprehensible network of underwater walls and control gates, all operated from a concrete building on tiny Johnnies Cay, a white spider sitting in a huge web of life and energy.

Susan rubbed her hands together and bitterly stared about her small house. Four months, and she knew nothing about this place, these people! Her book on Shastri cycles untouched. Her U.N. duties carried out just as perfunctorily as the locals could hope, from an uninvited snooper checking to see that UNESCO money wasn't decorating casinos or whore houses.

She had made only a few friends, and most of them among the Israelis, the other arrivés. Face it. Frank Albury was the only Abacoan who called her Susan. That's why they sent him this morning.

She rubbed her hands back and forth across her eyes until the flashes and spots came behind the lids, and she thought about taking the drug. She probably couldn't help them anyway; she hadn't done her homework on Abaco. Yet her only possibility would be to vector for them. She drew back and remembered her lover, intense, brilliant, corrupt Jamie. She had used the drug with him, but he did not believe in Shastri Vector Space. And he had told the committee she was addicted to cocaine. She lost the chairmanship. That bastard . . . ! She still couldn't reconcile his tenderness and strength with. . . .

Oh, hell. She was going to dress and ride to the Marsh Harbor ferry. But just before she stepped out the door, she swallowed two small pills and popped the tiny box, not knowing what might happen or for how long, into her skirt pocket.

Pedaling south the mile to Hopetown harbor on her bike, Susan saw no one until she arrived at the ferry dock. There, several young Israelis and black Abacoans

were wrestling some generator parts off a Wind Commune barge. The Donnie-Rocket glided into the dock
right on time and disgorged several wind workers and
some school children. Everything seemed very ordinary
and peaceful, but the drug was doing its work and
Susan vectored on the suppressed excitement among
the children.

She waited quietly while they revved up the flywheel
on the ferry, listening carefully to the children as they
babbled, walking off down the dock.

"I is in D-south tracker, Joan!" said a little black
boy excitedly. "Dat's de whole *end* of the system. I is
bound to get some tracks." The boy looked back, saw
Susan staring at him and abruptly and silently ran off
the dock. The very incomprehensibleness of his con-
versation rang alarm bells in Susan's head. What in
God's name were they up to? She turned back to watch
the repowering of the Donnie-Rocket.

The large island of Abaco and its chain of cays to
the north and east were linked and looped together by
the ferry system. Originally, the Donnies had been
I.C.-engined cabin cruisers, twenty to thirty feet in
length. Then in the late seventies, the gas-turbined
hovercraft, the Donnie-Rockets had arrived, spectacular, high speed, and kerosene guzzling. Although the
relatively new Swiss flywheel boats now ran in total
silence, the name, Donnie-Rocket, had stuck with them,
for they still went like blazes, up on their stalky foils,
forty feet of praying mantis doing thirty-five knots.

The captain of this Donnie-Rocket was skinny, fourteen-year-old Gerald Beans, black as night with a head
like a chestnut burr. He cut off the magnetic clutch and
signaled the dock superintendent to hoist the torque
bar out of the Donnie's engine compartment. Down below, in a hard vacuum, six tons of steel flywheel spun
in perfectly vibration-free gas bearings at over twenty-

thousand revolutions per minute. Captain Beans noticed Susan's intense inspection of the Donnie-Rocket's power plant and flashed her a great many large white teeth. "Plenty of crayfish to buy that wheel, Dr. Peabody," he suggested.

But Susan, fully into the drug, suddenly, blindingly saw how incredibly little she had seen in Abaco. These children and their talk. A fourteen-year-old ferry captain. This incredibly diverse technology. The Israelis, their energy communes, Governor Munoz and Fidel Castro. She was staggered at the vector complexity, and yet the alarm bell in her head was clanging continuously. She suddenly realized she had not thought of Jamie for at least ten minutes, and she smiled, really grinned in fact, at Captain Beans.

The Donnie-Rocket ambled out of Hopetown Harbor as a displacement boat, past the tall, old red-striped lighthouse with its 130-year-old Trinity House lamp and spring-driven occulting gear. Then Captain Beans clutched the propellers into the flywheel more strongly, and they rose up and scooted for Marsh Harbor. The only other passenger, an Israeli computer specialist whom Susan hardly knew, was studying an instruction manual. So Captain Beans turned to Susan. "Did you see that crazy Abaco independence man on TV, Dr. Peabody?"

Susan shook her head. "I didn't watch it last night, Gerald. Is he really nutty?"

Gerald Beans whistled and nodded his head. "Mad as can be, I think. But he's not the real one, I think. Those politicians want us . . . Abaco. All these kilowatts!"

"Yes," said Susan. "We Americans had all the toys, but they've gotten broken and we waited too long to fix them. All we can see to do is steal from somebody else."

"Those folks up north, with the snows. Who are they going to steal from?" asked Captain Beans.

Susan, distracted in her attempts to vector Abaco and its problems, looked at the boy sharply. "They'll steal from each other, I suppose, Gerald. We had it awfully soft for a very long time."

"Then," said Captain Beans inexorably, "why won't Abaco get the same way?" and Susan found she had no answer.

The Donnie-Rocket made a side trip up Sugar Loaf Creek to drop Susan at the big dock of the Wind Commune Headquarters. For the first time she saw a group of young Abacoans with side arms and some Uzi whistle guns on slings. One of them, a customs agent in fact, detached himself and nodded politely. "They've been waiting for you, Dr. Peabody," he said. "Let me show you the way."

She followed the soldier in his short khaki pants and knee socks up a path brilliant with bougainvillaea, the soft coral crunching underfoot. As she walked, Susan watched a big instrument kite leave its launching rack on the top of the building and climb into the sky. The local wind communes in the South Abaco area were fed data from here, and from similar installations on Man-o-War and Hopetown. On-line computers continuously load-matched the entire system and updated weather predictions. Susan tried to remember who had worked the kites out. The Swedes? The French?

The soldier held open a door and Susan stepped into a large, dim, air-conditioned room with picture-window views of the entire horizon. Around the walls under the almost continuous windows were the various consoles of the wind engineers: instrument boards, video read-outs, and interactive computer monitors. The entire center of the room was now filled with a long plain table at which sat perhaps twenty people. Susan looked at her watch. It was just ten. "Sorry," she said to the seated people, "Frank Albury told me . . ." she noticed Albury in a chair. . . . "You told me ten, Frank."

Albury popped to his feet and the other men followed. "You're right on time, Susan. We haven't started." They had, of course, started. They had been talking about her. Susan looked curiously around at the Abaco Defense Council and selected a chair next to Jerry Ravetz, towards which she walked. She was fully vectoring now, and selecting that chair had involved a certain extension of mental activity. She suddenly realized that Ravetz, with whom she was friendly, was perhaps the most important person in the room. Provost of the Abaco Technical College and called Jerry by almost everyone, Ravetz seemed to represent all the Israelis in Abaco in some generalized and unstructured way. And much of the new technology of Abaco, the energy farms, the huge, still-building thermocline system, the tidal impoundments running laminar-flow, low-head turbines, the crayfish farms, all were basically Israeli-engineered. As she mentally projected various vector trees, she began to see how it must have developed. Kilowatts were not the only problem!

"Hi, Jerry," she said firmly.

Ravetz smiled cheerfully. "Hi, Susan, sorry to bother you, but we do seem to have this little . . . ah . . . problem with the State of Florida." Several of the men around her grinned.

"You've got plenty of problems, Jerry," said Susan, and she did not smile. As was often the case of retrospective vectoring, the picture was clearing even as she spoke. "For one thing, you should never have left Fidel out of all this. Who else is Munoz thick with? There's some kind of Washington connection in this, Jerry."

Ravetz, a stocky, crew-cut man in his forties, wearing white tennis shorts and a purple T-shirt, blinked and let his smile slip away, turning to peer more carefully at Susan and her bright, sharp eyes. "It's a little late to get geo-political, Susan. We may be under attack before dark."

At that moment a tall black man in the same simple khaki uniform as the soldiers walked briskly into the room. He was about forty, lean and muscled, and it was perfectly evident that now he was in charge. Susan looked and looked, then turned to Ravetz. "Who is that, Jerry?"

Ravetz smiled again. "Colonel John Gillam, C. in C. of all Abaco defense forces and presently the acting military governor of Abaco," he whispered.

"Jerry," said Susan rather more loudly than she intended, "that's my garbage man!"

Colonel Gillam turned and smiled frostily the length of the table at Susan. "I do the garbage when things are quiet, Dr. Peabody. It's a way of . . . keeping an eye on things. I'm sure we'll have this Florida business under control in a day or so. Don't worry about the Friday pickup. I'll get your stuff." His voice was like ice. His eyes glinted and his big fat lower lip jutted red and wet at her. Susan flinched at the shock of his hostility. Here was one real hard conch eater, a North American hater. She was at this table over his dead body! He had obviously refused to even be present when they discussed what to tell her.

Jerry Ravetz pulled awkwardly at his T-shirt with its pink, Day-Glo words, "Crayfish Need Love Too," an obscure logo popular with biotechs. "Johnnie," he said quietly, "could we sort of get people introduced and go on?"

John Gillam sat down at the head of the table and pulled a sheet out of his briefcase. "Well, OK, Jerry." He looked around. "Most of you know each other, but

maybe some of you don't know who it is you know."
He grinned at a young Israeli across from Susan. "Now
Marv there is our boat man, kind of our admiral. He
bosses the Donnie-Rockets, work boats, and the rest."

The Israeli grinned back. "Just so I don't have to
go outside the reefs, John. I'm the Dramamine kid, you
know."

"Communication," said Colonel Gillam, "is Frank
Albury. You all know him. At ten this morning we put
all C.B. on scrambler and took the lid off the broadcast
power."

Frank looked around and gave them all a gentle
smile. "John," he said softly, "could we have a short
prayer before we get into this?"

Colonel Gillam shook his head. "You're the chap-
lain, Frank. But the time for that is when they're on
the screens. OK?"

Several other men were introduced, and Susan suddenly noticed that there were only two other women in
the room: Dr. Francis Foot, chief of the Abaco hospital; and Frank's niece, Mary Albury, whose main
function seemed to be to select which computer out-
puts would be displayed and where. Susan looked at
Gillam's coal-black face, the flat nose and high, shiny
cheekbones. A black honky-hating macho garbage man,
just what the crisis doctor ordered!

Colonel Gillam finally turned to Susan and said
evenly, "Dr. Susan Peabody is a newcomer. As most
of you know, when Professor Hollister of Princeton
retired here, we approached him to advise us in our
political relations with the U.S. Dr. Hollister had a
stroke last month and this, ah, problem required us to
bring in someone not familiar with our situation." Gillam paused and looked at some notes. "Dr. Peabody is
a professor at Harvard and one of the founding members of the Department of Contemporary Politics, a

current academic euphemism for crisis management. Dr. Peabody has come to Abaco as a U.N. Fellow and will make a report to UNESCO on the economic and political effects of our energy program and other developments."

The room suddenly became very quiet, and Susan realized they were waiting for something they had been told by Gillam would happen. The colonel looked at her steadily. "Before we go on, I'd like to ask you a couple of frank questions, Dr. Peabody. If you don't like them, or you don't like this situation, please feel free to go back to Hopetown. OK?"

Susan looked at him as evenly as she could. He radiated anger and resentment at her. She was suddenly standing in for Castro, Governor Munoz and God knows who else. "Shoot, Colonel."

Gillam took a deep breath. "We're probably going to be attacked by American forces today. If you have any doubts about which side you might be on, or if you think you might play U.N. lady bountiful or peace dove, please just go away."

Even the whites of his eyes were brown. He was a most thoroughly colored man. Susan looked steadily into the brown-on-brown eyes. "My tenure with the U.N. is six months, Colonel. They've already forgotten I'm here. As far as any choice between you or Governor Munoz, I'll take you and the rest here, even though you hate my bloody guts and wish I were dead."

That was vector talk, right down the middle. Colonel Gillam looked at his papers. "I don't hate you, Dr. Peabody. I don't know you."

Susan shook her head. "You can't imagine why we, and I mean Harvard and the State Department and all the big shots who have patronized and snooted you here for years, are now throwing you to Munoz and

Castro. Because it's coming apart up there, Colonel! President Childers is yellow to the core and incompetent besides. We counted on more time than the Arabs gave us, than the Arabs could ever give us. Do you know there's a cruise missile battalion in north Florida? Munoz hasn't got much now, but give him some successes, and who knows? Federal troops have gone over to a state before in our history. So hate away, all of you!"

Jerry Ravetz sat up in his chair and cleared his throat. "Johnnie," he said plaintively, "don't we need all the help we can get? There's nobody else here who knows the U.S. situation like Susan. You said yourself, her professional field is crisis management. What do you want, somebody in English lit, for heaven's sake?"

Colonel Gillam nodded grimly. "Welcome to the Abaco Defense Force, Dr. Peabody," he said evenly. Then, "OK, Frank, let's show everyone last night's TV spec."

Frank Albury nodded to an assistant at one of the consoles and a big, flat solid-state screen dropped over the north window and began to flicker. "You mostly saw this before," said Frank.

The TV tape cut into the eleven o'clock news and a black woman who gave a short spiel on the Abaco Independence Movement and introduced its leader, one Basham Kondo, dressed in flowing robes and a bushy afro. Basham had hardly gotten into his slurring, high-speed speech about the enslaved blacks of Abaco and the many Alburys and their Yiddish masters from across the sea, when the screen blanked and retracted. "Sorry," said Frank Albury gently, "but the prime minister is coming down on the roof."

The swish of big rotor blades above slowed and then they heard a flurry of footsteps. The far door opened and in swept Prime Minister Sean O'Malley and an entourage of two uniformed and two seer-suckered assistants. The old man walked rapidly over to Colonel Gillam and briskly shook his hand. O'Malley was light coffee-colored with a white, kinky poll and a grandfatherly look. Susan suddenly remembered parlor car rides on the New Haven Railroad with her father when she was a very little girl. There was always one porter who was sort of the Old Boss Man, the Chief, and they had all looked exactly like Bahamian Prime Minister Sean O'Malley.

"Colonel," said O'Malley, "don't let us interrupt or slow you up. This is your battle. I'm here if there should be any policy problems." Susan tried to remember what sort of strength the Bahamian navy possessed. Customs and fishery protection vessels certainly, but with what caliber arms? If Florida had a DE. . . . No, no, there was much more to this. These men weren't fools. Susan vectored continuously but the tree was too open, too diffuse. She had been all over Abaco. Where could they have the emplacements? The magazines? What about aircraft? Susan looked up startled to see Ravetz and O'Malley bearing down on her.

"Dr. Peabody," said the old man, "Jerry tells me you've agreed to help us and that you're a crisis expert. You couldn't be in a better place!" He shook her hand strongly. "Jerry," he said, "can't we get back to whatever you were doing? I know you have plenty of things to get ready."

Colonel Gillam beckoned for more chairs. "We were watching a replay of last night's extravaganza."

O'Malley's face registered the distaste of a man handed an overfilled diaper. "Well, I've watched it twice, but once more can't hurt."

Everyone adjusted chairs, the screen came down again, and that great lover of freedom and justice, Basham Kondo, told south Florida the way it was.

When it ended, Ravetz turned immediately to Susan. "How in the devil can he go on with that Yiddish and Zionist masters baloney? Don't the Jews in Florida listen to TV or vote?"

Susan shrugged. "Demographics. The old old Jews are dying off and the new old ones don't come down any more. Munoz and his Cuban gang disavow the worst stuff, but they know how the Sunbelt is going." She turned and looked directly at Colonel Gillam. "Is that man, that Kondo, an Abacoan, Colonel?"

Gillam snorted in disgust. "He worked here as a crayfish harvester but his work record was hopeless. We think he was born on the Berry Islands and his name was Smythe, but it's hard to trace drifters like that. He has perhaps two dozen with him, similar types, misfits from the out islands."

"He wasn't much of a find for Munoz," said Susan thoughtfully, "but I suppose he was the only game in town. Mr. Prime Minister, what steps are you taking in the U.S. about this fleet?"

O'Malley turned to Susan in surprise. "Why, my ambassador to the U.S. is carrying a note of protest to the Security Council this morning. . . ."

"Good grief," said Susan impatiently, "I don't mean that Tower of Babel. Why they won't even know where Abaco *is,* with no casinos, race-tracks, or fancy houses. I'm talking about Federal District Court in Miami. Don't you have a law firm there that can get on this for you?" She looked around quickly. "Does anyone have a copy of the Florida state constitution? I'm sure you can nail Munoz on at least a dozen violations of his authority in Dade County. With a federal restraining order, the Coast Guard will have to function. Furthermore, you can get injunctions so that Federal marshals and state police must keep his Guard planes on the ground. They couldn't be coming over with a fleet and no air cover. These are simple, traditional thinkers, Mr. Prime Minister. Break this chain anywhere and they'll crawl back into the woodwork!"

The room fell silent as everyone looked at everyone else. Colonel Gillam looked grimly at Susan but said nothing. Finally Prime Minister O'Malley's ancient face broke into a grin. "I'm chagrined, Dr. Peabody, that we did not think of that," he said gracefully, then turned and nodded to an assistant in a seersucker suit. The man rose and hurriedly left the room. Frank Albury also stood up, smiling at everyone. "I'll make sure he gets through on priority to Miami," he said. "We have protected channels through the satellite link." And he dashed out.

For the next hour they watched the successive satellite transmissions of high-magnification video showing the invasion fleet assembling in calm waters off Palm Beach. There were Naval Reserve and Coast Guard vessels from Port Everglades, National Guard tank-landing vessels from Fort Lauderdale and Miami, and a collection of state fishery and patrol craft. A young Abacoan stood up and gave the intelligence appreciation; twenty-nine craft, approximately twelve hundred crewmen and about fifteen hundred troops, tank personnel, and drivers. E.T.A. at present course and speed, assuming a Marsh Harbor destination, eight p.m.

While they were awaiting an update from the satellite, Prime Minister O'Malley slipped into a chair next to Susan. "Dr. Peabody, at what level of combat do you think the U.S. federal government might intervene?"

Susan looked sideways at the shrewd old face. "That would depend on who was winning, Dr. O'Malley."

O'Malley looked at her very piercingly, as though seeing her for the first time, and then smiled thinly. "Let's assume we are overwhelmed here and Fidel takes a hand at New Providence, Andros, and points south."

Susan jerked her head around and spoke fiercely, directly at him. "That *must* not happen. You must *never* count on Washington! Don't you understand? That's exactly what they want!"

Her vehemence startled O'Malley. "Who, Dr. Peabody? Who would want that?" he asked softly.

"Munoz's friends, of course. You don't think he got this together without help in Washington, do you? He's being used!"

"But, Fidel?"

"My God, the same! Fidel's a puppet, a decoy. He's their next step. The Bahamas, Abaco, mean nothing to them. Dr. O'Malley, have you ever heard of Shastri cycles . . . ? No, no, let's not get into that. This may be blunted." Susan shook her head, staring at the old brown man.

"Do you have any idea who these people in Washington are, Dr. Peabody?"

Susan nodded. "Yes, but there is nothing you can do here and now about this, Dr. O'Malley, except stop the war. And if it starts, win as quietly as possible."

Susan was vectoring powerfully. She had never achieved this formidable a high, and the great integrating power of her amplified consciousness created clouds of possibilities, the Shastri vector trees, growing and bunching in the created spaces of her mind. The whole development was transparent to her, Munoz, Castro, the cabal of horrible old men in Washington, made by disaster and uncertainty into monsters more fearsome than the rawest, maddest S.S. camp commandant in the worst days at the end of the last great convulsion of a Shastri cycle, over forty years ago. But through some incredible chance (or mischance, that would only vector clearly after the attack was met), these Florida amateurs had decided to drown a pussy cat that was looking more and more like a hungry tiger. As she waited in an ecstasy of speculation and computation, she thought briefly again of Jamie, naked, his cock wilting that night she had dazzled him with the theory of the Shastri cycle. She realized suddenly that he had never been even close to her in intelligence or ability, and it seemed odd that she had never seen that now-obvious fact.

At that moment, Frank Albury said, "Governor Munoz is on Channel Seven, impromptu news conference on the capital steps." The screen flashed in bright color, and there was Munoz, a short, stocky brown man with a thick mustache and receding hair, waving at some supporters. Around him were his guards and staff, black, brown, and white, as befits the modern Southern governor.

"Governor, is it true the State of Florida is supporting an invasion of the Bahamas?" The question came from off screen.

Munoz passed a hand across his brow. "We're not supporting anything. As I understand it, there may be a volunteer group attempting to liberate certain islands in the Bahamas group. In all fairness, I think. . . ."

Another reporter shouted, "Is it true that John Amsler of Amsler, Bigelow and Parke is in Federal District Court right now getting a restraining order on moving those ships into Bahamian waters?"

Munoz shrugged. "That's between the feds and their people. If they can't control discipline on the cutters, that's hardly Florida's problem."

Now there were several reporters shouting at once. "Governor, what if they get an order in Dade County restraining the state and National Guard boats?"

Munoz held up his hand. "Look, let me make a statement. It's simply this. Washington, the federal government, is no longer able to protect or even deal with regional interests. When we had everything, it was easy to resolve these differences. With the price of oil at its present level, it's become impossible. Now, the State of Florida has no intention of encouraging a foreign power, a very controversial and bloody-minded foreign power . . . I'm talking about Israel. Let's please get that straight . . . to penetrate to within one hundred miles of the Florida mainland, displacing as it does hundreds of poor blacks and disturbing the only friends who count today, and I obviously mean the Arab nations. The health, safety, and good life of all Floridians is the only thing that motivates me. This administration is. . . ."

Suddenly a small young woman popped into camera range, her pad pointing and waving at Munoz. "Then you intend to violate the law, Governor? You intend to defy any court order to ground the Guard jets?"

Munoz shook his head mildly but his magnified eyes were as thin and cold as a snake's. "I have no such intention. This office will obey all federal and state laws and orders of the courts. This office. . . ."

A red light over the C.B. speaker rack went on, and all sound in the room went suddenly dead. Then came a cool young voice on a C.B. monitor. "Attention! Attention, Abaco! This is Argus North. I have twenty-six single-seat bandits leaving the Florida coast. Estimated flight time to Little Abaco, seventeen minutes!"

Susan took an involuntary deep breath. Governor Munoz would evidently obey the courts' orders by flying his weapons before the orders arrived.

Colonel Gillam made two long steps to the C.B. center and pressed a protected red button. Priority lights shone all across the monitors and Gillam's voice was multiply projected, still clear and sharp. "This is Big John. Prepare for air attack. All trackers make final calibrations now. All protection vessels, put to sea at once. Argus North, take direction. Execute!"

"Ten-four, Big John. Trackers all, this is your Argus North. We will number targets consecutively and assign you in groups. Report your calibrations to subdivision leaders as available. I repeat. . . ."

John Gillam turned and grimly nodded at Frank Albury. "Time for that prayer, Frank," he said softly.

Albury stood up and looked out over the room. "Please bow your heads, whatever you may believe," he said in his gentle voice. "Dear Lord, we do not kill and maim our fellow men in Thy name, but because Thy Kingdom has not yet been achieved on this sinful world. Forgive us our pride and our cruelty, for we are imperfect seekers after Thy Truth, and though our sins offend Thy sight, bless us in simple love, we Abacoans and our friends from Thy ancient lands of Israel, Amen."

"This is . . . your Argus North. Our bandits are dividing their forces. We anticipate twelve to attack north from Cherokee Sound. E.T.A. Cherokee, nine minutes."

Colonel Gillam turned to Frank Albury. "Picture, Frank!" The big screen showed a radar presentation, a glowing map of the Abaco chain. "Project that squadron at twenty-X, Mary," said Gillam.

Twelve bright dots, moving far faster than in real time, swept across the southern Bight of Abaco and out over Tilloo Cay. "Argus South, are you tracking?"

"I see the picture, Big John," came a new voice. "Trackers all, Marsh Harbor and south, this is your Argus South. We will number targets consecutively. . . ."

Susan watched all this intently. By God, they *could* keep a secret here! What in hell? "Jerry," she started to say. . . .

"Urgent! This is Argus North! Enemy in sight! Six bandits on the deck! Numbering consecutively: target one, batteries A and B; target two. . . ."

Colonel Gillam peered out the window to the north-west. "Frank," and now he could not conceal the tight-ness in his voice, "optical blow on these first ones."

The screen flickered and then a projected telescope image showed two large jet aircraft head on, their images made wavery by the intervening hot air layers, growing in size slowly. Suddenly the closer one's wings showed two bright flashes. "He's firing rockets, John-nie!" Susan could hardly recognize Ravetz's voice, it was dry and tense. Colonel Gillam grinned fiercely.

"This is Big John. All shutters open! Execute!"

Susan looked out at Man-o-War Cay and she seemed to see a glitter, a sudden flash as though lightning had darted across the distant low land. The two jets came at 600 miles an hour southeast down the Sea of Abaco just off the water and heading for Marsh Harbor, a huge, growing roar. In an instant the leading plane cartwheeled and splashed gigantically. His wing man went into a sudden vertical climb, up and up north of them, and Susan could see without magnification that the plane was glowing red. Smoke began to plume from the entire fuselage, and the pilot ejected, a black bundle. But the bundle smoked too, and when the chute opened, it was no more than a bag of tatters.

Now the C.B. monitors were alive with urgent talk. "Track! Track! Carol! Hold your target!"

"Harden my focus, Benji!"

"Left, B Battery, Left!"

Planes were coming in on several angles now. One of the southern group went directly over them and crashed within a hundred yards of the harbor at Man-o-War. Two more went south on fire, and a third was glowing so brightly that it simply blew apart before ever smoking at all.

Susan turned to Ravetz, her surprise unconcealed. "Solar weapons, Jerry! You're using the mirrors on the energy farms!"

Colonel Gillam turned and his smile was now cruel and twisted. "Not quite what UNESCO had in mind, eh, Dr. Peabody? But on the right day, a nasty toy. You see, even if we don't hold them in the mirror battery's focus long enough to cook them, it's usually long enough to blind them. Of course, if they had brought welding goggles they might stop that, but it's hard to strafe nigger conch-eaters when you're wearing welding goggles!"

"This is Argus South! Batteries M and N, redirect to target eleven. You're tracking too fast, Dawn!"

"I got two already, Argus!" The girl's voice was high and tense, total excitement. "Harden my focus!" she shrieked; then: "Mine's on fire! Mine's burning!"

"Jerry," said Susan thickly. "That's Dawn LaVere! That child is only fifteen! What in hell are you doing here?"

But now Ravetz looked at her coldly and his voice was low, yet as hard as Gillam's. "Cut the shit, Susan! Don't you see it yet? This is a Shastri community. We're living what you people gave seminars on. You've been too close to it!"

And Susan, watching horrified another ejection at one hundred feet, this time the pilot enclosed in a bright orange tongue of flame, suddenly saw the whole puzzle unfold and, in chagrin, put all the pieces into place.

A jet came over Matt Lowes Cay firing cannon at Marsh Harbor, and Gillam raged into the mike. "Argus South! We're being hurt by target sixteen!"

"A-OK, Big John! We're tracking sixteen! Carrie, you're too low! Track! Track!"

The plane continued over the town and crashed into the Bight of Abaco to the west.

Susan turned firmly to Colonel Gillam. "Colonel, stop! Let some of them go home, for God's sake!"

Gillam whirled on her. "To their fucking subdivisions and their insurance offices? To their darky baby-sitters and cleaning women!" he shouted.

Susan shrank before his anger, but she stared resolutely back. "Probably a third of those pilots are black, Colonel," she said bitterly. "You're living in another age. I don't give a damn about those men, but if you kill them all, if you win absolutely, it's almost impossible to vector the effect!"

She whirled on Ravetz. "Jerry, you fool! What would Shastri have said? This is a Shastri community? Bullshit! You're all on raving ego trips!" She spun again, frantic. "Dr. O'Malley! I said you must win, but *quietly!* Don't you understand. . . ."

But it was too late.

"Trackers all, this is your Argus North. We have zero . . . repeat zero targets! We are checking the tapes now, hang on. . . . Trackers all! We have twenty-six kills! We wiped the sky clean!"

The C.B. monitors lit up like a Christmas tree and a confusion of shouts and cheers burbled out. To the north, several huge meteorological balloons surged upward carrying fluttering Bahamian and Israeli flags. Wind-pattern smoke rockets flew skyward from Marsh Harbor and Hopetown, painting sudden red vertical columns as high as the eye could see, and over it all came the high, sexy, excited voice of Dawn LaVere. "Ohhhh, Big John! I got five! I'm an ace . . . an ACE!"

Susan felt a real chill of panic. She looked around the room at the arrested figures, many of them still unable to believe what they had done, yet already believing and starting to live in a world in which it had happened.

"Well," she said soberly, suddenly remembering with a real pang of love her cheerful, gentle father and one of his favorite Yankeeisms, "You all really pissed on the stove this time!"

Cleaning up after the great battle consisted mainly of locating the pilots' bodies or getting them out of the sunken planes, and this grim business was taken in hand at once by Marv, the Donnie-Rockets, and the biotech scuba teams.

"For," said Colonel Gillam to Susan in as deliberately callous a way as possible, "we wouldn't want any missing-in-action problems, would we? All those wives petitioning your Congress? They're going to get everything back, the charcoaled remains, the dogtags, and the TV tapes showing just how and where we put the sun in their cockpits!"

Susan, sitting slumped in a chair, shook her head. "Come off it, Colonel!" she said with irritation. "Neither the Florida National Guard nor the Pentagon is going to want to talk about this very much. Those widows will be an embarrassment to Munoz, all right, but the press will probably represent the pilots as undisciplined and incompetent adventurers. No, no. You're missing the point. Once the power centers hear that an exuberant bunch of thirteen-year-old colored kids and sexy-poos like Dawn can total two squadrons of jets without a single local casualty, they're going to look much closer at Abaco and this Israeli thing. They've been looking and thinking plenty already, and I specifically mean Fidel."

Prime Minister O'Malley, who had watched, wide-eyed and silent, the first great battle of the Abaco reefs, now turned to Ravetz.

"Jerry, I think this is all unbelievable, too miraculous to take in. But I find Dr. Peabody's words more and more disturbing. Could we talk . . . ?"

"Hang on, everybody!" Frank Albury dashed into the room with some tapes. "It looked like the invasion fleet had stopped, but now it's headed our way again."

The cheerful chatter in the room stopped abruptly. "E.T.A., Frank?" said Gillam.

"Hard to say, John, right at this minute. They aren't really up to speed yet."

Susan started. She had completely forgotten the fleet! Hastily she rose and located a ladies' room and went into the toilet to take two more pills. This continuous confrontation with Gillam was wearing her down. She sat, resting and alone, on the cool john and rubbed her eyes. How was it possible that a Shastri community . . . for Ravetz had been absolutely right in so describing Abaco, she saw that with blinding clarity . . . could trigger a Shastri cycle? Or, as Shastri had called it, a spasm, for completed cycles were always accompanied by a multitude of unvectorable changes. Ravetz was right. In the seminars you could always keep things in their compartments; but the moment the insights became more than theoretical, the moment you built a community, weapons, life patterns, tools, ideals, then you rippled the pond; and the more successful and radical the insight, the more ripples there were. Susan gave herself five minutes of luxury, a mental vector investigation of the mirror weapon in all its Shastrian ramifications. Ravetz, or someone in Israel . . . or, what the hell, Archimedes if you like! . . . had achieved an almost perfect Shastri null-weapon. A weapon so totally integrated into the community that it had no vector strength whatever in most of the critical and dangerous areas. Such as standing armies and their officer corps, almost always more destabilizing

than the real and imagined enemies they faced. And
all the idle, extraneous, deadly hardware. Susan wondered how much extra it cost to turn the solar heating
mirrors into weapons; they had to move in altitude
and azimuth to track the sun anyhow. Ten percent for
the control stations, logic chips, and hard wire con-
nections? Probably not even that much. And the beautiful, Shastrian idea that in destroying the weapon, an
attacker would be destroying the very reason for his
attack; the booming energy wealth of the Bahamas in
a world of dry oil wells. And the fact that it could only
be used part of the time and only for defense, a fatal
flaw no doubt in the tired imaginations of the old in-
competents at the Pentagon, was completely in accord
with that essential, really primary Shastri vector: self-
realization and the necessity for diverse answers in a
society.

The greatest enemy in the Shastri canon was traditional systems analysis, the so-called single-vector
analysis in which cost, profit, growth, safety, or some
other single value dictated a decision. Of course, without the drug they really had to use single-vector analysis; they could not control the vector tree, could not
see the cloud of, not end points, but *extensions of
now*. Susan suddenly grinned. How it worked! Gerald
Beans went to school, but he captained a high-speed
foil boat of the most sophisticated sort. Dawn LaVere,
with her pouty red mouth, melon breasts, and tanned
white flanks that Ravetz had described as simultaneously a treasure and a disaster . . . she with five kills
against modern aggressively flown jets. The vector tree
always showed that there were several equally good
solutions to a problem. This diversity led to wealth
and to more diversity, to a social system in which
almost everyone could gain somewhere a sense of
themselves and their integration into their community

The children were cast in that role by age, but they were also full-fledged and useful members of Abaco society. Doubtless the Israelis had found their tracking reflexes superior to any adults. Susan had to agree, Shastri would have absolutely approved of that! It totally nulled the whole hero, macho, glory, bravery vector so excruciatingly dominant in war-beset, single-vector societies, so utterly useless in a Shastri society where heroes were replaced by experts, by persons whose confidence comes from their heads, not their balls or that mystical "backbone" her New England father made reference to when he really had no idea why someone behaved, or failed to behave, in a particular way.

But there was still a problem with the children! That most elusive of all vectors, ethics, the vague, but powerful human-based standards, how a society thinks about itself. Five dead men, fathers of children like Dawn LaVere, but prepared to kill Dawn and her black and Israeli friends from on high, impersonally as pilots always did. Dawn knew she directed the mirrors because she, and that little boy at the dock — God, twelve? thirteen? — they were the best in the community at that task. *They* knew and the *community* knew, that was important. And, yet, the children also know, may never be able to forget, that they burned those men! Susan rubbed and rubbed her eyes. Will Dawn love differently, or not be able to love, because she burned five pilots? Five bastards! Five of the main fucking reasons why there's burning in the world. . . .

The ladies' room door opened. "Susan, you OK, honey?" It was Mary Albury.

"OK, Mary. I sort of fell asleep for a sec."

"Oh, don't I know it! This is really too much for everybody. Listen, honey, the new stuff on the boats is coming in, and Dr. O'Malley wondered if . . ."

"Be right out, Mary. Thanks." Susan washed her hands and thought of Frank Albury and decided she would take up the matter of the children with him.

They were all seated when she returned, watching a blow-up of the satellite pictures of the fleet, which was apparently steaming at about eight knots so as to bring it into Abacoan waters well after dark. Susan saw that Dr. O'Malley was now across the table from her, and as soon as the pictures ended, he turned to Colonel Gillam. "I think I'd like to hear Dr. Peabody's appreciation, Colonel," he said a trifle stiffly.

Colonel Gillam inclined his head, and O'Malley turned immediately to Susan. "Why are they still coming, Dr. Peabody?"

"At what level do you want to discuss that, Dr. O'Malley, the fleet itself, Munoz, or his helpmeets in Washington?"

"All three, if you please," said O'Malley.

"Well, as to the fleet, I would imagine they left Florida with all communications, especially receiving stuff, radios and TVs, ripped out and confiscated. The one thing you folks didn't think about, Federal District Court, would be the *first* thing to occur to Munoz's gang. So they would have perhaps one man per ship with ways of talking either to the mainland or at least to a central communication vessel. That way, some judge can't get them on contempt, for failing to obey a court order which they claim they never got because they had twenty-nine busted radios. For this, the Coast Guard writes each captain a letter asking him to do better next time. Of course, they've been warned, through whatever hidden radios are left, about the solar weapons. So they're coming in at night."

O'Malley looked at her and shook his head. "They wouldn't be so stupid as to think we had no other arrows in the quiver? Master Kondo is doubtless a psychotic, but it defies belief. . . ."

Susan shook her head. "Who knows what even Munoz's closest man in the fleet actually has found out? I'm sure the news and TV stations are filled with rumors of death rays and general wild talk. . . ." She looked over at Frank Albury, who grinned and nodded vehemently. "The more important question is, why is Munoz still at this?"

"Exactly!" said O'Malley in a tense voice.

"Two reasons, I think. First, because he's already in plenty deep. If they could have gotten most of the pilots back, the thing might have dribbled away, a flaming sensation and nuisance, but something that could be handled. But all twenty-six . . . that's what I was trying to tell you . . . absolute victories are . . . absolute. They have nonvectorable elements. Munoz is the gambler suddenly in over his head with one last buck in his pocket." Susan looked around the room and even Colonel Gillam sat silent.

"The second pressure is the scary one, the one on Munoz from Washington. He's had to have help all along, and he certainly couldn't keep the fleet coming without both help and, probably, pressure from that same direction. Do you see what that means, Dr. O'Malley?"

The old man nodded at once. "I do. It means they don't care whether they lose the fleet or capture Abaco. That has become irrelevant."

"Exactly!" said Susan, and the room became silent for many moments.

"Dr. Peabody, do you use political cocaine?" said Colonel Gillam. "Specifically, are you on it now?"

Susan flushed involuntarily and turned to face him. "I am, Colonel. I wouldn't dare attempt vector analysis without the drug."

"Dr. Peabody, I spent three years with the C.I.A., and much of my time was spent working with Shastri vectors," said Gillam coldly. "They established that the drug was not only unnecessary but gave erratic results. Crisis experts in Washington vector using computer branching and cluster algorithms."

Susan curled her lip. "Right! And look at the U.S. political turmoil! The reason, Colonel Gillam, that your beloved C.I.A. could never really work in Shastri vector space is that in 1981, President Carter suddenly eliminated the Drug Enforcement Administration, by then an international scandal, and turned the whole, nutty U.S. drug hunt over to the C.I.A., thereby making it absolutely impossible for them to make any serious studies of drug-enhanced decision-making."

Jerry Ravetz ran his hands through his crew cut and pinched his pudgy nose. "Well, this is my fault. I didn't take my pills today, Susan. Believe it or not, the first Shastri null-weapon battle, and I thought it would be so simple I wouldn't need all that vectoring. I wanted to savor it emotionally instead of being endlessly into all that damn thinking."

"I didn't know you used the political cocaine, too, Jerry?" said Colonel Gillam stiffly.

"You never asked, Johnnie, and I didn't offer to tell," said Ravetz quickly. "The point is, Susan was right this noon and she's right now. We're in the initial stages of a Shastri cycle. Somehow the Abaco community has triggered it, chance, something else, I just don't know."

"Yes," said Gillam angrily, "providing we all believe in this drug-fevered hokum! Jerry, the C.I.A. used Shastri's stuff all the time, but they vectored on a computer."

Ravetz shook his head firmly. "No way! Johnnie, the C.I.A. showed you a lot of useful stuff, but you can't vector in real time on a computer. It's simply impossible. It takes weeks to write even a rudimentary program, and by then the crisis, decision, or whatever is past."

"Jerry, this drug, what is it anyway?" asked Sean O'Malley.

"Okay," said Ravetz, turning to look at everyone. "Quickly, here it is for those who don't know the story . . . or have the wrong one. Bar Singh Shastri was an Indian pharmacologist and general all-around genius working in a London hospital on synthesis problems. He got into cocaine as a recreational drug in the early seventies, but it had the same effect on Shastri as on Freud. He gained intellectual power, or at least felt he did, and set about searching for that part of the cocoa plant that carried the intellectual part of the high. Well, eventually he managed to isolate and synthesize a group of alkaloids that apparently reduce the time delay at the nerve synapses. They do other things as well, but the effect is that the mind can carry many more coherent thoughts simultaneously, in parallel, and can process thoughts more quickly. Short-term memory is also enhanced. Interestingly, even though Shastri was a really top-level scientist, he immediately recognized that his enhanced abilities under the drug would be most extended and useful in a political context. He ran for Parliament and spent three years forming a brilliant political career, then dropped it all and went to Israel, becoming a recluse to study and write. Shastri was far beyond becoming the first Indian prime minister of Britain. He had found a way to reorganize the world using vectoring and the vector tree. Most of you know where the theory leads: null-weapons, multiple, labor-intensive energy communes, decisions based on vectoring a cloud of factors."

Prime Minister O'Malley rubbed his cheek and

shrugged. "Well, Dr. Peabody, what projection do you . . . ah . . . see? Why do they attack us but not care if they win?"

"A Shastri cycle," said Susan, "can progress in two ways. With primarily external vector interactions, such as Europe in 1914, or with primarily internal vector interactions, such as Germany in 1939. We are in an internal cycle, in which a small, very powerful group in Washington is attempting to escalate a twenty-six plane raid on Abaco into, I'm afraid, an open-ended, transcontinental-level nuclear strike interchange. If you defeat the Florida navy, and especially if you defeat it as decisively as you did the jets, they will attempt, and they obviously have considerable hope of doing it or they wouldn't be taking these risks, to induce Fidel to fall upon you. Or at least make demands upon you."

Susan looked from Ravetz to Prime Minister O'Malley. "The Bahamas government has an agreement with Israel to accept some substantial number of refugees, if the Palestine situation becomes irretrievable. That's correct, isn't it?"

The room now remained very quiet for some time. O'Malley's face flushed darkly, but then the smooth brown calm slowly returned. "You know, Dr. Peabody, that was a very carefully held confidence between our governments that you perceived."

"Yes," said Susan coolly, "but Fidel perceived it too. I won't attempt to guess how many might come, one hundred thousand perhaps? But it would totally transform the Bahamas, this end of the Caribbean. And now Fidel sees that these Israelis, far from dancing the hora and raising yummy crayfish, have the strike of a cobra. No doubt your plans for the Florida navy are equally spectacular, and Fidel can watch them on his own satellite link, and what do you think will happen after that? All of you?"

Susan looked around. She had to vector them too. They must be led to this, inescapably. She looked at her watch. Four thirty, and the fleet here a little after midnight! She took a deep breath. "Munoz's bosses in Washington, through some ghastly chance, have stumbled into something that could be an all-win situation. If Abaco falls, Munoz will taste blood and go for Freeport. Fidel will have to move or have a far more hostile and expansionist neighbor than yourself, Dr. O'Malley. If, as they now probably expect, Florida goes down to defeat, they throw Munoz to the wolves, who will really be howling at this point, and panic Fidel with now-documented stories of Israeli superiority and hegemony in the Caribbean.

"In either case," and Susan paused and looked around the silent room, "the end result is a move by Cuba against the Bahamas followed by a spasm strike from the U.S. to protect freedom, save Jews, stop Communism, or whatever best serves them. One of the first conclusions Shastri came to when he began to use drug-enhanced analysis was that once the cycle reached a nuclear-explosion level, it could be driven to conclusion. The very fact of a burst over, say, Havana or Miami, would enable a leader to induce other crews and commanders to fire, whatever the dampers or restraints."

Sean O'Malley nodded. "And so, Dr. Peabody?"

"And so, Dr. O'Malley, we must immediately attempt to get Fidel here, tonight . . . to Abaco . . . and let him watch the big show. And, Jerry, you must decide how to get your government to send Israeli energy communes to Cuba and, I suppose, how to convince them to go."

"It's impossible!" spat Ravetz in sudden anger. "There's no way to vector that through, Susan. Cut the crap! You know what Cuba's like!"

Susan stared calmly at him. "What's it like, Jerry?"

Ravetz spluttered, "Phony elections, snooping! Secret police! Come on, Susan!"

"Listen," said Susan. "Cuba has softened and Fidel is old. And you Israelis have something big to offer, bigger than anyone else can offer. A transformed society *within* Communism! Shastri showed that multivector planning *requires* a collective approach. Everybody has to give somewhere in this, Jerry. The point is, once Fidel sees a Shastri society at work, he'll be like a child after candy."

"That bastard won't come here!" said Colonel Gillam. "Mr. Prime Minister, I'll resign if. . . ."

Sean O'Malley looked darkly at Susan. "Even if I were willing to see the man, what could we offer him? It may be possible in your computer crisis-gaming to call up dictators and have them run over, Dr. Peabody, but in the real world such talks require weeks of preparation. . . ."

"Nonsense!" said Susan fiercely. "Fidel is aware of Shastri concepts. Say that you'll talk with him about sharing all this. Just talk!"

O'Malley, flushed and angry, shook his head. "You don't understand. What do I do? Call him on the C.B.? I tell you. . . ."

"Dr. O'Malley," said Susan, "if Frank Albury can get me Major José Martino at the Department of State in Havana on diplomatic channels, that is guarded channels, it may be possible. But you've got to agree. . . ." She turned and looked at Colonel Gillam, her lips a thin line. "Before you resign, Colonel, you might consider that Fidel will certainly be more fascinated by your efforts than, say, me. The Cuban military forces are . . . crack. If those had been Cuban jets, you probably wouldn't have burned them all and you would have lost some mirrors too!"

"Who is this Major Martino, Dr. Peabody?" asked O'Malley and he suddenly sounded worn and tired.

Susan smiled. "A Shastri scholar. He studied with Shastri the same time I was in Israel. He is close to Fidel, Dr. O'Malley. Nobody is handing the Bahamas to anyone, just remember that. What it really amounts to is you extending your good offices to assist in getting energy communes into Cuba. Of course Jerry is right. There are political problems aplenty. But *they won't get smaller!*"

O'Malley squared his shoulders. "All right. Let's try it. Mr. Albury, my Mr. Steen will assist you in putting through the call." Steen, a middle-aged black in seersucker shorts, walked to a communications panel on the west wall and began dialing on a picture phone.

Susan turned and stared coldly at Colonel Gillam. "I've been assuming through all this that there will be a show for Fidel tonight, Colonel, and I don't mean a rifle regiment runing ashore on Elbow Cay!"

"That," said Gillam bitterly, "is the one and only certainty in any of this. If the bastards come ashore, they'll be swimming!"

"Susan," called Frank Albury, "Major Martino is on the hook!"

Susan jumped up and ran across the big room, dropping into the seat vacated by Steen. "José, how are you, old friend?" said Susan quickly, looking at the thin officer's image, with his slicked hair and tiny pencil mustache, smiling primly at her.

"Hello, Susan. I knew you were on Abaco and I hoped we would talk." Susan took her deepest breath of the day and held it for a moment.

"José, we may have a chance to socialize but there is now an urgent problem. A Shastri cycle has begun, José."

She watched his brown color fade on the screen, and

then he blinked several very long blinks. "Abaco . . . Susan? . . ."

". . . And Cuba," she finished relentlessly.

"I cannot see it, Susan. I sensed there were deeper problems when you burned the Florida planes, but. . . ."

"But you don't have all the vectors, José!" said Susan, looking at him intently. "Cuba is to serve as an excuse for a destabilization strike from the U.S.A. That is all I can say on electronics, but it is true. We are in deadly danger, José."

The little Cuban wiped his forehead and patted his thin hair. "And so. . . ." he almost whispered.

"Prime Minister O'Malley has agreed to invite Fidel to Abaco, to watch our defense against the Florida navy. We can talk about it all, José: the cycle, the Israelis, the energy . . . it can be worked out, José!" God, she was sweating in this cold room! She took more deep breaths.

Major Martino nodded. "Hold the channel, Susan. I will ring Fidel. We have been approached. . . ." He paused and thought a moment. "Hold the channel!" and the screen went bright and empty.

There seemed to be nothing much to do at that point but have supper, and most of them straggled down to the wind engineers' dining room, one flight below. Ravetz and O'Malley disappeared to some private place, while Colonel Gillam and some of his young staff and engineers ate in a quiet, closed group.

Susan sat down at a table alone with her tray and picked at the fried chicken. She sighed and rubbed her eyes.

"Cheer up, cheer up," said Frank Albury, putting his tray down across from her. "Moses never stepped on the soil of the Promised Land, but he knew his people would, Susan." His soft eyes peered into her shadowed, pinched face.

"Oh, Frank." She gave a deep, shuddery sigh. "This morning before you came I was sitting in a dirty dressing gown feeling sorry for myself. Now suddenly I'm telling everyone how to run the world. These are your islands, your technology, your weapons, and in a few hours I've . . . Oh, hell, Frank, of course Jerry doesn't want to put Israelis into Cuba, to deal with all that political hassle on top of the whole Shastri and technical thing. And Prime Minister O'Malley, after eight years of stiff-arming Fidel, suddenly has to face him under the worst kinds of pressures and dangers, no agenda, no plans, no data."

She rubbed her cheeks hard. "And Colonel Gillam. The miracle worker, the one man in the world who translated a lot of theoretical, academic hokum into a pure Shastri defense. And by carping and needling him, I've reduced his miracle to crud. He's better, more honest than I am, Frank. He always knew what was right and what needed doing, and he did it with his supertoys and his wonder children . . . and, oh, Frank. The children. I can't make them fit. I just can't!" And she wiped her eyes on her napkin and stared at her plate.

Frank Albury rubbed his pink knees and cleared his throat several times. "I'm not sure I can make them fit either, Susan," he said finally. "But David was a young boy. God needed David, not only to kill an enemy of his people, but to teach a lesson, to men, to us."

Susan nodded. "Oh, I know that. I've thought about that. David is very much a Shastrian figure. The small, confident expert facing macho bluster and baloney."

Frank nodded hard. "Susan, the Shastrian society is, at its base, a meritocracy structured to continuously maximize diversity, to maximize the ways in which merit can be achieved. To use adults for tracking aircraft when the children test better would simply admit they were less than full members of the Abaco community."

"Yes, Frank. It's all true, I see it now. But to kill so easily, like a contest or game. To kill with such glee. What if it hardens them, turns them callous, Frank?"

Albury nodded. "And if those troops were to land tonight and rape Dawn LaVere," Frank colored a bit thinking about that, "would she be less hard afterwards because she hadn't killed any of them? Or wouldn't she be both hard and a victim besides?"

A young man dashed up to their table. "Frank! We've got Castro on the wire! I've sent for the Prime Minister!"

Frank rose at once. "Coming, Susan?"

Susan shook her head. "I've meddled enough, Frank. Either Dr. O'Malley sells it or he doesn't, and all I could do is watch and fidget. Frank?"

He nodded, looking down at her. "I know you pray for us all the time and I don't believe a word of it, but . . . don't stop, OK?"

At almost ten that night, the huge Cuban VTOLs settled down out of the dark to crouch on their tails at the Marsh Harbor airport, their jet-prop engines whining shrilly. Susan and Ravetz stood in the floodlit landing area, in front of two dozen Abaco civil police who held back a mass of gaping Marsh Harbor residents, come to catch a glimpse of the terrible old man.

"It's like the three-shell game," said Ravetz. "You never know which one he's in until they open the doors."

But only in the first, upthrust fuselage did a door slide back and steps swing down, and Susan saw Major Martino start down the ladder. In that instant,

Frank Albury was at their elbow. "Susan! Jerry! We got it off the diplomatic wire ninety seconds ago, and now it's coming over the commercial channels! President Childers has been assassinated! His helicopter was attacked by some kind of missiles, wire-guided or heat-seekers, they don't know which yet, just after he took off from the White House!"

"Oh, my God, Jerry," breathed Susan and she began to shiver. "I've never been so scared, never!"

"Look!" said Ravetz tensely. "They've just gotten the news too!" Major Martino had been followed down the ladder by the old man himself, white-bearded and wearing an O.D. baseball cap, but then two more Cubans ran down the steps shouting and all four clustered at the bottom of the ladder.

"Jerry," said Susan suddenly. "They mustn't go back! Not now!" And she ran across the asphalt waving and shouting, "José! José!"

The dapper thin Cuban turned and watched her come up. "Ah, Susan, how fine. . . ."

"José! You've heard about Childers? Do you see now how it's happening? José, the cycle will diverge. We must all talk!" The shadowy figure behind Major Martino stepped up beside him and Susan suddenly gulped. Close up, Fidel Castro looked like an aging Ernest Hemingway, the same round beard and shape of face. She blinked and shook her head. "Dr. Castro! Within an hour, Vice-president Demarest will be sworn in. He is mad, sir! A manic-depressive who can barely be stabilized on lithium!"

The old Cuban looked at her coolly. "Dr. Peabody, José has told me about you and your call this afternoon. But, sane or mad, what is that to us?"

Susan pushed a strand of hair back. "Dr. Castro, have you ever heard of the Last Mile Study?" The old man shook his head. "Sir, the study was kept very secret because of its monstrous conclusions, but basically, Last Mile proved a number of things, all based of course on defective, single-vector analysis. First, they showed that the U.S. total-war capacity could only slip, was slipping, with time in relation to Russia and the Third World. Second, they claimed that in any all-out nuclear war, and especially a rapidly opening one, the Russians would be revealed as far weaker than believed. Third, that the longer the war continued, the greater would be the U.S. relative strength at the end." She paused and swallowed to moisten her dry throat. "The . . . the loss of life in Asia would be . . . beneficial, reducing the population pressure and breaking down super states like India that have become ungovernable. Even in the U.S., the tremendous damage and horror would turn people to the federal government for help, give it back its old clout. . . ." She shook her head angrily. "Oh . . . I won't give you any more of that horrible nonsense, Dr. Castro. It's just that President-designate Demarest believes it all, and all his advisors are ready to try it out if they can just get the first one to go off! Cuba, then the Soviets is their sequence."

Major Martino turned to the old Cuban excitedly. "Fidel, that is why they offered . . ." but the old man's narrow and snapping eyes stopped Martino instantly.

"Dr. Peabody," he said, "you urged this meeting tonight to insure that these people could not possibly connect me with this invasion?" Susan nodded. "But that was before this murder. Cannot Demarest do whatever he chooses? To Cuba or anyone else?"

Susan shook her head vehemently. "There has to be a context, Dr. Castro. A logical development. Don't you see that to even get the lowest commander to fire his own missile involves a whole mass of intangibles. What sergeant, no matter how plausible the codes and signals, would fire his missile when he's watching a Lucy rerun on Miami television with no sign of war or sense of trouble?"

Castro pulled his white whiskers and looked at Major Martino. "José?" he asked softly.

Martino nodded. "She is right, Fidel! Now we see many things that we did not see before. We must at once null the political vector between the Bahamas and Cuba. We will force this man Demarest to look elsewhere for his provocations."

"Oh," said Susan, taking long breaths in sudden relief and really smiling at the two men, "I expect Demarest will be dealt with almost immediately, providing our friends here in Abaco can carry out their part tonight."

Castro, Ravetz and O'Malley left the airport in a staff car and went into private sessions for an hour, when suddenly all arrived back in the window-room center of the Wind Commune building. It was almost midnight when Frank Albury said, "Hold it, everybody," and the big screen slid down. "Here's Channel Two."

The inside of the newsroom behind an open-shirted young black at his desk looked, for once, authentically busy. "Continuing Channel Two's coverage of the incredible Abaco and assassination stories," he said excitedly, "we have learned that Prime Minister Fidel Castro, Cuba's aging patriarch, has made a sensational visit to the Island of Abaco, scene this noon of an air battle involving renegades of the Florida Air National Guard and elements of the Abacoan defense forces. Cuban Radio announced that the prime minister wished to demonstrate his solidarity with other island nations who, Dr. Castro was quoted as saying, must now contend with the fall and death throes of the entire Yankee elephant rather than just the tramplings of his large and careless feet, unquote. Channel Two has also learned that the extraordinarily effective Abacoan anti-aircraft defense, which registered a sensational one-hundred-percent kill against the Guard jets, was not a laser weapon as first thought but a solar mirror concentration system that can be rapidly tracked. Channel Two also. . . ."

The breathless disclosures continued, but the old, white-bearded Cuban sat quietly down next to Susan and whispered, "That was what you wanted, was it not, Dr. Peabody?"

Susan nodded. "Thank you, Dr. Castro, and . . . sir?" He looked at her and nodded. "Shastrian ideas can work in Cuba. I. . . ." But he only smiled distantly and held up his hand.

"I know all about that from José, Dr. Peabody. We will see how it all works out."

They continued watching the developing stories on the Miami channels when Ravetz suddenly spoke. "Hush, let's catch this!"

"We have learned," said a frazzled young lady staring down blearily at the prompter readout in front of her, "that Israeli Ambassador Mishka Gur is attempting to see the new president in his Camp David retreat. Sources at the Israeli embassy say that Ambassador Gur is attempting an eleventh-hour appeal to stop the continued Florida-based attacks on the Jewish settlements in the Abaco Island group. Sources at Camp David have refused to comment on the appeal and say that President Demarest is in seclusion with his closest advisors."

"What's that all about, Jerry?" asked Susan, suddenly puzzled, but Ravetz, his face grim, only shook his head. "Johnnie," he said, turning to Colonel Gillam, "we can't win too big tonight. There's no limit on this one!"

Gillam laughed bitterly. "I thought absolute victories were a Shastri no-no, Jerry?"

Susan spoke up. "This noon that was true, Colonel, but not now, not with the fleet. The cycle may be damped, but Demarest is still as dangerous as a mad dog. Nothing will help his enemies more than total victory here." Gillam said nothing and Susan noticed that Castro was watching them with quick narrow eyes.

Suddenly, they all turned to stare at the lighted C.B. monitor board. "Attention! Attention, Abaco, this is your Argus North. Our pirates have increased their speed to twenty knots. E.T.A. Man-o-War, entrance-channel buoy, fourteen minutes."

Colonel Gillam jumped up and peered out the north windows. The moon was less than a quarter full and the Sea of Abaco was dark, only an occasional navigation marker winking or glowing along the five-mile channel leading in from Man-o-War to Marsh Harbor. "Infrared, Frank," said Gillam.

The big screen lit with a faint eerie light and in the center was a detailed whitish image of a destroyer escort bow on, with a black bone in her teeth. "She has a missile battery amidships, Jerry," said Colonel Gilliam softly. "We mustn't provoke her as long as she. . . ." He lifted up the mike. "Man-o-War Traffic Master. This is Big John. Prepare for lamp messages. Send at the DE, the leading vessel."

"Ten-four, Big John. We're waiting."

They were all waiting now, everyone frozen in the room, watching the infrared, magnified images of the incoming ships. "They're pretty well bunched, Colonel," said a young Abacoan operating the search radar. "Except for the last one. He's hanging back."

"He won't come," said Susan suddenly. "That must

be their communications center. They wouldn't want to lose their main radio contact with Florida."

"Imagine," said Ravetz in wonder. "Just plowing in here like that. Of course they have acoustic front-scanning so they can see the channel is clear, but after what happened this noon, it just. . . ."

The DE was heading directly for the lighted entrance markers at twenty knots. Colonel Gillam picked up the mike. "Traffic Master, this is Big John. Send in plain English the following: Welcome, please identify yourself. Repeat it over and over. Execute."

"Will do, Big John. Commencing message: Welcome, please identify yourself."

A signal lamp flickered at the north end of Elbow Cay, although they could only see it at Marsh Harbor on a video picture of the entrance area. Immediately the DE began signaling rapidly back from its bridge toward Man-o-War.

"Big John, this is Traffic Master. We are getting return signal lamp traffic as follows: The Abaco Independence Movement reiterates its solidarity with its . . . oppressed black brothers of the Abacos . . . we emphasize our peaceful intentions to all. . . ." Colonel Gillam pressed the priority button and silenced Traffic Master.

"Thank you, Traffic Master. Continue sending our message without change. Crawdaddy North?"

A new voice of a young woman came out of the monitor. "This is Crawdaddy North, Big John. We see your targets."

"Crawdaddy North. Is Harmon tracking?"

"Positive, Big John. Harmon is accepting targets."

The great Sea of Abaco, stretching forty miles north and ten south of Marsh Harbor, lay in faint moonlight. The small cay towns of Man-o-War and Hopetown were completely black, as was all of Marsh Harbor.

Susan peered out of the dark room at the dark water, and far across the flat sea she suddenly had a sense of motion, of activity.

"He's entering the channel now," whispered Gillam. "Here they all come. Crawdaddy North, do we have a wave simulation yet?"

"Hang on, Big John. Here is Harmon's proposed wave now. This is a thirty-x projection."

The big screen suddenly lit up with an outline map of the Sea of Abaco from Treasure Cay south to Cherokee Point. A thin green line starting at Treasure Cay moved south across the image, shifting in shape and thickness until it reached the Marsh Harbor area, where small green ship targets were also moving more slowly in an irregular line. As the green line passed across the ship pips, they winked out, one after another, and the green line continued past Marsh Harbor and disappeared.

Gillam watched the simulation scan closely. "Crawdaddy North. How soon until decision-zero time?"

"Harmon says four minutes, Big John."

"Crawdaddy, I don't like the north end of the wave. See if Harmon can truncate it."

"Will do, Big John. . . . Stand by, here comes Harmon's new try."

This time the green line did not overlap Man-o-War at all, but passed directly centered over the line of ships. "Crawdaddy North. This is Big John. I like that simulation. Put Harmon in real time and turn him loose."

"Will do, Big John. Harmon has control . . . now!"

Susan turned to Ravetz in puzzlement. "Who is Harmon, Jerry?"

"The hydrodynamic computer," said Ravetz with a grin. "The only self-adjusting, boundary-condition simulator in the world. But Harmon isn't just a thinker.

When he gives us what we want, then we let him go ahead and do it."

Susan looked at Ravetz and then at Gillam. "You're going to pull the plug on them, aren't you, Jerry? Empty out the bathtub?"

Ravetz grinned again. "We couldn't keep you guessing very long on this one, Susan."

"Big John, this is Crawdaddy North. Harmon is dumping now."

Gillam peered and peered into the night.

"This is Crawdaddy North. The basin is down five feet, and the sinkage is accelerating."

"That DE should touch anytime now," said Gillam tensely to himself.

Susan looked down from the considerable height of the Wind Commune building and gasped. The land beneath her had suddenly increased. The revealed sand and coral bottom stretched out away from the shore and into the night, no water in sight anywhere. "But, Jerry," she asked, "how do you get it to come back as a wave instead of just rising and floating them again?"

From way across the water there was a sudden, grinding, crashing sound. Ravetz cocked his head. "The DE wouldn't float again anyway. She's just ripped her bottom out hitting at twenty knots." He pointed to the projected map of the Sea of Abaco. "We pump down the tidal impoundment basin north of Treasure Cay, which is also dredged deeper for load-equalization on very low tides. The water surges into it when the gates are opened by Harmon, gaining velocity so that when it strikes the north end of the basin it builds into a south-moving wave. It isn't a wave really, but a bore, like in the Bay of Fundy, maybe twenty-five or thirty feet high."

Fidel Castro, one liver-spotted hand rubbing his thin

white hair, pointed to the screen. "And this, Professor Ravetz, is also a Shastrian weapon. Useful, community integrated, all the other things you have told us about?"

Ravetz nodded. "Quite practical really. With the entire Bight of Abaco, our backside, turned into a solar pond for the thermocline system, approach to our mainland really has to come across the Sea of Abaco."

"But amphibious vehicles, Professor Ravetz?" said the old man.

Jerry Ravetz smiled. "Reserve judgment on that question until our defense is ended, Dr. Castro."

"Big John, this is your Argus North. We believe all vessels numbering twenty-eight are now on the ground. We can see no movement anywhere."

"Argus North. Light up the sky!"

Immediately a series of pops sounded far to the north and the first parachutes opened, sending brilliant white light flooding down from the sky above the Sea of Abaco. Ravetz leaned toward the old man and spoke softly. "We're using the Swedish day-night battlefield system, Dr. Castro. The pyrotechnic projectors are programmed to provide a continuous, shadowless carpet of light for as long as we choose. This part of our operation requires much light."

Brighter and brighter still glowed the once-green Sea of Abaco, but now without its water. Out as far as the eye could see were pools and puddles, but no continuous sea at all. And to the north, in its dry center, were the distant ships, an irregular line of beached and heeled craft of all sizes. And in under the high ceiling of flare lights that continued to fly up popping and bursting came three big Bahamian army helicopters. Susan could readily make out what the massively amplified voice said, over and over, booming downward on the little ragged line of doomed ships. "Put on your life jackets. A tidal wave is coming. Do not stay below. Put on. . . ."

Susan gave a sidelong glance at the old Cuban Prime Minister. His mouth was open. He was thunderstruck, transfixed by the scene. This was going to work out. Oh, dear God, this was going to work out!

And now Colonel Gillam turned on the room. "We must have absolute quiet now! Please, all of you!" He picked up the mike. "Crawdaddy South, this is Big John. Is Harmon working on Wave Two?"

"All right, Johnnie. He's working but we've hardly accessed Wave One." It was an ancient, cracked, crotchety voice, a voice Susan knew belonged to eighty-six-year-old Professor Stephen Morheim, of N.Y.U. and the Trondheim Institute for Hydrodynamic Research, long retired to Abaco where he taught physics and calculus to the freshmen of Abaco Technical from a wheel chair.

Gillam leaned forward, tense, his voice low. "Crawdaddy South, we have only three point seven minutes until decision zero on Wave Two."

"Harmon knows that, Johnnie. He's working out the best initial condition within the solution-time restraint. Now you just lay back and. . . ." The irritable old voice trailed off and they heard him muttering to himself near the open mike. "Harmon, let's depth-average and get Johnnie something before he craps his pants. Forget those higher terms, Harmon. . . . All right, Johnnie," the voice got suddenly louder again. "Here's your projection. Fifty-x, since you're in such a raving hurry."

The screen still showed the southern part of the Sea of Abaco, and again they saw a green line projected on the map moving southeast toward Marsh Harbor from Treasure Cay, and as it moved south a second line of green detached itself from the Little Harbor Impoundment and moved north. The two lines came together between Hopetown and Marsh Harbor, and a third, fainter and more irregular line moved northeast over Johnnies Cay and into the Atlantic. But the original line, now very faint and tenuous, continued southeast to Elbow Cay. "This is Big John. Crawdaddy South, that was a simulated seven-foot runup on Elbow!"

"I know it and Harmon knows it. He's correcting, aren't you, Harmon? Let's delay opening on the west end, Harmon, and phase shift the stream function. . . ."

Susan leaned close to Ravetz and whispered in his ear. "Does he really . . . talk to Harmon, Jerry?"

Ravetz turned and whispered back. "He claims he does but John thinks it's just his way of thinking, of organizing himself."

"Here comes a better one for you," came the creaky voice. This time there was no discernible wave hitting Elbow, the entire result of the collision running northeast out over Johnnies Cay.

"Crawdaddy South. That was perfect! Put Harmon on line, we've only thirty-six seconds!"

"Don't get so danged rushed, Johnnie. Harmon wants to bifurcate the outrun and keep the blockhouse dry. Now you give the boy his chance. . . ."

Gillam suddenly turned and thrust his fingers through his kinky hair. "Jesus, God, Jerry. What . . . ?"

"Here's the wave, Johnny." And this time the green resultant line actually dimmed in the center as it reached Johnnies Cay and left the basin in two strong surges.

Gillam dropped his hands to his sides. "Oh, hell. They're actually going to do it!"

"Seven seconds, Johnnie, and I'm putting Harmon on line. Three seconds. Gates are opening. This is Crawdaddy South, Johnnie. Your Wave Two is off and moving!" And the old voice was firm and filled with powerful satisfaction.

Castro leaned towards Ravetz. "The second wave is to prevent the first one from doing damage within the sea, Professor Ravetz?"

Ravetz nodded. "The basin turns south at Marsh Harbor. So we have to modify the first bore by cue-balling a second one into it. The control station on Johnnies Cay is designed to go completely under water, but apparently old Prof Morheim and Harmon have the resultant bore splitting and going out on either side. Well, we'll see. . . ."

But Susan now gave a great gasp, for the northern bore was in sight! A great steaming, thundering white wall of water, it stretched almost from one side of the Sea of Abaco to the other, over three miles of blinding foam running like an express train. And it was growing in size rapidly. "It's doing about thirty-eight miles an hour," said Ravetz to the awe-struck old Cuban.

John Gillam stared hungrily at the great bore. "Optical blow on the crest, Frank."

The big screen immediately showed a magnified and vastly foreshortened image of the crest. And riding back and forth along it were great insects, black and stalky in the intense light of the battlefield flare carpet.

"The Donnie-Rockets!" breathed Susan.

"Yes," said Ravetz. "Riding the bore to the ships to help pick up survivors. Saving these crews is the biggest systems problem of all, over twenty-five hundred people in the drink at once."

Marv Weinstein, the Admiral of the Abaco Sea, shouted into his C.B. excitedly. "Gerald Beans, Captain Beans! Get back off that crest! You'll skid to the bottom!"

"We riding just great, Marv!" came the high ecstatic

voice of Gerald Beans. "Oh my, Johnnie, we Israelites are coming with the Hammer of God!"

"Here's the picture from Gerald's boat," said Frank Albury, and now the big screen showed a blinding color view down the sloping, white, boiling front of the wave to the sea floor. There was no sense of forward progress, just the violent motion, pitching and rolling. The huge, smoking, everchanging face of the bore fell away in front like a living, steaming sand dune, and as Susan watched, totally transfixed, the first ships came into view, distantly at the top of the screen, small and leaning in hurt attitudes. Now she turned and looked out the window and saw the great white monster itself, gigantic in the brilliant flat light and moving with implacable, terrifying speed. Now, back on the screen was the bore's face and the DE growing suddenly huge beneath them and . . . The bore devoured it! Ate it completely in a second! Susan, shocked, looked again out the window and saw the monstrous, shuffling white confusion of the bore face vanish each ship in turn with no more effort than if they were seed pods or bits of driftwood.

"How Biblical, Jerry!" said Susan gaping. "You've outdone yourself!"

Ravetz shook his head. "This is completely Colonel Gillam's show. Once he grasped the idea of the Shastri null-weapon, he turned this one up. I never believed it would work. I still don't believe it will work!"

The great white bore swept, roaring, past them, the Donnie-Rockets falling back off the crest now to the sea behind that filled the basin from shore to shore with confusion, surge and chop.

But Captain Beans' picture still showed the gleaming lumpy sheet of the face and, now, something in the right corner of the screen! Wave Two!

Marv urgently spoke. "Lay back, Gerald, lay back! We want the picture, not you *in* the picture!"

"Oh, Johnnie, Marv, I hate to leave her. She's such a beauty! But there comes old man Number Two! Don't he look mean, ole man Two!"

The last Donnie-Rocket fell back off the crest and let it roll ahead towards its turbulent destiny at Matt Lowes Cay. The southern bore, not so high but vast enough indeed, had thundered and smoked up past Lubbers Quarters. Now it was abreast of the old striped lighthouse at Hopetown, and then. . . . The great meeting of the seas! A tumult in the basin, an endless roar, spume hundreds of feet high! On Gerald's video they saw the boil and literal explosion of waters in breathtaking close-up, but through the east window a grander sight still, for the entire sweep of the horizon was suddenly intruded on, fragmented by a volcano of white waters, tumultuous and blinding under the flare carpet.

Susan felt suddenly dizzy. Is there nothing we cannot try? An ecstasy in the sea itself!

"This is Crawdaddy South, Johnnie. You want to bet ten crays that we won't wet the top of that blockhouse, eh?" The old man was cackling and breathing heavily.

John Gillam grinned, his teeth shining. "I'd rather bet that the sun wouldn't rise tomorrow, you old. . . ."

"Well, Johnnie, there goes the runoff. You just watch!" came the dry crackly voice.

And sure enough, the Donnie-Rocket camera showed that the smaller, but still impressive runoff bore did bifurcate, quite magically in fact, and roll by on each side of the Johnnies Cay blockhouse, and although some spray may have touched the roof, no green water did.

The ancient voice really cackled in satisfaction now. "Thought we couldn't optimize in four minutes, eh,

Harmon? Why Johnnie was pissing his diapers when I was jumping Navier-Stokes through hoops. . . ."

But now the space north and west of them was blackly spattered with heads, and more were popping up every second. The Donnie-Rockets ran slowly into the thickest bunches, and Abaco police and troopers in bathing suits pulled the men aboard with desperate haste.

Fidel Castro, his face white with astonishment and shock under his white beard, suddenly turned to Major Martino. "José, how many guard machines do we have around Abaco?"

Martino looked surprised. "Why, eight, Fidel."

"Colonel Gillam, if we could help, we have eight sea-surface, rotor machines available to you. They might perhaps come down into the larger groups and hold men until the more mobile. . . ."

"We accept, Dr. Castro," said Gillam quickly. "This was always the biggest problem. We simply don't have the capacity to do this fast enough."

As Major Martino and Frank Albury contacted the Cuban machines, Susan watched close-ups on several small screens of the moment-by-moment rescues. The scuba teams were down on the wrecks attempting to free those caught below in that precious moment before the sea water irrevocably damaged their lungs.

Now the first of the big Cuban guard machines settled ponderously into an area black with heads. Frank brought the scene into sharp optical close-up, and they saw the first Cuban in white coveralls leap down a ladder onto the huge float and rip his clothing off in a single gesture, diving smoothly into the sea. His target was a head and hand slipping back into the emerald-green waves.

"He got him!" breathed Ravetz. But now more

Cubans were in the water, and still others were rigging nets and ropes for the men in the water to grasp. As the next two Cuban machines settled down into the light, their floats were already crowded with brown lean bodies that dove from great heights at struggling figures beneath.

Colonel Gillam turned and looked straight at Fidel Castro. "These men are a credit to your nation, Dr. Castro. Their flexibility is superb!"

The old man nodded, his color almost returned. "Oh, we have learned some things from your Shastri and from José, Colonel." The old man looked again out the window. "But we have still more things to learn, José, do we not?"

"Si, Fidel, si," said Major Martino soberly, but Susan saw his face was now alight with joy.

The continual rescue and transportation of the prisoners to shore occupied every eye, and Susan turned tiredly to Mary Albury. "Oh, Mary, I'll never get back to Hopetown tonight," she said in a soft whisper. "Is there any place I can lay my head?"

Mary smiled. "Sure, honey, the night-duty weather watch bedrooms on the roof. C'mon, I'll take you up. They don't use them much."

They climbed to the roof and found a cozy, breezy bedroom that overlooked the far-flung rescues still going on to the northeast. Susan sat down on the firm bed, looking out at the brilliant light, and hearing the distant excited sounds. Mary Albury looked down at her. "We're part of history now, aren't we, Susan? Really part?"

Susan nodded drowsily. "Oh dear, yes, I really think we are, Mary." And kicking off her shoes she rolled over and fell into a dreamless sleep.

At quarter to nine the next morning, they all reassembled in the window room of the Wind Commune building. Dr. O'Malley, who had watched the night's events from a Bahamian naval vessel, was already seated, as was Fidel Castro and Major Martino. Susan picked a chair as unobtrusively far back as she could and leaned over to Frank Albury at one of his panels. "How did it all come out, Frank?"

He beamed at her. "Over ninety-eight percent saved, Susan. You know, we never got better than about ninety-two percent in the simulations. Having the Cubans really made the difference. That's the answer, put as many swimmers in the water as you can."

"You mean . . . the next time you do it, Frank?" asked Susan seriously. Frank Albury giggled, then laughed out loud.

"Well," said Jerry Ravetz, "I'm afraid we're not quite out of the woods yet. That 'we' means humanity in general, not just Abaco. President Demarest is to address the nation at nine A.M. We've done all that could possibly be done on Abaco, and with the help of our Cuban friends." Jerry nodded at Castro. "But now the final act is elsewhere. To put this quite quickly, we are expecting Demarest to resign the office of President this morning, although not . . . ah, before certain unconditional pardons have occurred, I suspect."

Susan could not resist leaning forward. "Jerry," she said quickly, "what if he won't do it?"

Ravetz shrugged. "He must do it, Susan. Munoz has fled to Nicaragua where his kind can plot endlessly. Demarest's part in this is hours from exposure. And last night was a total disaster for him."

"But he is mad, Jerry!"

"Channel Seven looks good," said Frank suddenly, and they all stared as the big screen descended and flashed the image of the seal on the rostrum. From offstage came the heavy, stagy voice: ". . . the President of the United States."

"All my fellow citizens. . . ." Susan looked up at the jowly, age-sagged face, newly ruined by defeat and fear. But the eyes were bright, alive, darting about.

"Jerry, he's mad as a hatter. Look at the eyes!" said Susan quickly.

"Hush," said Ravetz. "Hush!"

"I bring you a brief, sad message, my fellow citizens. . . ." His eyes were darting even more, peering every which way, the hands fluttering, the cheek muscles jerking. "Last night a group of brave young Americans were brutally murdered by a cowardly, dirty kike trick. . . ." The screen briefly blurred for several seconds. Then the image skipped and steadied. "But I must now announce to you all, my beloved friends and supporters, that my health will not permit me to continue. . . ."

"That's an electronic dummy, a piece-up!" hissed Frank Albury. Fidel Castro looked at Frank.

"What is a 'piece-up,' Mr. Albury?"

"Taking snips of video tape with separate words, facial expressions, and gestures and building a completely spurious TV appearance electronically. It's easy to spot if you know the tricks."

"Turn it off, Frank," said Ravetz quietly.

"Off?"

Ravetz nodded and the screen retracted. "All right," he said, and took a deep breath. "President Demarest is dead. Whatever I say here, I'll deny absolutely I ever said . . . and I won't say it again. Is that clear?" He looked around the room. "When Demarest became Vice-president or as he was becoming, a person joined his group who gained Demarest's complete trust. That person, who will soon be identified with an extremist U.S. Jewish group . . . and you just had a scrap of Demarest on Jews . . . was given a radiation weapon, a no-blast neutron generator. This morning, Demarest was visited by Israeli Ambassador Gur and told that if he did not quit, his part in the Abaco activities would be revealed and the death of these sailors placed on his head." Ravetz paused, then . . . "I'm guessing on some of this, but it must have happened something like this. Demarest balked, so Ambassador Gur played his final ace. If the President did not announce his resignation within the hour, he would be killed, and if he attempted to leave Camp David, he would be killed. Demarest agreed, but he is mad, as you said, Susan, and they were waiting for him with the taped piece-up ready. When that 'kike' popped out, they knew there was only one way to end it safely and they pushed the button."

"And the rest of those at Camp David?" asked Castro quickly.

Ravetz shook his head. "Gone, of course. Sacrificed. Ambassador Gur, other good and brave men, some evil men, some innocent men."

The room was still until Frank leaned forward and said quickly, "It's true. They can't raise Camp David. Phones, TV. Everything's out there!"

Susan raised her hand diffidently. "Jerry, could I say one more thing?"

Ravetz shook his head and grinned. "Susan, you've never stopped talking since you got here, and thank God for that!"

"Well," she said, looking around at them. "Dr. Castro, Dr. O'Malley, the rest of you, it's just this. The person who damped this Shastri cycle was Colonel John Gillam and no one else. If Munoz had gotten his way here, none of the rest of this would have happened. This was an epic, an historic defense, not only of Abaco and the Bahama Islands, but of Shastrian ideals as well!"

"Hear! Hear!" said Frank Albury loudly, and they all stood and clapped, turning toward Colonel Gillam.

Fidel Castro nodded vigorously. "Dr. Peabody, I will second that. Colonel Gillam, the matchless professionalism, planning, and discipline of your action is eclipsed only by the skill and élan of your men." The old man looked around excitedly. "Shastrian ideals can adapt Communism to the new, to the technical present. The sun shines forever, Professor Ravetz! And Cuba too shall have fourteen-year-old men who drive great foil boats to the very rim of the maelstrom!"

So, in the end, it was black, skinny Captain Gerald Beans of Dundas Town who would change the Caribbean and perhaps the world. Susan stared, transfixed, at the excited old man, his white beard spiky and erect, now not only looking like Hemmingway, but talking that same romantic wild stuff about élan and style. Oh, how Shastri would have laughed at that!

Major Martino leaned over and whispered in Susan's ear. "We will make the step, Susan. Someday they will light candles to you in Cuba!"

But Susan looked down at her brown knees and blinked and blinked.

"Oh, José. Oh, I hope not, José," she whispered back.

The Cuban VTOLs took off at noon while all of Abaco buzzed, and met, and organized the victory celebration that night. After some excited C.B. traffic, Elbow Cay was selected as the site, since it had been in the thick of the air battle and stood the greatest risk of run-up during the use of the hydrodynamic weapon. Colored lights were strung in the small revival park and a parade, of sorts, organized before the crayfish barbecue.

The parade never actually ended but gradually metamorphosed into a kind of combination conga line and boogaloo that stretched the length of Hopetown and kept busy every instrument and player in the entire chain of islands.

At the head of the great writhing chain of Abacoans and Israelis, or really in the middle since the head and tail had long since merged, was that ace of aces, Dawn LaVere. Dancing nearby, Susan noticed, was Prime Minister O'Malley, his eyes popping as Dawn's long thighs and tiny ripped jeans shorts flashed like bonefish in the warm fitful light. The extraordinary tightness and brevity of those shorts suggested that they might not come off at all, a possibility Susan smilingly rejected.

She leaned against the fence at the rear of the field where the dancers dropped off momentarily to get food and drink. She was now without the drug and in full possession of the inevitable downer. Her moment, the greatest moment of her life, had just passed, but she had made no more friends, nor was she any more a part of this blooming Shastrian society than she had been yesterday morning.

Susan looked at the gyrating, grinning throng and listened to the blaring music. She sighed and rubbed her eyes and tried to tell herself, as Frank surely would have, that peacemakers were especially blessed. That didn't seem to offer much to a lonely, overeducated, out-of-place woman in her forties, playing a brief, impromptu role in some larger. . . .

"Dr. Peabody?" She looked up startled and saw Colonel Gillam, now neatly dressed in Bermuda shorts and a flowered sports shirt, standing before her. "I wanted to thank you for the speech this morning. We . . . ah. . . ." he rubbed his shiny black face with a big pink palm. "We both wanted the same things, Dr. Peabody."

Susan sighed deeply. "Yes, we did, and we do,

Colonel." She looked up at the shadowed angular face, the high cheeks gleaming in the dim light, the brown eyes large and soft. If you judged a man by his friends —Dawn LaVere, Professor Morheim, Gerald Beans— John Gillam rated tops.

Susan threw her head back and bit her lip. "Colonel, John . . . would you like to try some political cocaine with me?" She looked openly into his face.

He rubbed his chin slowly. "Well, uh . . . Dr. . . . Susan." He smoothed back his kinky short hair several times. "Ah, well look, frankly, you scare the hell out of me. I'm afraid I'd be sort of like a scoutmaster trying to keep up with Mata Hari."

Two bright tears popped into Susan's eyes and she made no attempt to wipe them away. "Oh? Well, I guess I really asked for that, John. We Peabodys aren't used to. . . . Well, look, just forget I said it." And she stared at his face made blurry with the tears.

John Gillam took her hand and smiled, his big lips just parting to show the bright teeth. "I've had my great victories, Susan. I guess I can stand a defeat," and she unashamedly gripped his hand in gratitude for that.

They walked north from Hopetown, hand-in-hand, leaving the shouts, the happy laughter, and the tinkling music behind. As they paused at her front door and kissed for the first time, the fitful east wind drove the ridge-mounted wind rotors behind them at subtly different speeds and the air throbbed faintly with the beat frequencies. "Shastri's heartbeat, John," she said softly. But now she saw his eyes were holding her and that they had gone muzzy and soft as his desire for her mounted.

John Gillam suffered no defeat that night. The great subjective time suspension possible with the drug not only drove him to the peak of sensation but held him in a timeless spasm out of which he perceived another Susan, her body in a tight, upward circle of ecstasy, her face rigid yet smooth and lost as a child's. The softness of her arms and her gentle breasts caught John Gillam in a spiraling rush of tender lust. "Oh, how lovely," he breathed again and again. "Oh, Susan," and it seemed impossible that the relief, and yet not-relief could last so blissfully long.

But Susan was riding a hard, upward-curving wave of white passion, a wave that would never break, or else break and break again forever. Her body lusted for John Gillam's strong core, and when she saw his black face, now soft and heavy with desire, her own lust flamed higher. In that wrenching, protracted moment, she remembered her father, the fairy tales, how they lived happily for ever after, and she knew that John Gillam and she would live *within this moment* for ever after, and that was better.

And in her final overwhelming submission to utter pleasure, Susan cried out, "Oh, Johnnie! Mine's on fire! Mine's burning too!"

When those words were spoken, the Battle of the Abaco Reefs came, as far as any such battle can, to an end. It was not the last battle in the history of the West, but it was one of the most decisive. And as Susan had sensed that night, she and John Gillam did live together within that moment, through the rest of their long and useful lives.